Killing Despair

Loser Mystery #3

By

Peg Herring

Killing Despair, The Loser Mysteries: Book Three is a work of fiction. The names, characters, and incidents are entirely the work of the author's imagination. Any resemblance to actual persons, living or dead, or events, is entirely coincidental.

ISBN: 978-1-944502-45-4

First published by LL-Publications, 2014
Edited by Leslie Lutz
Printed in the USA

Chapter One

The past is like a tiger you've put in a cage. You might think you've tamed him, but one day as you pass by, he'll reach through the bars and claw you bloody.

I'd spent the morning hoeing the weeds away from among my tiny, tender carrot and pea plants, and after taking a moment to admire the neat, pale green rows, I started for my kitchen and a glass of cold water. It was May. The sky was so blue it hurt my eyes, and the air smelled of growing things. When I came inside, blinking in the relative darkness, I almost tripped over Eddie, who sat with heels propped up on the table and my iPad in his lap. Frowning at a screen so smudged it was a wonder he could read anything at all, he asked, "Loser, who's Jacob?"

A familiar face rose in my mind, friendly in repose, determined on the job. "Used to be my partner."

"You got an email from him." His tone turned chiding. "It's two days old."

When I took on the role of Eddie's guardian, Eddie became my conscience. Since coming to live with me after his mother was murdered the year before, he'd made it his mission to turn me into a participating member of society. With a lack of empathy typical of teens, he'd insisted I attend parent-teacher conferences, science fairs, and track meets. At first, face-to-face meetings with the public and the talking they required had been a nightmare, but over time I'd adjusted. After nine months, I could face teachers, coaches, and other parents without my guts clenching, and my smiles were no longer mere twitches of reluctant face muscles.

An accepted and popular member of the junior class at Beulah High School, Eddie provided plenty of opportunities for me to overcome my discomfort with being around normal people. At his first track meet that spring, I'd begun at the back of the crowd, arms folded around my waist, but when he took the baton and moved into the lead on the last leg of the mile relay, I heard shouts of encouragement. It took a few seconds before I realized I was making those spontaneous, joyful sounds.

"Here." Eddie leaned back in the kitchen chair, tipping it onto two legs in order to hand me the iPad. I didn't bother to ask if it might be safer to get up and walk two steps. "Better see what he wants."

Glancing around at our slightly shabby but comfortable home, I thought about that. Jacob was a good friend, but he reminded me of what I'd come to Beulah to escape: the city that came to me in nightmares. I didn't want to know what was happening in Richmond, Virginia. Still, Jacob wouldn't contact me unless it was important. With a sigh, I took the iPad and touched the circled *1* that signaled an unread email.

> Beth,
>
> I don't know if this is the right thing to do, but I thought you'd want to know. A couple of our guys caught a missing person case last week, a prostitute named Carole Ann Minier. When they searched her apartment, they found a florist's card in the drawer of her nightstand that said, *I'm sorry. You're the only woman I really love. D.* They ran the card. The prints on it came back as belonging to Darrin Lousiere.
>
> The other weird thing, which might not connect at

all, is that a street person named Aisha Star was also reported missing last week. Apparently she's been telling the world that you and she are best friends. It might mean nothing, but the two disappearances coming at the same time is weird.

Let me know if there's anything you want me to do on this end.

I leaned against the wall, fighting the rush of memories that threatened to overwhelm me. I'd never heard of Carole Ann Minier, but Darrin Lousiere was once my husband. He and our infant daughter had been savagely murdered three years earlier. The trauma of loss combined with being the main suspect in their deaths had caused a mental breakdown that left me living on Richmond's streets for over a year. I'd met Aisha there, though she and I had not been friends. Abuse of drugs and alcohol had left Aisha in a state where she couldn't recognize the truth if it appeared before her with angel wings and a halo.

Two women were missing, one connected to me and the other to my husband. What did it mean?

"What does he want, Loser?"

I brushed a lock of hair from my forehead, pushing away the past at the same time. Richmond and the events Jacob described were far from here. People in my home town, Beulah, West Virginia, knew me as Beth Lousiere, not Loser. These days I knew the correct date and who the President was. I paid our bills. I looked after Eddie and Mabel, a friend from the streets who'd come here to recuperate after a car accident. A year later it appeared she intended to stay, and that was fine with me. Mabel and I had a fairly normal life now, and Beth was able to keep Loser in a far corner of her mind.

Thanks to invested insurance money, I had enough to live on. My home on the side of a mountain was comfortable, safe, and far away from the tragedies I'd endured. In the last year I'd re-learned how to live inside—at least during the daytime. I'd stopped counting how many words I spoke in a day. Answering a question didn't put me into a panic, and I could initiate a conversation if conditions required it. I could act like a normal person, though Beth always felt Loser watching, waiting for her to screw up her life again. Mabel still called me Loser, and Eddie followed her example, so I was Loser at home and Beth to the rest of Beulah.

Eddie clicked his tongue to remind me he was waiting for an answer to his question about Jacob's message. "He's just checking in," I said. Using one finger, I tapped out a quick reply. *Jacob-Thanks for the info. I'm good here. Best to Sasha, Beth.*

Chapter Two

A person can say she's not going to think about something. She can resolve to put it into the back of her mind, slam the door, and lock it away. But it isn't that easy. My voices hadn't spoken for months, but that night they invaded my sleep, constant and demanding. I couldn't tell if I was dreaming or awake as I lay on the wicker settee on my front porch, tormented by the past.

Beth, I'm sorry. You were all wrapped up in being a cop and a mother. I didn't feel like I had a wife anymore.

So it's my fault you slept with some other woman?

I didn't say that.

Really, Darrin? Then what did you say? I don't quite get how your screwing around is okay because I don't watch extreme fighting with you anymore.

I knew the voices came from inside my head, but they were terrifyingly real. It was me; it was Darrin. Even my beloved Kara, though she'd been too young to speak, asked in a small voice, *Why did you leave that night, Mommy? Why did you let the bad things happen?*

With the voices came images: Darrin's corpse, half in, half out of the downstairs bathroom doorway, ghostly pale except for bright red stab wounds that pierced his back. And Kara, looking as if she were asleep but so very, very still. As I saw them in my mind, their voices joined in a single question: *Why did you let this happen?*

I hadn't killed my family, though most of Richmond believed I had. The police rejected my claim that Darrin had a girlfriend, since there was no sign of her in our house, our car, or his office. The working theory was that, suffering from post-partum depression, I'd created the fantasy that my husband was cheating on me and killed him in a fit of rage.

I'd found my coworkers glancing away when I came near, unable to believe I could be innocent. I was placed on leave by the department. My partner Jacob, who would have stood by me, was fighting for his life at the time and could not help. My foster mother Marta, who came to Richmond to support me, died of a massive heart attack less than an hour after the funerals of my child and my husband. Alone and grieved beyond bearing, I'd taken to the streets, joining the lost of Richmond, not dead, but hardly alive.

I'd tried to put it all behind me, but the past was back. The tiger had reached through the bars of his cage and reopened old wounds.

When Eddie came downstairs the next morning, I was sitting at the thick, knotty-pine table, a mug of forgotten coffee cooling in my hand. "You look bad," he said. Trust a teenage boy to be honest.

He knew the public part of my story. An inquisitive kid, he'd researched me at the library and learned about the murders of Darrin and Kara and the suspicion that fell on me. He knew about my spiral into breakdown and my fifteen months on the streets, where I did odd jobs, slept in alleys, and answered only to "Loser." He knew about it, but he didn't know. People know what happened to you, but they don't get it unless it happens to them—and who'd wish that on anyone?

Opening the fridge, Eddie stared into it as if he'd never seen anything in there before. "No sleep?"

"Not much."

"Is this about that email yesterday?"

"Maybe."

Taking out a gallon of milk that had *Eddie* written on the side, he took a long drink. I'd begun buying him his own jug of milk after I caught him doing that more than once, though Mabel had remarked with a chuckle, "We did a whole lot worse than drink after somebody else back there." Setting the jug back in place, Eddie took a slice of leftover pizza and closed the door, leaving the empty plate inside. "If you want to go to Richmond, I'll come with you."

He made the decision sound easy, but it wasn't. I felt the city drawing me back, yet I dreaded the thought of returning. It had been good this past year to be a citizen of Beulah, a person known only as Marta's last foster child. The smart thing to do was to go on being Beth and forget the two missing women in Richmond.

But now that I knew about them, forgetting was impossible. The police would conduct investigations into their disappearances, which might cause them to re-examine Darrin's murder. I wanted to be there for that—at least, Beth did. Loser was terrified at the thought of returning to the cloud of guilt she'd carried for so long.

What can you do in Richmond that the police can't? Loser argued. Nothing, if I was honest. The police had the resources to find the women, and they'd do it if they could. How could I help with that?

That didn't stop me from wanting—no, needing to go. Even Loser knew I'd never be whole again until I learned why my husband and daughter had died. For the police, a missing prostitute wasn't unusual, nor was the disappearance of a homeless woman known for small crimes and big lies. I cared more than anyone on the force would, because it mattered to me.

Having been a law officer, I knew that practicality makes demands on the time spent investigating. Certain types disappear for their own reasons. Either of the missing women might be hiding from someone she'd angered. Either might have found a man with a little money and a lot of bad taste. The police would know they might spend days chasing them only to learn they'd moved to another town or decided to begin life anew with another name. Carole Ann Minier and Aisha Star's names would go on a BOLO list, but after the initial flurry of information-gathering, no one would actively pursue their cases.

So I was going to Richmond, though my body already predicted I'd hate every minute of it. My coffee tasted bitter, and the half-teaspoon of sugar I added made no difference. My neck felt like it would snap if I turned my head too quickly, and my hands ached from their death grip on the mug. To say the trip wasn't something I looked forward to was an understatement.

Eddie was watching me, awaiting a decision. "You can't go. You've got stuff to do," I told him. I couldn't lean on a seventeen-year-old for support, no matter how willing he was to help. Besides, Eddie didn't need to see where I'd been. What I'd been.

"Yeah, but—"

I counted on my fingers. "Finals. Track. Camping." Eddie and three of his friends planned to bike the North Bend Rail Trail, a seventy-two-mile trek from Parkersburg to Wolf Summit. They'd been anticipating it for months.

He gave me a look. "Okay, but I'm calling Alex to let him

know you're coming."

Alex Bronson, the entertaining sidekick to my ancient, genteel lawyer Bertrand Suggs, was Eddie's hero. "No," I said firmly. "I'll call them after I get there."

"Promise?"

I fought the urge to cross my fingers behind my back. "Did I stutter?"

I hate lies. Lies ruined my life: lies my husband told, lies from someone I'd thought of as a friend, even lies I told myself. I tried not to lie to Eddie, so in this instance I equivocated. "After I get there" isn't the same as "When I get there."

It would be logical to contact my lawyers, but I wasn't known for acting logically. I told myself that Bert Suggs, who'd forced the police to admit they had no proof I'd killed Darrin, was getting old. He didn't need the stress of knowing I planned to poke my nose into police affairs. Alex was a likeable guy—maybe too much so—who'd never known Loser at her worst, and I didn't relish the idea of him learning more about that pitiful derelict. Though he'd been my white knight in the past, it was best if I handled this quest on my own.

Eddie was reluctant to grant complete freedom. As if he were the guardian and not the other way around, he ordered, "Then call me every day—or text, since you hate talking on the phone so much."

"Okay," I promised, relieved he'd given up so easily. Sending my voice over long distance felt creepy while texting did not. Written words can be edited and erased. Crazy, I know, but I was tackling my fears one at a time.

"Every day," Eddie said firmly. "I want to know you're okay." With a little smirk he added, "Teachers don't like us checking our messages during class time, but there isn't much they can do about it."

Grinning as I took back a little of my authority, I told him, "I'll text. After school hours."

I left home just before 1:00 p.m., after spending the morning making arrangements. Mabel was capable of seeing to the household chores but refused to handle money, claiming her inability to deal with it was what had put her on the streets in the first place. At the local bank, I took out a healthy stack of cash and signed a form so Eddie could withdraw funds if necessary. I hoped to be back in a week, in time for the end of the school year, but if life had shown me anything at all, it was that plans for the future count for nothing.

Our goodbyes were brief, none of us being much for emotional farewells. After I tossed a small gym bag into the back seat of my car, Eddie gave me a punch on the arm and a terse, "See ya."

Mabel's malformed face squinted into an even worse expression. "You gonna be okay back there, Loser?"

"Yeah." There was no way to predict, but there was also no sense fretting about it ahead of time. "Jacob will help."

"Are you gonna see them at the All-Aid?" She meant the people we'd once called friends, the homeless and nearly-homeless who eked out a living in and around Richmond's Fan District.

I shrugged. Part of me wanted to know how Howard, Bubba, Screwy Lewis, and Penrod were doing. Part of me wanted to visit Verle's restaurant and see the old curmudgeon try to hide a smile when he saw me. The rest of me said, *Leave it alone. They don't need Loser in her mid-sized luxury car coming around to show off.*

My uncertainty disappointed Mabel. "You should." She pointed a finger at me, and I waited for encouragement to face the tragedies in my past. I should have known better. "Find Howard and give him the dollar I borrowed the day that car hit me." As I started the engine, she added, "And if you find that little slut Aisha, tell her I know she's the one took my green hat. She ain't as smart as she thinks!"

Chapter Three

The drive to Richmond was beautiful, as spring in the Virginias is required to be. If Eddie'd been there, he'd have asked a hundred flora-and-fauna-type questions. A city kid, he'd fallen in love with the country and wandered our hilltop whenever possible. I'd made it a point to go for walks with him some days, identifying the spring flowers: Dutchman's Britches, Trilliums, Smooth Solomon's Seal, and the shy Jack-in-the-Pulpits that hide their deep purple color on the underside of a cowl-like single petal. Wildflowers lined the roadsides, scattered into unplowed fields, and trespassed onto lawns. Most of the trees had already blossomed and gone green, but once in a while I spotted a dogwood in bloom, and what I thought were persimmon flowers showing pale yellow among the green of white ash, maple, and box elder trees.

Homeowners along the way had their gardens in, some neatly fenced and others edged with items meant to keep critters out: old milk jugs, crime scene tape, and even rubber snakes. Almost everywhere, flowers peeped brightly from under porches and along sidewalks. Hummingbirds no doubt visited those hanging planters, sipping nectar from begonias and fuchsias. Everything looked alive and vibrant, and my mood lightened a little. I was tempted to take side roads in order to see more garden glories, but impatience prevented it. Maybe on the way home I could savor the sights and smells at a slower pace.

Though I tried to keep my mind on nature, the past kept punching holes in the pretty scenery. The police had confirmation that Darrin had been seeing another woman, but that wasn't proof I hadn't killed him. Darrin's confession of infidelity had hit me hard, though I hadn't shared it with anyone. At work I'd been withdrawn, and at home there had been loud arguments, slammed doors, and threats that, in retrospect, sounded ominous. Neighbors had heard me shouting, threatening to end the marriage. Shortly afterward, death had accomplished that.

After a fifteen-minute interview consisting mostly of my sobbing, the department's psychologist had diagnosed post-partum depression. In her scenario, I'd smothered my infant daughter after killing Darrin, caught up in one of those "She's better off dead than living in this wicked world" decisions unbalanced mothers sometimes make.

Faced with suspicion, my mental state had deteriorated. First I'd found myself unable to return to the home where everyone I'd ever loved had died. I stayed for a while in motels, not caring if I showered or recalling when I'd eaten last. I stopped answering the phone, stopped listening to Bert's increasingly worried pleas that I call. After two weeks—maybe a month—I began sleeping wherever I happened to be when I got tired. Soon Beth Lousiere was no more. Loser took her place, washing up in gas station bathrooms, bedding down under bushes, and working at odd jobs to make enough money to buy a single meal each day, if she was lucky.

Loser encountered good people, however. Mabel had taken me under her wing. Penrod and Howard offered help and advice. Verle, the owner of a local diner, had given me work. Maybe Beth had chosen the wrong friends, just as she'd chosen the wrong man to love. Maybe Loser saw things more clearly, even when she looked at nothing.

As I left West Virginia and headed toward I-64, I asked

myself several questions. Was I returning to Richmond as Beth or as Loser? Did I want to vindicate myself before the world or merely learn the truth? Would I ask for help or go it alone? *Stay tuned*, I told myself. *All this and more will be revealed.*

When I reached Richmond just after 6:00 that evening, I headed directly to the Fan. This section of Richmond was known for its mansions, row houses, and historical sites. I drove down wide, dignified Monument Avenue, a little intimidated at the traffic speed after the slower pace in Beulah. Passing statues of Stonewall Jackson, Robert E. Lee, and others, I turned at the Monument to the Confederacy and wound through smaller streets, remembering one resident who'd let me rake his lawn and another who'd warned me to get my dirty hide off his property. In some spots the lots were generous, and the houses sat back from the road, allowing room for grass, flowers, and perspective on their splendor. In other places the homes were stuffed together like dominoes, perhaps twenty feet wide but ninety feet long and two, three, or even four stories high.

I went up to Broad Street and drove past the science museum, noting places where I'd sheltered from rain or sun. Turning again, I slowed to peer at the All-Aid parking lot. It was like looking at a movie I'd seen long ago, familiar but not real. There was Howard in his wheelchair, chatting with a customer who'd just left the store. He hoped she'd find a dollar or two for a friendly amputee, and he'd continue to believe it would happen, no matter how many times he was disappointed. People like us look for old-fashioned types who still carry cash.

People like us? How easily I'd slipped back into Loser's skin!

Turning again, I did what I'd probably meant to do all along and headed toward my former home. Shaded by trees, Grace

Street was a little cooler than Broad. The houses there were similar but not identical to each other, their facades well-maintained, their tiny lawns neat and prettily flowered. At my old home I went around twice, cruising the alley to get a more complete view. The house looked much the same as it had when I last saw it, which was understandable, since the historical committee had strict rules for residents concerning what could and could not be done to the homes within its control. Still, the place seemed warmer, as if new owners had dispelled its curse. The windows were lit with varying brightness: a TV in an upstairs room, a lamp in another, and a chandelier shining in the round window above the entry. According to Bert, a couple with two children had bought it. *Good luck to you,* I said silently, leaving the cobblestone alley for the narrow side street. *In fact, the best of luck.*

After my stroll down memory lane, I drove to Monroe Park, a place Loser had often used as sleeping quarters. Pulling my silver Envoy into a spot where passing police cars weren't likely to notice it, I texted Eddie: *Made it to big city. Study for chem final!* Then I climbed into the back seat, draped my jacket over me, and hoped dreamless sleep would come.

Alex Bronson waited outside a bar, patiently suffering the horrible noise its patrons considered music. He was a little nervous, but it was the good kind of nerves, the kind that kept a guy watchful. He was prepared for the possibility that tonight wouldn't be the night, since his quarry might leave with friends. Alex had located the man's truck, a shiny new Ford with all the bells and whistles. The man's wife wasn't allowed to drive it, ever. When Mrs. Berger had to go somewhere, she saved up the change from her grocery money for bus fare.

The image of her battered face appeared in his mind. "Please don't say anything," she'd begged. "It makes it worse if he thinks other people know."

Caitlin Berger had come to the law office a few days ago, seeking a divorce. Bert Suggs hadn't seen bruises, but he knew the signs, he told Alex later: restless hands, downcast eyes. She'd been scared to death. When Caitlin called to cancel her second appointment, claiming she'd changed her mind about the divorce, Melanie, the firm's receptionist, noted the caller I.D. and reported she was at Henrico Doctor's Hospital. At Bert's request, Alex had done some digging and learned she'd been admitted with a broken elbow that required surgery.

Since Bert was busy at the office all day, Alex had gone to see Caitlin. She was a mess, battered and broken with one eye swollen shut. At first she kept to her story that she'd fallen down the stairs, but when both he and the RN called her a liar, tears came, first a thin stream at one side of her nose, and then great rivers from both eyes. When she recovered enough to speak, four years of horror spilled out. She blamed herself for most of it. "I make him mad. I know I shouldn't say things that rile him up. I try to say it nice and calm, but—"

Alex would have bet what she wasn't supposed to say were things like, "Where's the money to pay the rent?" and "Please don't hit me in front of the kids."

A rectangular light appeared as the door to the bar opened, interrupting Alex's thoughts. Inside, people were standing, sitting, or dancing. Everybody was having a good time, it seemed, but not the woman he'd visited in the hospital today. Caitlin had pulled together the nerve to escape her awful marriage, but her decision had made her situation worse. She wouldn't be able to work for months. "Who wants a one-armed waitress?" she'd said, blotting tears from her injured eye. Wistfully, she added, "Maybe he'll be nicer now. He feels bad, you know?"

No, he didn't know. In fact Alex was almost certain that "nicer" and Berger didn't belong in the same sentence. Recalling Caitlin's look of resignation, he watched Berger lurch toward his truck.

When the door locks chirped, Alex stepped up to the man's side. He'd worn black clothes and a jacket with a hood. With his back to the street lamp, he was just a dark shape in the night. "Mr. Berger."

"Uh?" He was half in the bag, maybe more, but he sensed danger. "Who're you?"

"Your wife is leaving you. Let her go."

Berger's brows descended till his eyes were slits. "What are you, her new boyfriend? I'll kill you, you son of a—" His fists bunched and he swung at Alex, but he was drunk and slow.

With a quick, sharp move, Alex blocked the punch Berger tried to throw and hit him in the stomach, doubling him over. He stepped back quickly, which was a good thing, because a quart of beer spilled out onto the ground. While Berger was still bent over, Alex punched him in the face, knocking him into the pile of his own vomit.

Berger lay moaning on the ground, one hand on his gut, the other over his eye. Bending over him, Alex said calmly, "I'll give you until 5:00 p.m. tomorrow to call your wife—do not visit—and apologize for being an asshole all these years. Tell her you won't stand in her way, and you'll accept whatever custody arrangement she thinks is fair. Tell her you'll see she's got money until she can work again." He straightened. "If you so much as get within fifty feet of her ever again, I'll become your worst nightmare. You won't know where or when, but I'll give you what you gave her and more."

Berger's voice turned whiny. "I didn't mean to break her arm. I just shoved her a little and she fell."

"Well, it isn't going to happen again, got it?"

Berger nodded, and Alex turned away in disgust.

As he disappeared into the shadows, Alex had a tiny moment of doubt. Had he done the right thing? He was an officer of the court, sworn to uphold the law, not to beat sense into senseless heads. If he'd worked within the system, got a restraining order—

No. Restraining orders were useless against men like Berger, who saw their wives as their own personal punching bags. Alex shoved his doubts aside. All he needed to worry about was whether Berger was too drunk to retain the message. It wouldn't do if he woke up tomorrow and concluded that the aches and pains he felt were simply the result of a drunken tumble in the parking lot.

CHAPTER FOUR

My rest in the park wasn't completely peaceful, but it was better than the night before. I woke in the back seat of my car, aware that I'd taken a step my subconscious thought was in the right direction. Day was just dawning, and mist blurred the green around me to ghostly gray. Monroe Park, was one of the oldest municipal parks in the country. By day, VCU students crossed on their way to class or sat and enjoyed moments of peace or social interaction. Visitors came to see its sights, the Richmond Catholic Cathedral of the Sacred Heart with its cupola, towers, and graceful pillars; the Richmond Mosque with its decorative friezes; Johnson Hall, an example of 1920s architecture that was now housing for students, and Prestwould, a dark brick, castellated, courtyard building with slate gable roofs, also from the '20s. In addition to all that, there were fountains and statues and trees and grass. It was what a park should be.

Still, the park reminded me of my time as Loser, since it drew both homeless people and criminals along with tourists. A person crossing Monroe at night had to either be very watchful or have absolutely nothing anyone else might want. Loser had fit into the latter category.

Though I'd often slept in the park, I'd seldom spent my days there. Some of the homeless became a spectacle during the day, assisted by whatever mind-altering substances they obtained. There was often singing, dancing, and general clowning for the unappreciative crowds. Good citizens complained about the noise, bad language, and smell of pot. The police responded, but the Homeless Hobos always returned.

I'd preferred to be somewhere else when the disruptive ones took over, which was why I'd begun spending my days at the drug store with Mabel and the others who, at least to me, were the reputable homeless. We did odd jobs. We didn't make trouble. We tried not to give homelessness a bad name.

Reminding myself that those days were gone, I drove to the parking lot of an office building and left my car where it was one anonymous vehicle among many. As I walked to the All-Aid Drug Store, I wondered if anyone there would recognize me. I was neither Beth from the Fan nor Loser from the streets, falling somewhere between the young wife I'd once been and the outcast I'd turned into. In plain khakis, a cotton shirt with no stains or tears, and shoes that didn't require duct tape to hold them together, I looked respectable but hardly fashionable. As Beth I'd usually worn my long, blond hair pulled back in a style practical for a police officer. As Loser I'd covered it with a cheap hat pulled down as far as possible. In Beulah I cut it myself, snipping it off bluntly along the jaw-line with Marta's sewing shears so I could tuck it behind my ears when I needed it out of the way. It wasn't couture, but I looked neater than Loser ever had. Mabel claimed my posture had gotten better too. "You don't slouch like you used to," she'd said one day. "But you ain't got scoliosis, like me."

That was Mabel: a new disease every day of the week. She loved listing her symptoms for her friends, no matter how outrageous the possibility might be that she actually had typhoid or scrofula. The corner looked empty without her standing there waving at passing cars, her contribution to the happiness of the world. "People smile when they see me," she used to tell us. That was all Mabel asked of life: a smile and someone to listen when she talked.

Penrod knew me right away. He stood in his usual spot, one shoulder against the brick wall of the All-Aid, not for support, I knew, but to feel the assurance of something tangible. The fingers of one hand touched his lips as he repeated in low tones a phrase that kept him reasonably calm, "Choose an awkward moment." I doubt even he can explain what it means.

Though he didn't appear to notice anything, Penrod noticed everything. For my rail-thin, jittery friend, the world swirled in a dizzying cyclone, too fast for him to process. By clinging to a phrase that meant nothing and everything, Penrod tamed the tempest in his head enough that he could function minimally. If modern medicine could have devised something to slow his brain to a reasonable speed, I suspected they'd find genius within that turmoil. As it was Penrod did okay, holding down a job at a local grocery store, re-stocking shelves a couple nights a week.

I approached, stopping a few feet back so he had room to breathe, and waited while he repeated his mantra a few more times. Penrod put his other hand to his stomach and pressed as if to force the words out. "How you doin', Loser?"

Howard, who'd been talking with a man I didn't know, turned when Penrod spoke. I saw him check me out, but he waited until the stranger moved off before putting his motorized chair into gear and starting toward us. The machine bumped obediently across the pavement, but the motor whined with the strain of carrying him. While Penrod looked the same as the last time I'd seen him, Howard had gotten even bigger. His torso sagged over the chair seat and bulged through the spaces, making the stumps of his legs seem even shorter than they were. Enormous jowls hid his neck completely. Still, his smile was as welcoming as ever. Neither of my old friends considered me dangerous, though they no doubt knew my story by now.

Howard put out a hand, and when I took it, pulled me down for a hug. "What you doing around here, girl?"

I shrugged. "Gotta be somewhere, right?"

It was a joke shared after we'd been lectured by some citizen outraged by our idleness. "Why do you just stand here all day?" was the typical question, followed by suggestions that we get a job, get counseling, get into a program, or get out of Richmond. As soon as the advice-giver walked away, someone would ask, parodying his tone, "Why do you people just stand here all day?"

Whoever was present at the time was expected to answer in unison, "Gotta be somewhere."

Howard could have been somewhere else. A double amputee due to diabetes, he was considered disabled and lived in an adult foster care home, where in theory he was tended by certified personnel. In practice, the home was more of a holding pen than anything else, and no one there minded if Howard spent his days hanging out at the drug store. One less bell to answer.

When I spoke, Howard reacted with delight. "You never used to say it with us. You doin' okay, Loser. Doin' okay."

"Can I buy you guys some breakfast at Burger King?"

If they were surprised at the invitation, neither showed it. Howard accepted graciously for both of them, while Penrod turned the volume down on his calming command. As we started for Burger King, his lips moved, but only a whisper came out.

The guys chose a table outside the restaurant, where the sun had already warmed the metal furniture and dried the morning damp. I asked what they wanted to eat and went inside to get it. I'd been there many times as Loser, and it felt weird to not look to the little menu for something I could afford. There was no one behind the counter I'd seen before, but I held two twenties in my hand, clearly visible, to forestall questions as to whether I could pay for all that food.

As Howard ate his big breakfast of pancakes, scrambled eggs, and bacon, and Penrod wolfed down three sausage wraps, I caught them up on where I'd been. I was surprised, though I shouldn't have been, to learn they didn't know what had happened to Mabel after her accident. Howard had seen it, and he described the whole thing in great detail—twice. Some of it was wrong and some greatly exaggerated, but I listened politely. It was no doubt the most exciting thing that had happened to him in years, and it didn't matter if he told it his own way. Penrod's comment showed more humanity: "I'm glad she's with you, Loser," he said in his gulping manner. "She missed you pretty bad."

I felt a pang of guilt at having left my friends behind. Should I invite them to live in Beulah with Mable and me? Aside from Penrod's mental and Howard's physical challenges, they were decent men who didn't deserve the hunger, insults, and extremes of hot and cold that street people face each day. I set the subject aside for the moment. I had things to do here before I could issue any invitations. Besides, what would Howard and Penrod do on a mountainside in West Virginia?

"We got the apples you sent," Howard said, stabbing a bit of pancake. "I ate one every day for a week."

Last fall I'd sent Alex Bronson with a box of apples from my orchard to give to the gang at the All-Aid. Being a good guy, he'd done it without asking questions. "Fiber," I told Howard. "Good for you."

"The guy that brought 'em your boyfriend now?"

Alex's face rose in my mind. He was a good man, a good-looking man, and a man who liked doing good in the world. He made the long drive to Beulah every month or so, claiming he liked the view from my porch. I figured his real reason was pity—maybe his, maybe Bert's—for the client who tried to be Beth but couldn't escape Loser. We all enjoyed Alex's visits though, and I figured it was good for Eddie to have a decent male role model for once.

"No boyfriend," I told Howard. "He's my lawyer."

He nodded, wiping syrup off his Styrofoam plate with the remains of a hash brown patty.

Pushing thoughts of Alex aside, I asked, "Where's everybody else?"

"Larry's in rehab again. Screwy's in jail for disturbing the peace and some other stuff." Howard shook his head in disgust. "I told him save it for when it's cold outside, but that boy got no self-control."

That was certainly true. "And Aisha?"

His expression turned dark. "Missing, I guess."

Penrod's repetition sped up a notch, and I asked, "Anyone hear from her?"

"Nobody." Howard's round face took on a serious expression. "The cops came askin'."

"Know where she went?" They'd tell me things they wouldn't tell the police.

Howard shook his head, causing a minor quake around his

jowls. "I didn't think nothing of it when I didn't see her for a while, but then she missed free clothes Thursday at the Lutheran church."

"I need to talk to her."

Penrod pressed both hands to his abdomen. "Billy always knows about Aisha."

Billy, an unlikeable sort who lived in his car, was Aisha's sometime boyfriend. "Where is he today?"

Penrod shook his head and went back to "Choose an awkward moment," but Howard said, "His car was at the dealership on Main over the weekend."

Billy had a 1997 Dodge Avenger which, he often reminded us, had the Sport Appearance Package. That might have been impressive except for two things. First, the rear end had at some point encountered a hard, cylindrical object, so it was a mass of compressed metal. Second, Billy had no regular income, so he couldn't afford to actually drive the car. He left it in places it wouldn't be noticed: dealerships on weekends, city parks for a day or two, stores that were open 24/7, and driveways of houses with *For Sale* signs on the lawn and no lights in the windows. He kept just enough gas in the vehicle to change locations when necessary.

Since the trunk had to be chained closed, Billy's belongings lay in two untidy piles on the floor in the rear. He slept on the back seat when he felt the need to rest, but twenty hours a day, he hustled. Billy played pool at local bars. He took whatever wasn't nailed down from parked cars, coat pockets, and luggage left unattended at the train station. I'd heard he even snatched purses and knocked junior high kids around for the money they carried. So far, he hadn't been caught at those things, though he'd done minor time for drug possession.

The only person Billy had ever impressed with his car and his macho attitude was Aisha, who'd often shared the back seat with him on cold nights. She talked about it like it was a camping adventure in the wilderness, unconcerned that the car smelled like urine and seldom went anywhere. Aisha thought Billy was strong and tough. Everyone else thought he was ornery and mean.

I waited around for opening time for the Patriot, a dive decorated sometime in the 1970s to evoke the 1770s. These days, the fake lanterns' insufficient light hid how dirty and depressing the place was. Approaching the bar, I set a ten-dollar bill down and asked for a Coke. When the guy set the glass in front of me, his oversized paw cloaked the ten, hiding the denomination. Seeing the wheels turning in his head, I met his gaze and stared at him until he moved to the cash register and returned with the correct change.

Sipping at the drink I didn't want, I sat down at a table in the corner. It wasn't long until Billy came in. He'd already found a mark, a kid who strutted like he knew everything but obviously didn't know anything if he'd agreed to bet on pool with Billy. They went to the table farthest from the door, and the young guy paid for a game and racked the balls. I remained where I was. No sense putting Billy in a bad mood by interrupting his plucking of the young rooster.

They played three games, and Billy's nasal laugh got louder each time he made a shot. After losing the first two games, he appeared to get frustrated. He offered double or nothing on the third game, and the kid went for it. The kid broke, got nothing, and yielded to Billy who shot, shot, and shot again. It was only minutes until the eight-ball sank into a corner pocket and rolled its way to the bottom to join the others. The opponent stood watching, his disgusted expression revealing he knew he'd been had. Accepting the wadded twenty he shoved at him, Billy said, "Good game," with a smirk that indicated the complete opposite. The kid left the bar, his strut gone.

I picked up my drink and walked over to where Billy stood, chalking his cue to be ready for the next opponent. This corner of the bar was even darker than the rest. The traditional Tiffany-style lamp over the table lit the green felt brightly, but its upper surface was so dust-covered that those standing around were thrown into shadow.

"Hey, Billy." He turned, squinting to see who'd spoken.

Not the type women dream of, Billy had a homely face, an angry expression, and a physique no one would call manly. He got even uglier as he poked his head toward me, stretching the chords in his neck. "Do I know you?"

"Loser."

Anger turned to surprise, and he pasted on a smile as fake as a face-lift. "Hey, girl! Long time no see!"

I ignored his lousy acting. "Where's Aisha?"

He put a hand to his chest in a dramatic gesture. "I'd like to know that myself, Loser." Looking at the floor, he said sadly, "I hope nothin' bad happened to her."

"Where was she sleeping?"

He shrugged elaborately. "Far's I know, the same old places." One eyebrow quirked. "They said you wrote a book and made a lot of money."

I shook my head. "No book."

He thought about that. "You should write one." Pantomiming a banner over our heads, he quoted, "*Homeless Hero Saves Little Girl's Daddy from Murder Charge*. People love crap like that."

I gave him a level gaze. "Aisha?"

Billy set the pool cue into a rack on the wall, but I thought he was avoiding my eye. "She just left, that's all."

"Was she acting different?"

His bottom lip pushed out as he mimicked deep thought. "Nope. We hooked up maybe eight, ten days ago. She was fine." He sniffed, wiped his nose with a knuckle, and added, "I mean, fine for Aisha. Girl's a little off, but she's something when she gets going, y'know?"

I didn't, and I didn't want to. Aisha often spoke of free love, and Billy was proof she wasn't discerning in her choices. "Any strangers talking with her lately?"

"Don't think so." His eyes narrowed. "Speaking of talking, you didn't used to talk much. You on something?"

"No." He was fishing to see if I had any interesting medication, and I had no doubt he'd try to take it from me if I did. I repeated my question. "Strangers?"

"There was a reporter came around wantin' to write a story about you. Aisha talked to him a couple times." Billy's expression turned sly. "She thought it was funny to tell him shit, y'know? Shine him on a little."

"She and I are best friends?"

He chuckled. "Yeah, like that. Guy gave her twenty bucks."

"Anyone else?"

He shrugged.

"Things were okay between you and her?"

Something flashed in Billy's eyes. It wasn't guilt, because he had no capacity for that, but he was aware of something he wasn't going to share with me. Aisha had appeared with a shiner once that Howard attributed to Billy, and I'd sometimes noticed bruises on her arms that looked like they were made by fingers.

"I just want to talk to her, Billy. If you know where she is—"

He banished responsibility with a wave. "I ain't her daddy."

I thought of what might have happened to Aisha, from a beating to death. For most of them, Billy was the most likely suspect. Reminding myself that likely hadn't meant guilty in my case, I said, "Okay."

He looked me up and down once. "I could use a loan, Loser. There's this guy I owe money to, and—"

I turned away before he finished, set my half-full glass on the bar, and left. I heard Billy muttering at my back, and the word I picked out was "Bitch!"

The public library has long been one of my favorite places, sometimes for research, other times for a place to stay warm or out of the rain. When I left Billy, I headed to Franklin Street to look for the article Aisha had contributed to. It was comforting to climb the wide steps and pass between the huge square columns. Coming here as Loser had made me feel that I was still minimally connected to the world. I'd read, surfed, and even stayed in contact with Bert through the library's impersonal benevolence. As long as I behaved myself, the place offered peace, quiet, and answers.

It wasn't difficult to find the article titled, "What Happened to the Homeless Hero?" It was published in a third-rate e-zine called *Richmond's Hottest News* whose subhead claimed it portrayed "Life in the South's Greatest Jewel." Apparently, life in Richmond revolved around miraculous recoveries from catastrophic illness, military heroes whose wives cheated while they were overseas, and dogs who saved small children from drowning. The issue was over a month old, and the piece began with my lurid past.

> Suspected of murder, Richmond police officer Beth Lousiere became one of the city's saddest cases. Sometime during the night of September 12th, 2010, Mrs. Lousiere's husband and four-month-old daughter were murdered. Though Beth insisted her husband's lover was to blame, police suspected her from the start. Placed on leave by the department, her depression—or perhaps guilt—pulled her into madness. She took to the streets, joining the lost of Richmond as the anonymous Loser.

That much was true. In the span of a few days I'd lost everything. A stronger woman might have held it together. I had not.

The article continued with the "redeeming" part of my story, the fact that I'd helped to rescue a little girl named Bryn from her murderous aunt. The reporter offered his opinion that Bryn reminded me of the child I'd lost, but he also hinted I might have been trying to atone for suffocating my own baby.

After rehashing what had already been published in a dozen places, the reporter turned to Aisha's fabrications. According to her, she'd found me almost dead on the banks of the James River. Knowing I had "something good deep inside," she'd refused to let me "die on the streets like a dog everybody kicked around." My long trek back to sanity had begun with the help of my dear friend, who'd reminded me, "Each life is worth something. The world needs everybody."

With typical artistic license, Aisha had put herself into the role someone else had played. It was Mabel who'd supported me, and she'd done it without stooping to meaningless platitudes. Aisha's role had been more devil's advocate, with emphasis on the word *devil*. Entirely selfish, she stole from all of us when she could get away with it and lied when it served her purposes. I'd been her victim at times, but no more than anyone else.

At the close of the article, Aisha claimed we were still good friends. In fact, I'd offered her a home in the mansion I now occupied. She didn't mention the place—How could she when she didn't know it?—but claimed she was too free spirited to be confined to mundane life, no matter how luxurious. "I have to be free of society's rules and stuff. If everybody owned just what they can carry, we'd all be happy."

I sat back in the hard library chair, staring at the screen as the words blurred. Though false and downright dumb, the article had brought my name back to public attention. Soon after it appeared, Aisha had gone missing. She might be in a dozen places, but she'd never stayed away this long. Had her moment of fame brought someone looking for her, someone who might hurt her in order to hurt me?

CHAPTER FIVE

I'd texted Jacob to let him know I was in town, and his reply appeared when I turned the phone on as I left the library. *Meet me at Cleo's at 5:15. I'll buy you dinner.* Cleo's, a restaurant we both liked on the west edge of Carytown, was busy enough that no one would pay much attention to us, and far enough away from the Fan and the First Precinct that neither Jacob nor I would be recognized.

I spent the afternoon visiting places Aisha had frequented, posing as a relative worried by her disappearance. I went to the second-hand store where she often consigned things she "found." I visited the soup kitchen. I went to the little restaurant where she sometimes cleaned the floors and probably cleared out the pantry as well. Each time I got the same response. She'd seemed okay. No one had noticed she was missing for a few days, since Aisha wasn't what anyone would call predictable. That was all.

When I stopped at a storefront mission a few blocks off Main Street, I learned who'd made the missing person report. *Get Up!* the sign out front proclaimed, and I gathered from a brief study of the posters in the window that the purpose of the place was to help the disadvantaged move toward a better life. I went inside, thinking the problem was in the definition of "better."

The person in charge, a striking, whip-thin woman with beautiful eyes and lots of dark hair, told me she'd called the police when Aisha missed an appointment. "We were working to get her medical benefits back," she told me. "She'd failed to fill out renewal papers, and her case got dropped. I told her I'd help her get it straightened out if she came in that Tuesday."

"And you called the police when she didn't show up?"

My tone signaled doubt, and the woman explained, "Aisha was diagnosed with cervical cancer a month ago. She's going to need treatment."

That was certainly serious, but Aisha had trouble with the concept of doing something today to prevent bad things from happening tomorrow. Reading my thought, the woman opened a desk drawer and took out a necklace of green and gold beads. "She admired this when we first met. I promised I'd give it to her if she came in and did her paperwork." That was more telling. Aisha was a lot like a magpie, so a shiny incentive was a good idea.

I glanced at the nameplate on the desk, interested for the first time in the woman herself. *Jonanna Booker*, it said. Ms. Booker was apparently wiser than some who came down here to save the homeless. Well-meaning types promised future happiness, better health, and heavenly bliss, but they often had no clue what it was like to be hungry, cold, or lost in your own head. Intangible rewards meant little. A decent meal, a calming pill, or a pretty necklace was more likely to spark interest.

I wondered if Billy knew Aisha was sick. "Did she mention a boyfriend, or anyone she was seeing?"

Booker chuckled. "If I were new to this business, I'd have thought I stumbled on an angel. A virgin angel."

I had to grin. "Snow white and earnest, right?"

"Exactly. According to Aisha, she's on the streets due to a series of terrible events, a perfect storm that left her dazed and confused." Booker waved a hand. "Now she's ready to rejoin society and become a contributing citizen."

"With a small loan to get her started?" I guessed.

"That was it. I convinced her we needed to get her straightened around medically before we could tackle other issues." She sighed. "At least I thought I'd convinced her. The fact that she didn't return means I was wrong."

"Hey, you tried."

She smiled grimly. "Yeah, I keep trying. It's just hard, you know? There's never enough money to do anything decisive, so we put Band-Aids on deep, open wounds."

I ended up taking a short tour of the facility with Ms. Booker as my guide. The place had been here when I was Loser, but it had been purely religious, with watery orange juice and granola bars served with healthy doses of Hell to scare sinners away from sin. Under Jonanna's still-new guidance, the facility's focus had turned toward short-term jobs. "Our clients need to take small steps in order to gain the confidence to tackle larger ones," she told me. "We offer assistance with finding mentors, living quarters, meals, and decent clothing. It's been tough in this economy, and a lot of our funding has disappeared, but if somebody wants to get his life back together, we try to help."

"What would you do if you had more money?"

"Buy up old motels," she said quickly, revealing she'd thought about it a lot. "Fix them up and let people live in them, semi-independently. There'd be a manager in each one who'd monitor the clients, providing them with individualized support. If a man needs a job, we'd help him find one and get him ready for the interview. If a woman needs childcare so she can work, we'd find reliable caregivers. I'd hire problem solvers instead of bureaucrats, and I'd use students from the universities as assistants."

I was favorably impressed. Having seen the changes stability had made in Mabel, I figured there'd be modest success in her program. Despite the fact she'd never been homeless, Jonanna had a good grasp of the problem. I left admiring her enthusiasm and her empathy, but I had no idea where Aisha might be.

When Jacob entered the restaurant, I was already seated at a table in the corner. He squinted into the relative darkness, trying to locate me, and I waved discreetly to get his attention. As he shifted his way through the crowded tables, sending a smile ahead of him, I took stock. The brain tumor that had shattered Jacob's life was gone, at least as far as medical science could discern. He'd been declared tumor-free, and the moderate paralysis that had resulted was less noticeable than the last time I'd seen him.

When he got to me, Jake spread his arms, and without hesitation, I rose and stepped into his embrace. My former partner was one of the few people on earth I was comfortable hugging. Twelve years older than I, eight inches taller, and light years more confident, Jacob was a mentor and a friend. Richmond born and raised, he had two loving parents, still living and lively; three children; four brothers and two sisters, none of whom had moved farther than forty miles from home; and an assortment of nieces and nephews I'd never been able to keep track of.

At twenty Jake had married Sasha, and the love they'd shared for more than two decades was the type everyone dreams of but few achieve. Sasha accepted the cop's wife role without dramatics, and Jacob tried every day to live up to the image of him she carried in her heart. They knew how the promise of marriage is kept, though I doubted they ever discussed it.

"You look good, Beth," Jacob said, pulling the chair opposite me out with a scrape and plopping into it with a sigh.

"You too. Sasha and the girls?"

"Good. They're at her mom's this weekend, making centerpieces for Lydia's bridal shower. I was on my own, so I'm glad you called."

He caught me up on milestones, from his oldest daughter's upcoming wedding to Sasha's sudden interest in couponing. "I think she's a little scared of the empty nest," he told me. "She does a little web site design from home, but her life has been focused on the girls for twenty years. She's not sure who she wants to be now that they're grown up." He set his elbows on the table. "She's great with kids. I've been telling her she should volunteer somewhere, but she's still thinking about it."

As I listened, it almost felt like the old days, before life smacked us both upside the head with a reminder there's never as much time as we expect.

After he'd made me laugh a few times Jacob asked, "So how are things in West Virginia?"

"Good." I felt a pang of homesickness, wondering what I was doing here when peace was there. But it wasn't, I reminded myself. I couldn't pretend I didn't know about two missing women and what that meant for me.

Jacob reached into his pocket, brought out several sheets of paper, and slid them across to me. "That's what we know."

I took the pages and skimmed the information. Aisha rated a single page. She'd been reported missing on May 19th by J. Booker. Police had asked questions around the Fan and in her usual haunts—nothing. I learned that Aisha's real name was Barbara Cotter, and she'd been on the streets since being emancipated by the foster care system at seventeen. There were arrests for shoplifting, unlawful entry, and disturbing the peace. Each time she'd avoided jail by promising to change her ways. I paused, wondering if I'd been too tough on Aisha. Without Marta, I might have ended up like her, making my way by any means possible.

The prostitute, Carole Ann Minier, had been reported missing on May 20th by her landlord. Unanswered calls about the rent she owed had brought him to her place, where he'd found her mailbox overflowing and her cat screaming on the other side of the door. He'd opened the apartment and found everything in place except for a Lean Cuisine meal left sitting in the microwave. It had been heated but not eaten, probably three or four days earlier.

A waitress dressed in leggings and an oversize t-shirt that said *Cleo's: There's an App for That* stopped at our table with menus. Neither of us needed one, so she memorized our orders and went off to see to them. Jacob sipped the water she'd brought as I looked at the file.

The police had asked around. No one admitted knowing where Carole Ann might have gone, and she hadn't mentioned plans to leave town. She hadn't seemed nervous or scared. A search of her apartment turned up nothing unusual except the card from Darrin, which of course led nowhere, since he'd been dead almost three years. The abandoned meal was troublesome, but wherever she'd gone, Carole Ann had taken her purse. The investigator's note suggested she might have remembered an appointment at the last minute.

"An appointment she never came back from?" I asked,

looking up at Jacob.

He was staring at me, and he hadn't expected me to catch him. I guessed he'd been wondering how much Beth he was facing and how much Loser. "I'm doing better," I said.

"I can see that." He leaned closer. "I'm glad, Beth. Really glad." After a pause he said, "I felt like—I don't know. Like I let you down somehow."

"Geez, Jacob, you were in a medically-induced coma. Not much you could have done."

"I should have looked for you. When I got better."

"And that was how many months later?"

He smiled vaguely. "Well, I did have to learn how to walk and chew and swallow again, but—"

I licked my lips. "I feel like I abandoned you. You wish you'd contacted me. Let's move on."

Jacob dropped the subject, gesturing toward the report I held in both hands. "The guys think Carole Ann got an opportunity she couldn't resist." He shrugged. "You know, a guy calls, says, 'I've got two tickets to Paradise,' yada, yada."

"Which might not have been Paradise."

He nodded. "They checked the whole state for a Jane Doe corpse that might be her. Nothing."

I turned to the next sheet, which listed Carole Ann's arrests. Busted three times for soliciting, she'd never served time. There was a photo, and despite the general dreariness of mug shots, I could tell she was pretty, even after years of drugs and hooking. A pretty face couldn't cover the blankness in her eyes, however. *Not the sharpest knife in the drawer,* Marta would have said.

Carole Ann was a Richmond native who'd had a few short,

unsuccessful stints with respectable jobs but ended up making her living in the sex trade. A pimp named D'Nard Dobermeyer, a.k.a. D'Nard Doom, had won her heart, or whatever women like her give to a pimp, and in return for D'Nard's protection, Carole Ann got a life sentence on the streets, promising nameless men the night of their dreams for a fee.

As I scanned the second sheet, something caught my eye. Carole Ann's first arrest, which had resulted in brief detention and release, was signed by Officer Maureen Daley. I pointed out the name to Jacob. "I know her. She's the reason I was out the night Darrin was killed."

"Tell me," Jacob ordered. "If you recall, I was busy getting my brain reamed out."

I took a deep breath. While I was capable of explaining, long speeches still made my tongue heavy and my lungs tight, especially when the topic was emotional. However, Jacob's interest was neither idle nor ghoulish. He cared. Letting the air out, I began, "Maureen and I went through the academy together. She asked me to help her prove that some of the cops at the Second were crooked."

Jacob's brow furrowed at the idea of crooked cops, but we both knew such things were possible. "Why'd she think that?"

"She said they always sent her somewhere right after a bust, like they were getting her out of the way."

"So they could skim drugs or money."

I nodded. "There was a bust planned for that night. She asked me to hide at the warehouse and take pictures."

"And what did you see?"

I shrugged. "It never happened. I stayed till after four, and when I got home, I found—"

Jacob stepped in to prevent my having to say it. "Did you tell the detectives where you were?"

"I called Maureen and told her I needed to, but she said she'd deny everything. She was terrified of these guys."

"That's crap. If she was your friend—"

"It wouldn't have helped, because I couldn't prove I went there. She'd have destroyed her credibility with her guys, and I'd still have been Suspect #1."

At the time, Maureen's refusal to provide me with an alibi had been one more blow to my fragile mental state, one betrayal in a host of others I faced. I recalled her comment. "People don't get arrested for things they didn't do, Beth."

I hadn't been arrested, but it was because Bert Suggs had turned from wills and trusts to save me from criminal prosecution. Bert had kept me out of jail. It wasn't his fault I'd fallen apart afterward.

Jacob had turned pensive. "Maybe Maureen would be willing to clear things up with the RPD now."

I spread my hands, palms up. "I haven't spoken to her in years. And like I said—"

Jacob held up a finger to stop me. "They've got Darrin connected to this Carole Ann. If Daley places you on the South Side, they'll have to take a fresh look at the case. Let's at least see if we can find her." Reaching for his phone, Jacob made a call. "Connie, I need some info on one of Richmond's finest."

While he was on the phone, I considered what I knew of Maureen Daley. We'd met during training and stuck together, being the only two women in the class. What I remembered most was how she'd stood up for herself against the men who enjoyed harassing the female candidates. A few times she'd stepped up to protect me too, though I'd never asked her to. A guy named Manville, no giant himself, had claimed I was too small to be an effective cop. He'd made life miserable when he could, but what woman hasn't dealt with jerks like that? I'd have ignored it, but Maureen didn't do things that way. Manville got a faceful of trouble from her, and he backed off.

Though she liked me, Maureen and I never became particularly close. I had Darrin, and the house in the Fan took up a lot of our time. I wasn't looking for a BFF. The few times she asked me to go for drinks or meet for lunch, I'd declined. If Maureen was offended, she never said so.

Jacob hung up, reporting, "Either she isn't a cop anymore or she's gotten married and changed her name. The records are supposed to be updated, but you never know. Connie's going to check."

The waitress brought our meals: a Cobb salad for me and a messy-looking pulled pork sandwich for Jacob that no doctor would approve. By tacit consent we spoke of inconsequential things as we ate. Jacob asked a lot of questions about the house in West Virginia, the town of Beulah, and my adventures with Mabel and Eddie. My terse descriptions didn't do the past year justice, but I did what I could, ending with, "You should visit."

"Sasha would like that. She says mountains are God's best work."

When the check arrived, I succeeded in snatching it from Jacob's outstretched hand. Putting a couple of bills inside the fake-leather presenter, I handed it right back to the waitress, who recognized we weren't dessert types and removed herself.

"What are you going to do?" Jacob asked. We were back to my reason for coming to Richmond.

Since I didn't know, I couldn't share, even if I'd been the sharing type. "Nothing that will make trouble for you."

He gave me an eye-roll. "You wouldn't. I know that."

I picked up the salt shaker he'd used to make his fries even less healthy and turned it in circles on the table. "Loser might find out things the cops didn't."

Jacob's expression turned wary. "Loser? Beth—"

"It's not me anymore." As I said it, I hoped I was telling the truth.

We both knew a little about undercover investigation, though neither of us had ever done it. It was hard to miss the cops who showed up at work only rarely, looking skuzzy and haunted. Working undercover meant looking at life from a different viewpoint. Some criminals are scary; others are forgivable, pitiable, and even likeable. Like those cops, I'd seen the other side of life, but as one of the lost, I'd been unable to step away.

Jacob leaned forward, resting his forearms on the table. "I can keep you in the loop."

"Will that make trouble for you?"

He shrugged. "Why shouldn't I be interested in my old partner's case?" He chuckled. "Billings is the boss these days, and he's busy counting paper clips and sending out daily three-page memos reminding us not to waste paper." He related a story of mild incompetence and dumb mistakes, the sort of things cops tell other cops, things not to be aired in public but too funny not to share.

Chuckling at Jacob's parody of the pompous Billings, I felt a twinge of nostalgia. We'd been well suited as partners. In our clunky old Ford with A/C that worked sporadically at best, we'd talked about anything and everything, disagreeing sometimes but never on anything that mattered.

The only niggle of irritation Jacob had ever caused me was his avoidance of Darrin. If I mentioned my husband's name, Jacob's gaze slid away. When I told stories about home, he listened without comment and then changed the subject. And on occasions when I asked him and Sasha to go out with us or come over, they'd always had a prior engagement.

Putting the salt shaker back in its little basket I said, "You never liked Darrin, did you?"

He looked uncomfortable. "It wasn't dislike. He just wasn't—" He fished for the right words, couldn't find them, and gave up. "Sasha wants you to come to dinner tomorrow."

Rising to go, I gave him a smile and the answer he probably expected. "Maybe later."

Standing off to one side of Bert's office, Alex watched as his partner explained to Caitlin Berger that her divorce would be uncontested.

"Really? He just agreed to everything?"

"Mr. Berger called yesterday and explained that an opportunity has opened up for him in Montana," Bert said. Earlier, he'd confessed to Alex that the call surprised him. "The man has a bad reputation, but he was cooperative, even polite."

"Interesting," Alex commented. "You can never tell about some guys."

Now, watching their client's shoulders relax a little, Alex smiled to himself. Caitlin had begun to let herself believe.

"Mr. Berger will send child support monthly," Bert told her.

Fat chance, Alex thought, but she didn't seem concerned.

"As soon as my arm is better, I'm going back to where I worked before," she told them. "My mom will watch the kids. It's just that we were worried before that he'd—" She stopped, embarrassed. "That he'd do something mean."

Bert glanced at Alex. "He seemed sincere, ma'am."

As Bert and Caitlin concluded their business, Alex excused himself. He'd only wanted to see her face when she got the news, and it had been worth it. Caitlin would never know why her sadistic husband caved so easily, but it was enough that he had. His first venture as a white knight had been successful.

Second venture, he corrected himself. The idea had taken root a year ago, when he'd learned that Beth Lousiere was in trouble and gone to find her. On a hilltop in West Virginia, they'd succeeded in stopping a murderer and his thugs, and Alex found he had a taste for it. His law degree sometimes helped him right the injustices of the world by taking the bad guys to court or threatening to, but there were times when the law wasn't very effective.

For every action, he thought, *there is, or there should be, an equal and opposite reaction.*

In West Virginia, Alex had used both mental and physical skills to oppose evil. Ever since, he'd missed the thrill of combining the two. The law required mental acuity, and he had a little of that. But at times life called for something else. Some evils responded best to a little physical education.

CHAPTER SIX

After a quick text to Eddie and a fairly restful night in William Byrd Park, I took the Powhite Parkway, heading to where Maureen Daley lived when I'd known her. Once when something had happened to her car, she'd called and I'd driven out to pick her up. I didn't recall the house number but thought I remembered the way.

Like many old cities, Richmond is a puzzle to newcomers, a maze of highways, neighborhoods, and bridges. In theory it has quadrants: north, south, east, and west, but in practice, they were fuzzy around the edges. The James River made the north and south part easy, but the West, North, and East sections were all north of the river, which took a steep turn south at the city's center.

I'd lived and worked on the north side of the river, and over time I'd learned terms the locals might use—Carver might be referred to as Sheep Hill, for example. The East End, where Jacob and I had been assigned, included more than a dozen neighborhoods such as Church Hill, Chimborazo, and Oakwood, with non-city areas from eastern Henrico or Hanover Counties often included. The fact that the boundaries of Richmond's four police precincts bore little resemblance to the city's quadrants had made it tough for a newbie cop from the sticks to get oriented.

The South Side was least familiar to me, and that was where Maureen had been assigned as a patrol officer. A century ago, Manchester had been a city of its own, and some contended it still should be. Other South Side communities with evocative names like Westover Hills, Forest Hills, and

Woodland Heights spread west from Manchester, each with its own character and historical significance.

I passed them all, heading to an area that had run down during the '90s but was experiencing a rebirth as people looked to save on gasoline. Old and new mixed. Many of the homes had modern siding, fresh landscaping, and obvious add-ons while others were in dire need of all of those things.

Maureen's house looked the same, but the one next to it, a nice little two-story, practically glowed with a new, cheerful aspect. The place belonged to her landlords, who'd bought two properties, one to live in and one to flip. It looked like they'd finished their own place, and as I turned into the shared driveway, I saw that the door of Maureen's house had been removed and the frame replaced. On the porch, building materials waited: lumber, a step ladder, and piles covered by tarps. Apparently it was time for the rental to be upgraded.

When I stepped onto the porch, I could tell the house was empty. Maureen must have moved somewhere nicer. I turned to the house across the driveway. The landlords might know how I could find her.

The pretty woman who answered the door was pregnant, maybe seven or eight months along. "I'm sorry," she informed me in a pronounced drawl. "Maureen moved out last year."

"Do you know where she's living now?"

She laid one hand on her belly. "Are you a friend of hers?"

"We went to the police academy together."

Her face lit with pleasure. "You must be Beth!" When I nodded, too surprised to answer, she gestured an invitation. "Please, come in! I'm Helen Franklin. It's so nice to finally meet you."

I followed her inside to a large, open living area and a bright, modern kitchen with a marble-topped island in its center. In one corner of the living room, a toddler slept on a blanket on the floor. His blond curls were stuck to his forehead with sweat, and his soft lips gaped slightly as he breathed in and out.

I looked away. *Think about something else.*

"You have a beautiful home."

She smiled at the compliment. "Thanks. You should have seen it when we moved in. All chopped up into little, dark rooms with crummy wallpaper and dingy carpeting, you know? We opened it up, laid down wood floors, took out the yucky velvet drapes—" She waved a hand. "Making it ours, you know?"

"Yes." I swallowed a lump that formed in my throat. Newly married, Darrin and I had bought the house in the Fan and begun renovating it. Sanding, painting, sweeping up. Working together. I remembered Darrin laughing at a spot of paint I'd smeared on my chin. *You match the dining room,* he'd told me. I'd thought we were blissfully happy. That hadn't turned out well.

Helen was focused on her story. "—this house and the one next door from an old couple who wanted to move into senior living. They gave us a really good price." Stopping in front of a rocker that had a knitting basket beside it, she pointed me toward the couch. "Now we've got this one livable, we're starting on the other place. I won't be able to help as much with this, but I'll do what I can. Ken does all the heavy work, but I can be the gopher, with a papoose on my back."

That too I remembered. "Great."

"Before I sit down, would you all like some iced tea?" Swiping the back of a hand across her cheek, she added, "I'll turn on the air. Ken doesn't think it's necessary until afternoon, but he isn't carrying twenty extra pounds around."

"Please."

Helen turned a knob on the wall and walked behind the bar to fill glasses with ice. As cool air began to battle the stuffiness, she moved about the kitchen. Other than her big belly, she was trim, medium height, with jet black hair and large green eyes. She seemed perfectly calm, which I thought was odd. If she knew who I was, she must know what I'd been accused of.

Maybe Maureen had convinced her I wasn't a murdering maniac. I noticed touches of religion in the room, a picture of Jesus with children, a wooden sign that said *Pray Without Ceasing*, and a shelf of books that all seemed to have *God* in their titles. Maybe her faith required her to assume a person was good until she demonstrated otherwise.

Helen raised her voice over the clinking sounds she was making. "Sugar?"

I shook my head. A benefit to being Loser was I'd lost my taste for added sugar. Helen added two spoonsful to her own glass and stirred. "I'm surprised you found us way out here." The spoon clanked as it dropped into the sink.

"I picked Maureen up once."

"Of course. She said you two did stuff together all the time. I just never saw you before."

"Actually, we didn't spend a lot of time together."

"Really?" Her face twisted. "I thought you and her were good friends. She talked about you a lot."

I shrugged. "We lost track of each other after my husband

was killed."

Her eyes got even larger. "That was horrible. I was glad for you when they cleared it up."

From that I surmised that Helen, like many good citizens, assumed that if I'd been guilty, I'd have been arrested, tried, and sentenced. Since I hadn't, I must be innocent. Leaning over clumsily to hand me the tea, she said, "God's hard to understand sometimes, but I know He sent angels to comfort you in your sorrow."

If you count Mabel and Penrod as angels. "When did Maureen move out?"

"Let's see." Setting her tea down and easing into the rocker, she rubbed her chin with her fingers. "Last June, somewhere near the middle of the month. It was kind of a surprise, because she was paid up until July 1st."

That was just after the stories about the Homeless Hero appeared in the news.

Helen glanced out the window at the homely house across the drive. "She probably found a better place. We told her before she ever came to Virginia that this house needed work, but she said she didn't care." After a sip of tea she added, "You never could talk Maureen out of anything."

I must have looked confused, because Helen smiled. "She never told you? We grew up next door to each other in a speck of a town in South Carolina." She lifted her mane of hair, which must have felt like a wool scarf on a day like today, and held it off her neck with one arm. "I'm a couple of years older, but we knew each other our whole lives."

I didn't recall Maureen mentioning her background. "I came from a small town too. Great way to grow up."

A tiny frown line appeared between her eyes. "It wasn't so great for Maureen. They had this little house, and there were kids everywhere." Touching her stomach, she said, "I want a lot of kids, but I would never make the older ones into miniature babysitters."

"Like Maureen was?"

She grimaced. "Her momma was always too tired to do anything, and her daddy was never there. When Linda told him she was pregnant for the ninth time, he left and didn't come back. I guess that's why Maureen's always taking care of people. She's just used to being a little momma."

A lifetime of responsibility did help to explain Maureen's efforts to protect me from Manville's harassment at the academy.

"How'd she come to Richmond?"

Helen turned her glass, sending rivulets of moisture down the side. "I guess I had something to do with that." She leaned against the chair back and shifted her legs. If she didn't have company would she put her feet up on the coffee table? The heat and the extra weight were no doubt making them swell. Mine had.

Helen was talking, but the words had turned to a hum in the background of my thoughts. I forced myself to listen. "—moved here after high school, intending to become a lawyer and show the world what a woman can do. After about six months, I met Ken, and all thoughts of higher education left my head." She nodded toward a photograph on the end table beside me. It was a photo of her in a dress like a birthday cake, standing at the front of a church next to a stern-looking, handsome man in a tux. She gave a self-deprecating grin. "Now I'm happy to be plain old Mrs. Ken Franklin."

"Yeah," I murmured. I remembered finding happiness, finding Mr. Right. It hadn't been real, but maybe Helen had had better luck. "So Maureen came here because of your friendship?"

Something came and went in Helen's eyes, but it was quick and I couldn't read it. "She called me right after she graduated high school. My mom mentioned to her mom we had a second house, and she asked if she could rent it." A frown creased her forehead again. "We had Delia by then—she's at her granny's right now—and I was pregnant with Gilbert. I couldn't work, and the economy had started going bad. We figured her call was God's way of helping us out. Like I said, she didn't care how junky it was. I think she just wanted to be somewhere besides Meyer Corners."

"So she moved here and entered the police academy."

Helen nodded. "Maureen said a woman can move up fast on the police force if she's tough and smart." Her expression turned sad. "It was quite a blow when she lost that job."

"Maureen isn't a cop anymore?"

"No. I guess there were some layoffs. This economy is just awful, isn't it? Things will never be right until this country wakes up and turns back to the right path."

I interrupted to forestall a political or religious rant, possibly both. "So what's she doing for a living?"

"I don't know." Helen set her tea on the table beside her. "It's just too bad. She always wanted to be somebody, you know? She thought becoming a police officer was going to be her ticket to success."

That was why Jacob hadn't found Maureen in the department records. She was no longer a cop, at least not in the city. I hoped he'd be able to find out more before we met again.

"Would she have gone back to South Carolina?"

Helen shook her head emphatically. "She'd never do that. She said she had a better chance of finding a new job if she lived closer to downtown." Helen pointed a finger at me. "I think she was going to look for you too. She kept wondering where you'd gone and how you were dealing with—" She stopped, unsure how to describe my life as Loser. "I'm sure she wanted to help you if she could."

"Do you know where I can find her?"

"She said she'd send an address, but she never did. I have a phone number, but she doesn't return my calls." She plucked at the hem of her top. "I just hope she isn't mad at us."

"Why would she be?"

She fluttered a little. "Ken says I'm silly to worry, but I felt like she was disappointed in us. She came to Richmond thinking I was headed for law school, and here I am just a dumb old housewife. And then Ken—well, he can be direct sometimes, and people don't know how to take him." Smoothing her skirt with both hands, she added, "He didn't grow up with Maureen, and he thought she was pushy." With a weak smile she concluded, "Ken isn't shy about expressing his opinions, you know?"

I rose to go. "Thanks for seeing me. Good luck with the renovations and the new baby."

We walked to the door together. "The rental house has taken longer than we expected. After Maureen moved out, someone broke in and trashed it." She glanced out the window. "We were at church, and somebody broke all the glass, knocked holes in the walls, and I don't know what all. It was so bad Ken wouldn't even let me see it."

"Did you call the police?"

She shook her head. "He said it was kids. We don't have insurance on it, so he went right at it and fixed it himself. Still, it set us back."

"Thanks for the tea."

"It was really nice to meet you," Helen said, resting both hands on the convenient shelf at her front. "Maureen was always bragging on you. 'Beth did this' and 'Beth can do that.' She was real upset when those awful things happened and you disappeared, but I knew the Lord would make it all work out right."

Yeah, I thought as I headed for my car. *I was upset too.*

Once I was away from the Franklin house, I pulled off the road and texted Jacob to let him know Maureen was neither with RPD nor at her old address. It would be a while before he could answer, so I returned to the reports he'd given me, looking for a different path to investigate.

Carole Ann Minier had a cocaine problem she'd never conquered, apparently because she didn't want to. A staffer at a halfway house quoted her saying, "It makes me feel good and helps me get shit done, so what's the problem?"

I tried to picture my husband with a woman like that. It was hard, maybe because I didn't want to, but also because Darrin had been pretty much a law-abiding citizen type. How had he met a prostitute from Bellemeade? What had he seen in a woman who saw no harm in abusing drugs? A sex partner who sold her body to other men? It was the opposite of everything I knew of Darrin, everything I'd been as his wife.

Maybe that was what he'd wanted: the opposite of me.

The report listed Carole Ann's address, an apartment building in a South Side neighborhood that had a bad reputation. Police questions had turned up nothing, but I thought someone inconspicuous might learn more. Not middle-class Beth, who had no excuse for being there. Someone like Loser, who hardly amounted to a blip on the radar.

Jacob texted that he couldn't find Maureen's current address. *Wll kp lkg,* he promised. While Jacob did his thing, I decided to learn more about Carole Ann.

Leaving my car in a shady spot, I started for Bellemeade, which meant a succession of buses. At a transfer along the way, I visited a musty, overstuffed secondhand shop along the James River and chose clothes that would mark me as a nobody. The outfit smelled a little too clean, but the pants were suitably faded and spotted with grease stains. Despite the warmth of the day, I layered several shirts and pulled a shapeless knitted hat over my hair. On a rack along the wall I found a pair of suitably-worn shoes, and from a bin of underwear I dug out a pair of grayish socks to put over my own to help keep the shoes on. From some knapsacks hanging on a nail I selected the worst one, sun-faded and heavily pilled, and took my purchases to the counter. Once I'd paid, I went into the dressing room, put on the things I'd bought, and stuffed my own clothes into the knapsack. It was as close to Loser as I could get without giving up showers for a month. I can't describe the look on the clerk's face when I emerged, but it was priceless.

Travel seemed to take forever, and as I waited at the bus stop, I realized I missed having direct access from Point A to Point B. *How soon we forget,* I chided myself. Motorized transport had been a luxury for Loser, who'd often walked half a day to get somewhere she needed to be. First fruits of re-joining society: impatience.

Stepping off the bus I'd found more noxious and noisy than I remembered, I stopped for a moment, taking in the ambiance of Bellemeade. I paid particular attention to the idlers, knowing I'd be spotted as a stranger. Street people had turf, not in the sense gang members do, but they paid attention. As I walked I felt eyes watching, but when I turned, they looked somewhere else.

On the way south I'd thought about how to get information from the locals. I'd decided on free food. Almost everyone likes getting a gift, and if a person has to answer a few questions to get it, it's not much to ask. At the second bus transfer I'd stopped at a McDonald's and bought a handful of ten-dollar gift cards. I should have done it before changing clothes, because the McClerk checked my fifty-dollar bill twice with her magic pen.

The second time around a three-block area, I located Carole Ann Minier's address. The building, renovated within the last decade, was rapidly sliding back into decay. Rents were low, nuisance levels high, and the inhabitants were used to violence on their doorsteps and drugs everywhere.

Entering the building where a faded sign said *Homeland Apartments*, I searched out *14A*. My footsteps were quieted by a carpet that felt lumpy underfoot and didn't smell so good. I couldn't imagine Darrin setting foot in such a place. Though he hadn't minded what he called "old dirt," the stuff we found as we renovated our home on Grace Street, he'd often railed against "lazy dirt," the kind that wouldn't exist if people cleaned their bodies and property from time to time.

Where had he and Carole Ann met for their trysts, if not

here? An image of Darrin ushering his sleazy girlfriend into my home hit me in the gut like a flying brick. Had he taken her up to our bedroom? To our bed? On the night he died, had Darrin made love to her there, punishing me for leaving when he asked me not to? When he went downstairs to shower afterward, had she followed and stabbed him, over and over? I didn't have to imagine how he'd looked when it was done.

He'd asked me to give him another chance, asked me to stay home that night, but I'd refused, unwilling to grant him any concession. If I'd done as he asked, the whole thing might never have happened. Maybe I deserved to be Loser. I'd certainly been a loser as wife and mother.

Leaving Carole Ann's building, I stood on the sidewalk for a few minutes, trying to decide what to do next. On a porch across the street, an old man sat in a beat-up wicker chair, watching the traffic and smoking a cigarette. His hair was kinky and white, a stark contrast to his ebony skin. Next to him was another chair, just as ratty but straight-backed, probably the last survivor of a dining set. After waiting for a panel truck to pass, I headed in his direction. He took note of my approach but gave no sign of it until I spoke from the sidewalk. "Afternoon."

He glanced at me, never meeting my eyes, and nodded a silent greeting.

"Mind if I sit?"

His brow furrowed slightly, but after a drag on the cigarette, he nodded again. I stepped onto the porch and took a seat. We looked outward for a while, noting the world moving around us. He remained quiet, smoking and watching. If he was waiting for me to start the conversation, he had no idea who he was dealing with. Loser could keep quiet for days.

"What you need?" he asked when the silence had grown

too long for his taste.

"Do you know Miss Minier?"

The frown returned. "That ain't no Miss Nothin'. She Carole Ann."

"So you know her."

One side of his mouth lifted in what might have been a smile. "Everybody know that girl, one way or 'nother."

"She's gone missing."

His eyes slid toward me, assessing. "That what they say."

"Anybody say where she might be?"

His head turned and he looked at me full on. "Why you askin'?"

I groped for a way to convey the importance of the question. Should I say she was the woman who'd ruined my marriage? "I need to ask her some questions." It sounded weak, even to me.

His eyes turned toward me, though his face remained forward. "Even if I did know where she is, she wouldn't want me tellin' it to no white woman with a list of questions."

He was one hundred percent correct, and a sense of failure dropped on my shoulders like a wet wool sweater. What had made me think people here would tell a total stranger Carole Ann's secrets? She was theirs, however flawed she was, and I was not. I slumped in the chair, held in place by inertia. I couldn't come up with a good reason for him to help, but I couldn't gather the energy to walk away, either. To my surprise, the man said softly, "D'Nard might know."

I recalled the name from Carole Ann's records. "Her pimp?"

That got me a glare of disapproval. "He her man, has been since she's fifteen."

"I see."

He grumbled something incomprehensible, adding, "Some people got different ideas about things, that's all."

If D'Nard was behind Carole Ann's disappearance, he might have taken her somewhere, might have married her, might have beaten her so badly she was in a hospital or in hiding. All those things were possible in the relationship typical of a pimp and his girl, the relationship my companion seemed to think of as love.

"I need to ask her about a man she used to see," I said, choking on the euphemism that might mean anything from dinner at Applebee's to fevered sex in anonymous hotel rooms. "He died, and I need her help to find out why."

His eyes softened. The emotion in my voice had revealed more than the words. "Don't nobody but D'Nard mean a nickel to Carole Ann. If your man was seein' her, it was strictly business."

That seemed to be all he had to say on the matter. He ran his tongue around in his mouth a little, dug out another cigarette, and lit it from the butt of the dying one. Thanking him with one of the gift cards, I rose and moved on. The street was active with cars and pedestrians, and I wove among them, looking for someone who might add to my impression of Carole Ann. I passed two women carrying tote bags filled with groceries, three young men with pants hanging low on their hips, and several lone men carrying boxes or packets. The shops I passed were small and varied in purpose. A barber swept up tufts of hair in his tiny square of space; farther on, revival posters covered the plate glass windows of a storefront church; and a dark, narrow restaurant beyond that promised the best in southern cooking, though it looked like it had been closed for a long time.

Looking down an alley, I saw a woman sitting on the ground, her head resting on the brick wall of the empty building. Beside her was a battered suitcase. Her expression was blank, but there was awareness in her eyes. Not under the influence, at least not at the moment.

Entering the alley, I sat down near her, keeping my distance. She tensed, as Loser would have, but I held out a gift card. "I'll give you this if you answer some questions."

Her eyes took in the golden arches, and hunger lit in their depths. "Okay." Her voice sounded croaky, like she hadn't used it much lately. She'd tell me anything to get the card. The question was whether she'd tell me the truth.

"What's your name?"

She took a few seconds to consider her answer. "Pat."

"How long have you been on the street?"

Her shoulders shifted in a tiny shrug.

"I'm not from here," I volunteered. "I stay near the Fan."

Slight interest showed in her eyes, probably because I wouldn't be competing for resources.

"I'm looking for a woman named Carole Ann. You know her?"

She shook her head, apparently unaware of the negative gesture. "Sure."

"Here." I showed her the photo from the missing person report. "Do you know her?"

"I seen her around." She sounded relieved that lies wouldn't be required. "Cops are lookin' for her." She frowned. "You a cop?"

"No."

She nodded, looking doubtful.

"She was sleeping with my husband."

That got her attention. "Yeah. They do that."

"Who?"

"Women. They'll take a man if they can."

A story spun out in my mind. She'd been one of those women who thought a man would always be there for her. Betrayal had caused a slow slide into despair. Realizing I was describing myself, I focused on here and now.

"Maybe you saw something you didn't tell the cops," I said, holding the gift card under her nose. She put a hand out as if to take it, but I pulled it back.

She made a quick gesture, almost anger, mostly frustration. "That one never talked to me. Always had her nose in the air."

I nodded. It was funny how people who were damaged tended to look down on those with a different kind of damage. "Anything you can tell me about the time before she disappeared? Something or someone unusual?"

She shrugged, but a light passed behind her eyes that made me lean closer. "Anything. You get free food either way."

"It wasn't nothing." Her eyes focused on the card. "I saw them that day. Carole Ann was talking real fast, like she does, and they went off together."

I sensed there was something more to it than that. "Was the other person someone you knew?"

Her face creased with doubt. "I thought it was a cop from down here, but it's hard to recognize them when they ain't in uniform." Her hand reached out, and this time I gave her the card. As I rose to go, she added, perhaps in an attempt at full disclosure, "I ain't sure that's who it was. It was just funny, Carole Ann all cozy with a cop."

I left the alley with my mind on what I'd learned and not on my surroundings. I was dimly aware of passing the barber, now sweeping the sidewalk in front of his shop. He was well-groomed, about fifty, wearing black trousers, a bright white smock, and highly polished wing tips. Nodding at me, he said, "Mornin'."

I smiled absently and continued to the bus stop. The bus was due in fifteen minutes, and I stood waiting, mulling over what I'd learned. Carole Ann cozy with a cop? What did that mean? It was a sure bet D'Nard wouldn't like it. Had Carole Ann stirred her lover's wrath by snitching on him?

"Hey." A hand grabbed my arm, and I was jerked almost off my feet and pushed into the doorway of an empty building. I tripped on the uneven concrete step and went stumbling into the battered frame. When I turned, I faced three men. One of them was almost certainly the guy I'd been thinking about.

D'Nard Dobermeyer stood before me, flanked by two big men who blocked the view from the street—if anyone cared enough to risk his own health to investigate. He was almost pretty, with smooth skin and large, liquid eyes that, at the moment, shone with malice. Probably less than twenty-five, D'Nard appeared at least twice that in mean-living time. The guys with him were younger, but neither had much to commend him: flat eyes, tattooed necks, and wide bodies that would soon run to fat unless prison time gave them incentive to get back in shape.

"You been askin' questions."

Lie? Tell the truth? Keep my mouth shut? Any of those could get me into trouble. I chose the latter.

"What you lookin' for Carole Ann for?"

When I didn't answer a second time, D'Nard slapped me so hard my head smacked against the door behind me. His expression showed neither enjoyment nor anger. It was just business. "You come 'round here asking questions, somebody gonna tell me real quick, so that ain't smart." He repeated his question. "Why you asking about my girl?"

"She knew my husband," I said through lips that were already swelling.

D'Nard stepped closer, his face inches from mine. "You think she run off with some white guy?"

Before I could answer a voice said, "What you punks doin' over here?"

All of them turned, and the one on my left took a step back. It was the barber I'd noticed earlier. Something about the line of his shoulders and the muscles in his arms told me there was more to the man than haircuts and eyebrow trimming. He'd taken an aggressive stance, holding his broom like a cudgel, and he spoke in a firm voice. "This neighborhood bad enough without scum like you stoppin' women on the street." He clipped one of the younger men on the thigh with his broomstick. "Richie, I tell your mother you hangin' with D'Nard again, she gonna send you to boot camp." Turning to the other, he said, "Ain't you on parole, Winston? You lookin' to go back?"

D'Nard jutted his jaw like a stubborn child. "This ain't none of your bidness, Gilbert." His tone sounded whiney, and Gilbert glared him to silence.

"You all get outta here, now. Let the lady be."

To my amazement, they didn't argue, though D'Nard grabbed a handful of my shirt and threatened, "When I find

Carole Ann, bitch, you better be nowhere around!"

They walked away then, bodies bobbing and elbows out in an attempt to pretend they hadn't just been scolded by the local barber. He watched them go, his steely gaze meeting D'Nard's when he turned back to frown at me. After they disappeared around a corner, my rescuer gave me a little bow. "Need a smack upside they heads, them boys." Shaking his own grizzled head, he added, "The younger ones, they might be okay, but stay away from D'Nard. He just plain bad."

"Thank you," I said, wondering what made him capable of facing three toughs with only a broom for a weapon. Guessing that a McDonald's gift card was an inappropriate reward for a knight in shining smockage, I repeated, "Thanks," and headed for the bus stop, where my escape from Bellemeade was just pulling up at the curb.

Chapter Seven

As I rode, transferred, and rode again, I put together what I'd learned. Carole Ann had a boyfriend/pimp who used violence as his preferred method of problem solving. If Darrin had become more than a customer to Carole Ann, D'Nard might have killed him. I made a mental note to ask Jacob if D'Nard was known for using a knife. Killing Kara made no sense, but if the man was a serious drug user, bizarre acts wouldn't be unusual. I bit down hard on my lower lip at the idea that my child might have been suffocated on the whim of a jealous coke freak.

The problem with the theory of D'Nard, or even Carole Ann, committing the murders was that they'd been done with a cleverness one wouldn't expect. No evidence of a stranger's presence was found in our home. However, the killer had been assisted by my coworkers' leap to the conclusion that I was guilty. The easy answer, post-partum depression, might have curtailed a thorough investigation. They'd tried to bully me into confessing, and it might have worked. Without Bert's intervention, I might even now be housed in some mental institution, convinced I really had killed my own family.

Bert's success in preventing my arrest had not convinced my so-called friends on the force that I was innocent. Or Darrin's parents. Or his co-workers. Or the newspaper-reading public. Everywhere I'd gone in the days after Darrin's death, I felt people staring at me, judging me. That was when I'd begun to disappear.

It was after five when I reached my car. Without Eddie to remind me, I almost didn't remember my phone, which I'd turned off and stowed in the pocket of Loser's pants. As I changed into Beth's clothes, I noticed the weight of it and checked. There was a message from Jacob. Good, I had information for him too.

What I read stopped me cold. *Carole Minier found in the James this p.m. Stabbed, prob. last night, thrown off the Manch. Brdg. Meet tomorrow, same time & place.*

I closed the phone and sat for some time in the overheated car, trying to absorb the news. My husband's lover had been missing for a week, but she'd died last night. Could it be a coincidence that she was murdered so soon after I came back to Richmond? I doubted it.

"What do you think, Alex? Do you like the lilac better, or should I go with the magenta?"

Bronson, more than competent in the courtroom, was stymied by color questions beyond what he'd learned in elementary science, ROY G BIV. Pointing vaguely to the blouse on the right, he said, "That one?" The uncertain tone came from his belief that when a woman asked a man for fashion advice, it was to convince herself to buy the other item.

Christina wasn't like that, though. Nodding agreement, she draped the blouse he'd indicated over her arm. After putting the other one, which he guessed was magenta since it didn't look like any lilacs he'd seen, back on the pile, she leaned forward and kissed him lightly on the cheek. "I'm sorry. I know it's torture for men to shop with women."

It really wasn't torture to shop with Christina. In the first place, she was gorgeous, intelligent, and funny. In the second place, he'd volunteered. Their busy lives left them little time together, and Monday she was headed to Detroit to do a presentation on some aspect of advertising he barely understood. Tonight, during a leisurely dinner at a trendy restaurant in the Shockoe Slip, she'd mentioned that the trip would take longer than she'd first thought. "There's some kind of ceremony on the last day, so I have to stay."

"Something fun, I hope," he'd said.

"Probably not. It's a dinner—with speeches. Which means another outfit," she said with a sigh. "I should have bought something, but I just found out today, and there's no time."

That was when he'd offered to take her to the mall to find something. Work was simpler for men, he thought, a suit, a crisp white shirt, and a choice from an assortment of ties. For women, a new event required planning equivalent to the D-Day Invasion.

The exception to that rule, Beth Lousiere, came to mind. Alex had met her through Bert Suggs, his employer and mentor, but she'd quickly become more than a client. Beth was different from any woman he'd ever met. Questioning Bert and reading newspaper accounts, he'd pieced together the tragedies that had sent her over the edge and left her living on the streets of Richmond for over a year. From the first he'd felt drawn to her, to the innocence that lingered despite all she'd seen and experienced. Loser despaired, but Beth persevered. Loser drew back, but Beth reached out to those in need of help. Loser survived, and Beth made surviving worthwhile.

Neither of them, however, was looking for a relationship. Alex had—well, right now he had Christina, beautiful, intelligent, and entertaining. Everything came naturally to her, from the clothes she wore to conversations about current events, and her insights were always thought provoking. Tonight she looked stunning, as usual, in a wine-colored dress set off with just the right amount of gold jewelry.

Alex had never seen Beth wear jewelry, and he guessed she seldom bought new clothes. He found himself wondering what it would be like to treat her to a whole new outfit, complete with all the things women were supposed to love. Would she be secretly pleased or openly horrified?

"I'll meet you at the front entrance," Christina said. As she went off to pay for her purchases, Alex left the store, wandering aimlessly along the display windows lining the wide hallway. What had brought Beth to mind? Probably the fact she was so different from Christina, from all the other women he knew. An attractive woman, Beth displayed few feminine traits, as if being a person was all she could handle. She was a puzzle, for sure. Maybe a bunch of puzzles mashed together.

If he was honest, Alex was used to a little more effort on a woman's part to attract his notice. Though she was friendly and seemed glad to see him when he arrived on her doorstep, Beth had never revealed the slightest interest in him as a man. She never flirted or seemed bothered if long stretches of time passed between his calls or visits. That wasn't great for a guy's ego.

His phone vibrated discreetly, and he slid it out of his jacket pocket. "Bronson."

"Alex? It's Eddie."

For no reason he could articulate, Alex's spirits rose. He hadn't been unhappy, but now he was happier. "Hey, buddy, how are things?"

"It's okay here, but I was wondering. Have you heard from Loser—from Beth?"

The feeling of happiness dissipated a little. "No, why?"

"That's what I thought." Eddie sounded disgusted. "She promised she'd call you when she got to Richmond."

"Beth is here?"

"Yeah. The guy that was her partner on the police force emailed to tell her a couple of women are missing. One she knew on the street, and the other is the one her husband was screwing."

Alex tried to recall stories of missing women in the news, but nothing came to mind. "Beth came to see what happened to them?"

"A street person and a hooker. She figured the cops wouldn't care." Eddie cleared his throat. "I think she's been working her way back to this, you know? She's a lot better than she was, and she can handle finding out what happened. She thinks."

"It doesn't sound like you're sure that's true."

Eddie sighed. "She's tough, you know that. But it's one thing to help someone else with their problems and another to solve your own."

Alex chuckled. "You're pretty wise for an eleventh grader."

"Hey, I'm almost officially a senior," Eddie countered, but when he went on, his tone turned serious again. "I'm worried, Alex. Loser said she'd text me every day around four, but I got nothing today."

"She might have forgotten." Alex checked the time. Eight fifteen. Four hours overdue. "I'll see what I can find out and call you." He wasn't sure where to start, but he didn't want the kid to worry.

"Thanks. It's been bad enough wondering what she's up to, and when she didn't call tonight—" Eddie lowered his voice.

"Mabel wants me to put an ad in the papers saying she's got Lyme's disease and Loser should come home."

"Lyme's disease. That's a new one, isn't it?"

Eddie sighed again. "I don't think she's ever had the same imaginary disease twice."

"Okay. You deal with Mabel, and I'll find Beth. Talk to you soon."

Ending the call, Alex stood staring down the hallway, seeing nothing except the images in his mind. In the military he'd met women who were tough, and in life he'd met women who were damaged. Beth was both tough and damaged. She often struggled to make a sentence. Her nods to convention were often grudging, and he'd seen the world differently since getting to know her. Loser had little patience for trivial conversation and frivolous pastimes. She couldn't have cared less what duchesses, movie stars, and other so-called celebrities said or did. She had no interest in what was on television, nor did she go to movies others flocked to see. She wasn't being rebellious. She just didn't care.

Hearing the click of heels on the tile floor, he turned to see Christina approaching. A shopping bag hung from one wrist, a green ribbon strung through the handles and tied in a bow. "Trouble, babe? You look worried."

"No trouble. I just spoke to a guy who needs to contact a mutual friend here in the city. I told him I'd see what I can do."

She smiled, revealing perfect teeth. "At least that will keep you from falling prey to some glamorous woman while I'm away."

"Right." Alex grinned weakly, acknowledging to himself he wasn't lying. No one, not even Alex himself, would call Beth

Lousiere glamorous.

I waited in the alley outside Verle's Place until everyone left, hoping the owner would be the last man out, as he often was. Verle was a bit of a workaholic, and it was his practice to open the restaurant in the morning, cook breakfast for his customers, leave around 9:00, and return at four for the dinner hour. Good business practice, but probably a strain on his two-year-old marriage. For me it was a good thing.

Twenty minutes after the *Open* light went out, I watched Sandra, Verle's longest-serving waitress, leave with a woman I didn't know. They headed for the bus stop, shoulders slumped with exhaustion. Another day of waiting tables finished.

I climbed the two steps to the kitchen door and peeked inside. Verle was writing on a pad, probably making a grocery list for the next day. I knocked on the door, and he turned with an irritated expression. When he saw it was me, the look melted away and he hurried to open the door. Unlike Jacob, this old friend didn't offer a hug. Instead he said, "Hey, Loser! Come on in."

I stepped inside, surveying the kitchen I'd come to know well. The place was pretty clean, though I saw areas that could use a little elbow grease. Pots and pans hung overhead like unimaginative mobiles. Coffee cups sat stacked atop each other, ready for tomorrow's breakfast crowd. A few bubbles clung to the sink drain, returning the glare of fluorescent lights above with a rainbow of color. Sniffing the air, I guessed today's special had been something with onions.

I wasted no time on how-have-you-been small talk. "I need a place to stay for a few days."

The grin on Verle's face was replaced by apprehension. He liked me, for reasons I'd never understood. He wanted to help me—had in fact done so before I ever knew he was doing it. But the question in his mind had to be what he'd tell Flo, his jealous wife. If he kept my presence a secret and she found out, he'd be dead meat. If he told her and she objected, he'd be forced to kick me out.

In a tone only slightly off, Verle said, "Sure, Loser. The apartment's just sittin' there empty." Leading the way, he snagged a key ring from a nail near the hallway entrance. "Not any prettier than last time, but livable." Unlocking the door, he handed me the key with a crooked grin. "The bed's musty, but I'm guessing you won't be spending any time there anyway."

I'd planned to continue sleeping in my car, but that was no longer an option. I'd soon be a suspect in Carole Ann's murder, so the police would find out what I was driving and broadcast a description. Anticipating that, I'd hidden the Buick in an abandoned garage Mabel had sometimes used as her home base. The upper floor had collapsed onto the lower one, making a mess, but there was just enough room to fit the car under the fallen beams. I'd slid out the narrow space between it and the wall, used some debris to hide it from view, and walked the dozen blocks to Verle's restaurant.

My phone and iPad were useless too, since they'd pinpoint my location. I couldn't text Eddie, which would worry him, but the police were sure to contact him. It was best if he could honestly say he hadn't heard from me since yesterday. In need of a place to hide, I'd thought of Verle and the apartment that had once been his bachelor pad. I'd feel as safe there as anywhere, and I could sleep in the alley once everyone went home.

Verle hovered in the doorway, watching me. "You want to tell me what's going on, Loser?"

I shook my head, and he nodded as if expecting that. "I'm alone in the kitchen most mornings from 5:00 to 5:30. If you need anything, you can catch me then."

"Thanks."

He jabbed a thumb toward the kitchen behind him. "Get yourself something to eat. You're still too skinny." A short time later, I heard sounds of the restaurant closing down: the snap of light switches, the sigh of unplugged appliances going quiet, and the grate of the back door closing. After that, a car started, reversed, and pulled away from the back of the building. I was alone.

I debated taking a shower. If I wanted to blend in with street people, I shouldn't, but the heat of the afternoon had made me feel grimy. I compromised by showering but not washing my hair. Barefoot and still damp, I put on my Loser clothes and padded out to the restaurant kitchen to check out the offerings. It was dark, of course, but there was some light: a slice from the street lamp out front, security lights in the dining room, and red monitor lights on several appliances. I opened a fridge and peered inside. Some chicken noodle soup in a large pot smelled good, so I helped myself to a bowl. While it heated in the microwave, I located a roll to have with it.

When I finished, I washed the bowl and utensils and put them back where I'd found them. Satisfied I'd covered my raid on the food supplies, I went back to the apartment, hid my knapsack under the bed, and went out the back door. Flattening a couple of cardboard boxes, I made myself a bed of sorts and lay staring at the stars, barely visible due to the city lights. Remembering how clear they looked from my porch in the mountains, I asked myself what I was doing in Richmond. If I retrieved my car in the morning and headed home, Mabel and Eddie would swear I'd never left.

It was a tempting thought. I was sorry I'd come, sorry I'd been unable to leave the past alone, and I sensed my arrival in Richmond had led to Carole Ann Minier's death. Aisha, too, might in danger, because she'd claimed to be my friend.

I slept, though not restfully and not for long. My situation was enough to delay sleep, and in addition, I was aware of the uncomfortable ground beneath me, the stinking trash nearby, and the sounds of Richmond traffic. Beulah had changed me, offering comfort, peace, and a new start, but it wasn't enough. I was no longer Loser, but I wasn't Beth, either. Whoever I was, trouble was looking for me.

Chapter Eight

Before dawn the next morning, I rose from my damp pavement bed and entered Verle's apartment. I needed no light to find my way to the old rocker, where I listened as the restaurant awoke. Verle's car pulled up outside, the kitchen door opened, machines groaned and popped to life, employees and customers arrived. I remained still and silent until the breakfast rush slowed, trying to figure out what to do next. I couldn't leave the investigation of Carole Ann's death to the police, since I was likely to be their prime suspect. If I learned something worthwhile, I'd turn it over to Jacob, who'd make the rest of them pay attention.

Again I considered asking Bert and Alex for help, but the conversation I imagined bothered me.

Bert: Beth Lousiere called. She's suspected of another murder.

Alex: I thought you said she didn't kill her husband.

Bert: I didn't think so at the time.

Alex: But now you're wondering.

Bert: Maybe.

Would Bert say that? Would Alex believe it? He'd never seen the worst of Loser, and I couldn't bear the thought of him investigating my past. How could he help but be disgusted by the thought of his client sleeping in alleys and eating what restaurant staff threw out at the end of the day? *I* was disgusted by it, and I'd done it. I had dim memories of those days, was aware that I'd been driven by hunger to do things I could never have imagined. There'd been days I thought I would freeze to death, but I don't recall that I cared much.

I didn't even remember the worst days, though there were flashes of horror: beatings, a near rape, and months spent out of my mind, talking to myself and sobbing, both in total silence. My odd behavior might actually have protected me, because people avoid the visibly insane. Only Mabel hadn't minded my antics. Shortly after we met, she'd taken me to a church where they gave away clothes and picked out the homeliest outfit she could find. "There," she'd said when I'd replaced the black dress I'd worn for who knows how many days. "You ain't so pretty now. That's good out here."

I'd looked at the forlorn figure in the mirror: breasts and hips concealed by baggy, shapeless clothes. Face obscured by dirt and a pulled-down hat. Eyes haunted by madness, lips cracked and scabby. *No one would want me*, I remember thinking, *and no one should want a loser like me.*

Remembering that time, I didn't want to put Bert and Alex in the position of having to bail me out of trouble again. Maybe later, if I had to.

At mid-morning the staff took a break from the kitchen, their usual custom, drinking coffee in the dining room and resting their feet in anticipation of the busy lunch hour. Wearing the decent clothes I'd brought from Beulah, I slipped out the apartment door. The alley was empty except for Verle's boat of a car, parked so close I had to sidle along in order to keep my clothes clean. On the plus side, it provided cover as I disappeared around the back of the building.

I planned to visit the All-Aid to see what my friends could tell me, but I took the long way around to prevent anyone connecting me to Verle's place. At best, Aisha might have turned up so I could question her. At worst, the police were waiting there to arrest me. It was a risk, going out in broad daylight, but they were looking for Loser, not a plainly-dressed, normal-looking woman. Besides, with the Fan's every hiding spot logged in my memory, I was cautiously confident I could evade patrol cars.

Ambling along like a student with no particular place to go, I sat down on the lawn of the Children's Museum. I'd brought along a book from Verle's man-adventure selection, and I took it from my backpack and pretended to read while I watched the street for half an hour. Nothing I saw indicated a stake-out team waiting for me to show up.

Satisfied that it was safe, I stowed the book, got up, and walked to the All-Aid. Again, it was Penrod who noticed me first. Leaning against the wall in his accustomed spot, his lips moved as he repeated his phrase, but his chin lifted in greeting. Howard, tuned to Penrod's shifts in mood, looked up, saw me coming, and smiled. As he opened his mouth to call out, I made a quieting gesture. His mouth and his brows closed together.

When I got close enough to speak softly, I said, "No names."

"Sure, L—Sure."

"Any word on Aisha?"

"Nope. Still gone."

It was a disappointment, but a relief too. At least there hadn't been word that she too was dead.

Penrod slid along the wall, keeping his shoulder against the bricks. "Manville stopped a while ago."

"Manville?" I glanced around, afraid my nemesis from the police academy was right behind me. When Darrin died, Manville had gone so far as to tell a reporter it was "well known" on the force that I'd been depressed and angry. "The spouse is the most likely suspect in a case like this," he was quoted as saying, "especially when there isn't anyone else who might have done it."

Arrest would be a blow, but it would be harder if it involved a man I despised. "What'd you tell him?"

Penrod grinned, revealing fuzzy teeth, and pressed his stomach. "He asked if Beth Lousiere has been around here. He said she killed some woman on the South Side."

Howard stepped in, unwilling to let Penrod tell the rest. "We said we didn't see no Beth. He didn't ask did we see Loser!" He raised a palm, and Penrod managed a high-five before returning to his usual closed stance.

My throat tight, I said, "Thanks, you guys."

Tilting his head, Howard asked pointedly, "Hey, Loser, you got the time?"

When I pointed to a nearby clock, he nodded. "Noon, straight up." He paused. "Yup, noon."

I got the message. They'd done me a favor, and it was payback time. "Lunch?"

Penrod smiled, and Howard spurred his chair forward a few feet. "Lead on, Macbeth!"

Without bothering to correct his misquote or point out he'd already taken the lead, I followed. "The Chinese place," he suggested, pointing. "We can take the leftovers with us."

I followed Howard down the street, hoping our odd little threesome wasn't too noticeable. Penrod bounced from building to building, letting go of one only to hurry on to the next. Howard jiggled along, a jumble of inexplicable objects protruding from the bag attached to the back of his motorized chair, including but not limited to a lamp, a stuffed alligator, and one high-heeled woman's boot. It was a relief when we reached the restaurant and entered the A/C cooled dining room.

We weren't greeted with open arms, but I flashed some cash and the waiter tilted his head toward a table in a far corner, ordering, "Sit there." It took a while to maneuver Howard's wheelchair up to the table and get Penrod seated across from me. I noticed a few of the customers staring and whispering indignantly. Our host took a pencil from behind his ear and waited, nose twitching, as Penrod and Howard made their way through each item on the menu, discussing with brutal honesty what sounded good and what didn't. Once they decided, the waiter wrote it down with angry slashes and stalked off toward the kitchen.

About the time things began to settle, the door flew open and another of my old companions appeared, blocking most of the sunlight as he paused like the villain in some old oater. Though largely harmless, Bubba was not on my list of favorite people, mainly due to his habit of calling attention to himself and everyone around him. In a tattered wool coat, zip-up boots, and a bandana that couldn't contain his mass of frizzy black hair, he looked like a cross between Jack Sparrow and the Gorton Fisherman. "Hey," he shouted across the room. "Penrod! Howard! What you guys doin' in here?" His eyes met mine, and recognition dawned. "Hey!"

Rising quickly, I approached, making a "keep it down" gesture. Bubba, who had the mentality of a seven year old and the voice of a boxing announcer, had no doubt seen us enter the restaurant and followed, hoping for a free meal. I didn't need him shouting my name to the world.

Taking his sleeve, I led him to the table. "Sit," I ordered. "I'll buy you lunch if you keep your voice down." Going back to the counter, I ordered another meal and more crab Rangoon. Bubba could neither be quiet for long nor make sense much of the time, but he could eat. His presence made discretion impossible, so I told the waiter to make our meal to go. He smiled for the first time. Well, almost smiled.

When I got back to the table, Howard was explaining my presence in terms Bubba could understand. "Loser's looking for Aisha," he told him. "She got a check that was s'posed to go to her."

"Yeah, they always screwin' up them checks," Bubba said, nodding wisely. "That 'cause the people in the banks speak Klingon 'stead of English." Bubba got most of his opinions from his sister, who let him sleep on her back porch like a stray dog she didn't want but couldn't drive away. From what I could tell, the sister railed against illegal aliens a lot, and Bubba, with his minimal capacity for understanding, had concluded from her complaints that everyone in a position of power, including our current President and most of Congress, was from another planet.

Across the room, the waiter cleared his throat, and I turned to see a neat stack of bags and boxes on the counter. "Outside," I ordered.

Bubba, whose heart is as big as his mouth, stepped ahead to hold the door open for Howard. I stopped and picked up the food, taking time to see that the order was complete before I left. No way did I want to have to return for plum sauce.

Bubba led us to the parking lot of a bank, empty since it was Sunday. I chose a place in the shade, out of view from the street. The concrete barriers made convenient seats, and we set out an impromptu buffet, avoiding the large cracks in the asphalt. The guys focused on eating, and for some time there was no conversation.

When his first plateful was gone, Bubba burped loudly, took up the box of shrimp fried rice, and said, "Aisha ain't been around for a while now." He launched into a story about his travels over the last several days. Most of us took care not to be nosy about each other's business, but Bubba was a curious sort who ranged widely through the city. He reported in detail the places he'd been recently that Aisha was not. We listened. When Bubba started, it was best to let him tell a story his own way, because he would, no matter what. At the end he said, "She been sleeping in the Hollywood Cemetery, but she ain't there now. I looked."

"Any idea where she went?"

Bubba swallowed a large mouthful of food. "I don't know where, but she's with a marine."

Howard turned the remainder of a box of sweet and sour pork onto his plate. "Aisha wouldn't go anywhere with no marine, idjit. She thinks everybody in uniform is a cop."

"That's what she tol' me!" Bubba was indignant. "I tol' her about this church that was having' a free supper, and she says, 'I can't go. I gotta meet my friend the marine tonight.' I figure they run off together, 'cause she never came back."

A thought hit, related to my visit with Helen the day before. "Bubba, are you sure she said 'a marine'? Could it have been someone named Maureen?"

His rubbery face went through a succession of expressions, and he scratched his eyebrow with the tines of his plastic fork. "I ain't sure, Loser."

I handed him the rest of my stir-fried beef and he dug in, forgetting the question as easily as a puppy forgets its manners. I tried not to watch him chew. Maureen's former landlady had said Maureen Daley was worried about me. Aisha had claimed to know where I was.

"Who's Maureen?" Howard asked. He'd been paying more attention than I thought.

"A cop from the South Side. Kind of a friend, I guess."

"From when you was a cop." Howard ran his tongue over his teeth. "She musta read that stuff in the papers and found out you're Loser now. Maybe Aisha's helping her look for you."

Searching the streets for Loser over the last year would have brought no results, since I'd left Richmond to escape the publicity that had lauded me as the Homeless Hero. But the article Aisha had contributed to might have brought Maureen back to the Fan to question my supposed friend. It was odd to think that Maureen might be looking for me right now, just as I was looking for her.

As the men ate their meals, I made a timeline in my head. Aisha had been reported missing six days ago, Carole Ann the day after that. "When did the reporter come here?" I asked.

Howard paused for a moment, holding his fork like a trowel. "A long time ago."

I sighed. To Howard, that might mean three days or three months. "How long?"

Pushing a mouthful to one side, he considered. "It was the same day Bubba got beat up."

I turned to Bubba, who swallowed before defending himself. "I wasn't doing nothing, neither."

I wouldn't have delved into that subject, knowing how

Bubba's mouth can get him in trouble, but he was anxious to establish his defense. "I was talkin' to Howard here, and Jimmy got all mad 'cause I said snakes ain't got no teeth, but they don't Loser. Honest. They said it on *National Geographic*."

Penrod stepped in to spare me the details. His meal had disappeared as if by magic, and I guessed he'd stored bits of it in his pockets for later, as Loser would have. "Jimmy went after Bubba, and he fell down trying to get away."

"Poked a big hole in his leg." Howard made a softball sized shape with his fingers. "Bone stuck right out, all crooked."

Noting Bubba's perfectly usable leg, I almost despaired of getting concrete information out of them. Howard inflated the smallest event into an all-out catastrophe. Bubba didn't understand most of what he saw. And Penrod's communication skills left much to be desired.

Loser isn't so great at explaining things either.

As I chastised myself for judging them, Penrod came through like a champion, gulping, "It was St. Patrick's day, 'cause a lot of people went into the store wearing green hats and stuff."

I left the guys with full bellies, entertaining themselves with an argument over the merits of steamed rice or fried. As I went, I tried not to jump to conclusions. There were lots of Maureens in the world, if Aisha had indeed said *Maureen*, not *marine*. Still, I couldn't shake the feeling that Maureen Daley was looking for me, hoping to help. She'd also known Carole Ann, at least as well as a cop knows the criminals on her beat. She might have learned something I could pass on to Jacob.

I'd moved into the Fan, where the streets were narrower and less traveled. It was a peaceful place. Traffic noises receded. The temperature cooled slightly as the shadows of massive homes and ancient oak trees dimmed the sun's glare. I slowed my pace, letting the familiar surroundings wash over me. The Fan wasn't home, but it soothed me somehow.

My reverie was broken by the sound of footsteps behind me. I slowed to let the person pass, turning my head away as if interested in the flowers on a bush along the way. He stayed a few steps behind me, and I could tell he was a mouth breather. From the clomp, I guessed it was a man, and I quickened my pace as if I'd remembered I had somewhere to be. The steps quickened, just enough to keep up. Along with the raspy intake and hissing outflow of air, I heard a tiny metallic clink every few steps, along with a quiet creak. Handcuffs shifting on a leather belt?

Though I didn't dare turn around, I was certain it was Manville. He was the type who'd play with me before making the arrest. He'd let me feel the dread, fear the result. The food I'd eaten lurched upward as if seeking a way out. At the next corner I turned. The footsteps followed. The metal-on-metal clink sounded. I felt his presence looming behind me. I heard him take a deeper breath.

Someone tapped on my shoulder. "Hey, Loser!"

Bubba. With a sigh that was part relief, part irritation, I turned to face him. "You scared me."

He was immediately contrite. "Sorry. I want to tell you somethin' without Howard around." Bubba's bottom lip jutted for a moment. "He makes fun of me, calls me a idjit."

"He shouldn't do that," I said, though I guessed the politically incorrect terms of twentieth-century psychology would have placed Bubba somewhere between imbecile and moron, not idiot.

"He's mean." I waited for Bubba to sort that out, but it took a while.

"What did you want to tell me?"

"Oh, yeah." Bubba's eyes went wide. "You're looking for Aisha, right? I can show you something I found."

I almost refused. He might lead me ten blocks away to see nothing more interesting than a pretty rock. "It's about Aisha?"

"Yeah. Come on." He turned and started off. With a sigh I followed, hoping for the best.

He led me to a spot under the expressway where I recalled seeing Aisha a few times. Unlike me, she enjoyed calling attention to herself. She'd set all her belongings out around her in a wide circle so she could touch and admire them. Until darkness made it impossible, she'd examine each item in turn as if it were made of gold. Though Aisha sold some items to make her meager living, she often kept the shiniest things for herself. Sadly, the things she was so pleased with often belonged to someone else.

Traffic roared around us, and I remembered it was the weekend. Normal people were going on outings, picnics, water parks, day trips. I wondered briefly what Eddie and Mabel had done with their time. Mabel, who'd settled into my little house and seemed uninterested in going anywhere again, had probably watched *CSI* reruns. Eddie might have gone fishing or swimming with his friends. I imagined them gliding along the lakeshore like the kings they were, for what small-town boy of seventeen isn't royalty as far as girls are concerned? I had to contact him somehow. Maybe I could use Verle's phone to send a text.

Out of habit, I looked around to see who was nearby before

following Bubba into the shadow of the overpass. His boots made a different sound as we left the pavement and crossed the sun-baked, brittle grass. Exit and entrance ramps twisted together, forming a hollow space invisible from most vantage points. Only by climbing a steep incline and shining lights under the bridge could the police clear the homeless from this haven of privacy, and they didn't do that often. We were allowed the narrow ledge of concrete for our beds, and more than one night I'd lain there, chilled by the stone beneath me and tormented by the rumble of cars above. Even that had been better than sleeping inside.

In the farthest corner of the space, Bubba reached up into the bridge's under-structure and pulled something out. I'd stopped on the concrete platform, and he brought his find to me, spilling the contents of a battered tote bag onto the ground. Bending, I saw a t-shirt with sequins, a sweater studded with fake gems, and Mabel's hat, adorned with a gaudy *Virginia Is for Lovers* appliqué. All of it was splotched with rusty-brown stains. It might have been paint, but I was sure it was blood.

I put the items back in the bag and told Bubba to return it to where he'd found it. It was Beth, not Loser, who promised him lunch tomorrow if he kept his discovery quiet. Beth even remembered the gift cards and gave one to him. But all the time, Loser was fighting for control. Once Bubba hurried off with his prize, Beth faded into the shadows of a mind beset by guilt and dread. I staggered back to the street, wandered blindly along until I found a few spindly trees beside a strip mall and sat beneath them, fighting off waves of nausea.

Aisha is dead, just like Carole Ann. Two more added to the tally—murdered because of you!

I sat there for some time, rocking a little and mouthing

words I couldn't say aloud. More lies. Aisha lied, told someone she was my friend, and it led to her death.

Loser! It isn't only the people you love who die. Anyone who comes near you is in danger.

I had a dim memory of myself—Was it after Marta's funeral?—lost in a world of woe, aware that I was poison to be around. Bert held my arm, holding me up, actually. He'd been concerned. "Go home for a while," he'd urged. "West Virginia, isn't it? Go back. Home will help you recover."

I'd promised I would, and Bert hadn't known for months that I was not where he thought I was.

Leaving everything I own in the house I can no longer bear to enter, I get in my car and start west. I try to tell myself that Bert is right, that I need to get away from my ghosts, but they call to me.

"How can you leave us behind? What kind of mother are you—what kind of wife?"

When I realize I can't leave Richmond, some innate type of cunning kicks in, and I realize I don't want Bert to know I'm there. He's been so good, but I'm nothing to him, and it's best if he can walk away. I pull off the freeway, leave the car in Oilville, and walk all the way back to the Fan. It's midnight when I finally reach my house, unable to enter but unable to walk away.

What keeps me here? I don't know, but I stand there for a long time, tears running down my cheeks. I don't even hear the man who comes up behind me and takes hold of my purse strap. Instinctively I grab it, holding on, but it's the worst thing I could do. He hits me so hard I cry out, falling backward onto the grass. He bends over me, pulls the purse away, and hurries off.

When he's gone, I do the only thing I can do. Holding the skirt of my dress over my bleeding nose, I curl up in the shadows of my front yard and lie there, waiting for sleep or death to overtake me.

"Are you okay, lady?"

A boy of about ten stood over me, a bag of groceries in each hand, one bulging in the shape of a milk jug.

I looked around in confusion, reorienting myself in the present. Through force of will I stopped rocking and mumbling. Those were Loser behaviors.

Loser had made my decisions for a long time—from the night I'd lost my money until—until when? Was I going to let myself slide backward? Loser would have responded to the boy's concern by turning away, but Beth answered, "I'm okay."

He glanced away, probably toward home and the tasks that waited there. "You sure?"

"I'm sure. But thanks for checking on me."

Shrugging to indicate it was no big deal, the boy moved off. I looked around, aware of my surroundings, aware that Beth Lousiere had things to do. Someone had to pay for these deaths—Aisha, Carole Ann, Darrin, Kara, and even Beth herself, who might never feel truly alive again. I would not drift into anonymity. I would find the killer and face him. Smoothing my wrinkled clothes as best I could, I started for my meeting with Jacob.

Chapter Nine

I approached Cleo's with caution, uncertain if coming was a good idea. I was wanted for questioning in the death of Carole Ann Minier, and it was Jacob's job to bring suspects in. Even if he could ignore that for old times' sake, Jacob might be under surveillance, since everyone knew he'd been my partner and friend. Meeting him might be the same as walking into police custody.

"Beth." A voice caught my attention as I stood at the restaurant door, unsure whether to turn the handle and enter. I turned to see Jacob standing nearby, facing away as if he were waiting for someone. He spoke without looking at me. "Head south. Wait for me at the end of the block and follow when I come by." He moved to the restaurant entrance, and I heard the little bell above the door tinkle as he closed it behind him.

Chastising myself for doubting him, I did as Jacob directed. A few stores down, I stopped at the door of a gift shop where a rack of tourist items caught my interest. Choosing a pair of oversize sunglasses and one of those sailor hats like Gilligan wore on the island, I went inside and paid for them. Hiding my hair with the hat, I put the sunglasses on and checked the two by four inch mirror. Not much of a disguise, but it made me feel a little less prickly at the back of the neck.

When I exited the store Jacob was passing, a take-out bag in his hand. I fell in behind him, looking down the side street as if trying to find my way. Keeping some distance between us I followed, turning when he made a left at an intersection and a right a block down. From behind, his limp was more noticeable. One leg moved normally, but he had to drag the other forward, making a shorter step. He didn't let it stop him as he moved purposefully through the crowd.

We came to a spot where a wide alley opened onto what had been intended as a chic pedestrian court. The fact that it was almost empty indicated poor planning on the part of the developers. Jacob turned through the wrought iron gateway and headed across the cobblestones. Most of the stores had closed down, an experiment in shopping that had failed. Only a shoe repair shop and a dry cleaner remained open, but in front of where a fake-French cafe had been was a stone table with two benches. While it wasn't completely private, it was hidden from street view.

Still paranoid, I stood for a few moments near the gateway. Jacob seemed to understand, because he sat down at the table and began taking food out of the bag, apparently with no thought in mind but a restful break from work. When I'd waited long enough to judge that no one had followed us, I joined him at the table.

"FYI, there's an exit through the shoe shop," he said, pointing.

"Good to know."

He nodded and began pulling food from the takeout bag. Jacob looked stressed, which was my fault. A by-the-book cop all his life, this was no doubt the first time he'd ever aided a fugitive. He managed a smile, however, as he pushed the take-out bag toward me. "I got myself a gyro and you a wrap. Hope you like jerk chicken."

"Thanks." My comment covered more than a chicken wrap, and he waved to show he got it. I didn't need to thank him for risking his job, and he didn't need to say he'd done it because we were friends.

"If I know you, you haven't had protein today," he said with mock sternness. "So eat!"

I took a bite of the wrap, which was as good as everything from Cleo's is. Though I didn't feel like eating, I did, reminding myself that my next meal might come on a tray slid into a jail cell.

Swallowing the first bite, I returned to a question left unanswered at our last meeting. "Jacob, why didn't you like Darrin?"

He seemed uncomfortable. "Beth, it doesn't matter."

I folded my hands together in front of me, willing myself to insist. "He's dead. You can tell me."

Jacob squared his shoulders as if absolving himself of blame. "I saw him once."

It felt like my concrete chair had been fitted with an electrical charge. "With the woman."

A nod. The tiniest one possible. "I went to one of those fancy restaurants down in the Bottom to make a reservation for our anniversary, and there they sat. He didn't see me, and at first I told myself she was a client or a coworker."

He stopped and I prompted, "But she wasn't."

"No. They were...affectionate."

Though I knew Darrin had been unfaithful, had in fact heard it from his own lips, I was still tempted to argue. It might have been—Who? Darrin's mother? He had no sisters, no cousins living in the area.

Seeing my disbelief, Jacob added in a regretful tone, "When I told Sasha what I'd seen, she said he—"

"He hit on Sasha?"

"Nothing overt. She just said he sent out signals, you

know?"

I felt humiliated, imagining Sasha and Jacob discussing my marriage between themselves, pitying me, wondering why I'd chosen a husband like Darrin. How had I been so blind?

He looked miserable. "Some guys are like that, Beth. They just don't get monogamy."

Darrin had been mildly disgusted by my pregnancy, and he'd been openly impatient when, after Kara arrived, I was captivated by her wonderfulness. It had been a mistake to start a family so early—

I stopped, forcing myself to face the truth. Over time, I'd seen that Darrin needed lots of female admiration. Chances were he'd never have been faithful, no matter how hard I tried. "Anything on Aisha?"

"No."

I told him about the bloody clothes and where to find them, and he made a call, saying he'd had a tip that evidence for a current case could be found at the overpass.

When he finished Jacob asked, "Do you think she's dead too?"

I shrugged. "If she is, they'll say I killed her."

He glanced around as if realizing how bad my situation was. "You should stay out of sight until they find out the truth."

"Who's looking for the truth?" I asked a little too harshly. "They're just looking for me." Fiddling with the dark glasses I'd laid on the table beside my sandwich, I let my anger subside. "I don't see how I can help myself by hiding in some dark place."

Jacob gave me a sideways glance. "Then maybe you should call your lawyer. He could put pressure on the department." Rubbing his nose between finger and thumb, he added, "You know I'll do what I can to help, but I doubt they'll listen to the old gimp who used to be your partner." There was no complaint in his voice, but I heard a note of frustration.

"Well, they should," I told him. "You're pretty smart for an old gimp."

Jacob grinned. "Will you call Suggs and tell him what's going on?"

I gave the same sort of evasive answer I'd given Eddie a few days ago. "As soon as I can."

"Good." He dug a piece of paper out of his pocket and slid it toward me. "Here's Maureen Daley's current address. It took a while to get it, because she's gone off the radar."

I stopped with the wrap halfway to my mouth. "Why?"

"The rumor is she was let go by the RPD for bad conduct. Her partner turned her in to I.A."

I recalled her words: *If my coworkers find out I suspect them, my life will be hell.*

"Can you find out more about what the charges were?"

He shrugged. "I can ask. You think it connects with Carole Ann and the missing homeless woman?"

"Maureen's former landlady, who's an old friend of hers, claims she was concerned about me."

"Why now, after all this time?"

I touched the pocket where I'd stashed the address. "Now that I know where she is, I'm going to ask her."

I rose, but Jacob stepped in front of me. "Beth, don't do this by yourself. Let me help."

"Grauman," I said firmly, "Don't jeopardize your job for me."

He raised his hands in a dismissive gesture. "I'm stuck behind a desk, so do me a favor. Get me fired."

Despite his attempt at humor, we both knew that losing his reputation, identity, and pension wouldn't be good things for Jacob. "There is something you can do." Taking out a pen, I wrote *edman14@yahoo.com* on a clean napkin. "That's Eddie's e-mail." The kid thought of email as right up there with chipping hieroglyphs into slabs of stone, but I thought he'd check for word from me. "Let Eddie know I'm okay, but don't give him any details."

I stepped past him, touching his shoulder in farewell. Anticipating his words, I said, "I'll be careful."

He spoke to my back, his tone uncertain. "We could do this by the book, Beth. You come in with me—"

"When there's no other choice." It came out stronger than I intended, but the prospect of being questioned, probably locked up, made the muscles in my body feel like ropes pulled taut.

"Wait." Jacob took out a business card and scrawled a phone number on the back. "Sasha's cell. Keep in touch."

"Thanks." I took the card, knowing I wouldn't contact Jacob again. Sooner or later I'd be caught and arrested, and I didn't want him involved. It was hard to walk away, but I did it without looking back.

The library was closed, but I went to an Internet café and I paid for an hour. When my turn came, I read every article I could find on the search for Carole Ann's killer. Though I wasn't mentioned by name, reports said the police were "pursuing strong leads" and hoped to make an arrest soon. One writer editorialized a little, stating that Carole Ann plied a dangerous trade and had trusted the wrong man once too often. Such comments soothed the nerves of normal people, reminding them that good citizens aren't murdered, prostitutes and their ilk are. His opinion soothed my nerves a little too. Though the reporter jumped to unwarranted conclusions, at least he had no idea I was the main suspect.

Carole Ann's lifestyle was indeed dangerous. Having met D'Nard, I could accept that "the wrong man" the reporter mentioned might have been the one she thought of as Mr. Right. It was possible she'd been killed by a client. But why had someone taken her, kept her alive for a week, and then murdered her? The answer to that might be too gruesome to contemplate, but the autopsy would tell. I tried to believe it wasn't about me. Both Carole Ann and Aisha took chances with their lives, and what had happened to them didn't have to be connected, either to each other or to me.

I heard a heavy sigh, and I knew where it came from without turning to look. Rolling my eyes, I relinquished my computer to a girl who'd been fidgeting in her chair, checking her phone every twenty seconds to see if my time was up, and closing it with an impatient snap each time.

Leaving the café, I began the long walk back to Verle's. I didn't mind walking, though my legs reminded me that concrete was harder than the soil at home. I twisted through the darkening alleys like a ghost, keeping to the shadows. Once a bus stopped ahead with a hiss and a cloud of black smoke, but I let it go on. I'd feel closed in, and too many people would see my face. Listening to my own thoughts, I shuddered. Loser had the upper hand, but then, Loser knew how to survive.

When Verle's sign out front went dark, I cut across the alley and approached the back door. His car was in its usual spot, and I slid past, fumbling in my pocket for the apartment key. After listening for a few moments, I opened the door, slipped inside, and closed it softly behind me.

"I thought you'd be along."

The unexpected voice scared me, and the key dropped from my hand, making a metallic clank on the linoleum floor. I made no move to pick it up. I knew who'd spoken, and it meant more trouble.

"Flo?"

There was a click, and a lamp lit one corner of the room. In the chair beside it sat Verle's wife. She looked me over critically, her fingers toying with a necklace of oversized beads. Not one to start a conversation, I waited to see what she had to say.

I'd seen Flo a few times from a distance, but now I got the chance to examine her as she examined me. About ten years Verle's junior, fifty or so, she had dark hair tipped with gold tones, expertly cut and styled in spiky tufts. She'd tanned too much for too long, but her skin looked okay except for one crepe-y spot above the neckline of her top. Her legs and arms were toned and thin, but a slight bulge under her silky shirt flowed over the top of her capris.

Flo wore a disapproving expression. Thinly plucked brows arched at the sight of me, an equally thin nose rose in disdain, and deeply red lips pressed together as if to hold back words of contempt. When she spoke again, however, it wasn't to berate me. "The police were here today."

I wasn't prepared for that. I slumped against the door, kicking myself for getting another of my friends into trouble. Like a little kid who always crouches behind the sofa for Hide and Seek, I'd returned to a spot where it was known I'd hidden before. *Dumb, Loser!*

"I'll leave."

Flo plucked a piece of lint from her pants. "Why does my husband go out of his way to help you?"

It wasn't for the reason she was thinking, but it wasn't easy to explain either. "He's a friend."

"He says there's nothing funny between you."

"You should believe him."

Flo had pretty eyes, but they focused on me so sharply it almost hurt. "He shouldn't make a fool of himself over a girl young enough to be his daughter."

"He doesn't."

Her gesture might have signaled anger, but it came across as pleading. "He believes you when everyone else thinks you're some crazy—"

"Loser?" I supplied. Flo nodded.

I glanced around the apartment. If the police had been here and found nothing, they weren't likely to come back. If I could win Flo over, maybe she'd let me stay. I could pay, or offer to work—

No. I'd traded on Verle's friendship, and within a day he'd had to lie to the police because of it.

"Sorry." I turned, stepped back outside, and closed the door behind me.

"Wait!" The door opened as I hurried away, and Flo called, "Beth? Beth? Loser?"

I didn't answer but faded into the Fan, where magnificent houses cloaked my escape. Once I was away from the sound of Flo's voice I slowed, walking the sidewalks and cobblestone alleys aimlessly. I was Loser again, and no one could afford to associate with me. Behind the windows I passed, people sat in comfort, watching TV, knitting, playing games, or surfing the Net. I passed my former home, where I'd often slept on the porch or lawn. There was no longer any solace for me there. Only the streets welcomed and protected me. Beth didn't belong on the streets, but Loser did.

That didn't mean the streets were safe. As I made my way down Mulberry, the growl of an engine caused me to turn. A car accelerated past and then turned sharply, cutting me off at the corner. A faintly familiar and unwelcome voice called out, "You! Stop right there." It was D'Nard.

He exited the passenger side and started toward me. He held something in one hand, close to his side. It looked like a ball bat. Inside the car the driver leaned out, craning his neck at me.

Turning, I began to run. Whatever D'Nard wanted with me, it wasn't good. I crossed the street, wishing I'd worn Loser's battered tennis shoes rather than flats. Dodging into the first alley I came to, I clattered down the cobblestones. It was me against two and a car, but at least I knew the territory. The alley I'd chosen opened onto a residential street where a dozen outbuildings offered shelter.

The car appeared at the opposite end of the alley and stopped with a squeal of brakes. While D'Nard followed me on foot, his companion had driven around the block, cutting off my escape route. I heard D'Nard's footsteps slow as he entered the alley. I didn't think he could see me in the dark, but I was trapped between him and his companion.

Willing myself not to panic, I weighed my options. There was a Dumpster ahead, delivery entrances for the buildings on either side, and a rickety metal balcony. I didn't think I could jump high enough to reach the balcony, and even if I did, it was sure to make noise. I doubted either of the doors was unlocked at midnight. That left only the Dumpster as a refuge.

"Did she go by you?" D'Nard called to the guy in the car.

"I don't know," the other answered. "I got around as fast as I could, but she might have."

As quietly as possible, I hoisted one leg onto the top edge of the container. With one hand, I lifted the plastic cover a little. The bin was almost full, and a half dozen smells rose to greet me. With agonizing slowness, I pulled my body onto the frame and into the bin. Spreading my weight as best I could, I laid myself out along the top of the garbage and lowered the cover gently back into place. Rolling to the back, I let myself sink between the bin wall and the topmost bags. If my pursuers took a good look inside they'd see me, but it was dark enough that I wasn't easily visible. Besides, I had no other options.

From my smelly haven, I heard the car door open. The two men approached each other, their steps echoing off the hard surfaces around them. One of the bin's two lids had been twisted out of shape by time and weather, and through the crack I caught a glimpse of a tiny flame. One of them was using a cigarette lighter as an impromptu flashlight. As the light came closer, I held my breath. It stopped beside the bin. The lid on my right opened, and I saw the outline of an arm and the silhouette behind it. The guy climbed onto the side of the bin to peer in. Looking up from the dark interior, I saw his face clearly in the light of the flame. I hoped all he saw was the trash that covered me.

Something in the vicinity was soaked with gasoline. My fear of discovery was amplified by the thought that I might soon be part of a well-fueled conflagration. If he brought the flame too close—

From a few feet away D'Nard growled, "Careful with that, Richie! You gonna set the whole alley on fire!"

"I'm bein' careful," Richie said. "Ain't nothin' movin' in here."

Would he shift the bags around and locate me? I lay tensed, ready to jump out and run, though I knew I was unlikely to escape them. Climbing out would slow me, and they'd catch me as soon as I hit the ground. The light moved back and forth, but Richie didn't seem willing to touch anything in the bin. Finally he climbed down, letting the lid drop back into place.

"She doesn't look very big," I heard him say. "You really think she killed Carole Ann?"

"The cops do. They been lookin' for her all day."

"Then they'll arrest her." Richie's voice turned resentful. "Why I gotta use up all my gas to find her?"

"Because there ain't no cop can find his ass with both hands," D'Nard answered. "Pat says Carole Ann was bangin' her husband. That's prob'ly why she killed her."

"And she lives around here?"

"Yeah." His tone turned harsh. "We almost had her. I oughta use this bat up side your head."

Resentment faded as fear took over. "I'm sorry, man, but she's pretty fast." Moving away from the trash bin, the smaller man added, "We can drive around some more. Maybe she'll show up again."

"We won't find her tonight," D'Nard replied, "but I ain't givin' up. I'll find her, and then she gonna be one sorry bitch."

CHAPTER TEN

Alex spent Sunday night trying to make himself believe that Beth was okay. A few hours' delay in messaging Eddie wasn't the end of the world, but he knew Beth tried to give the kid stability and certainty, knowing he'd had little of either in his life.

Monday morning as he dressed for work, he texted Eddie: *News?* Seconds later he got his response. *Nothing.*

Before their workday began, Alex told Bert about Eddie's call. He almost hoped his partner would chuckle at his fears, but Bert also saw cause for worry. "You know Beth well enough by now to realize she will never ask for help," he said, "though she must know we're willing. I think you should clear some time this morning to look for her. I can provide some places to visit and people you might speak to." Bert suggested he begin with Verle, who'd sheltered Loser before. Asking his P.A. to reschedule his appointments, Alex left the office.

Verle Gajewski looked like an extra from *McHale's Navy*. When Alex told him why he'd come, his disorderly eyebrows lowered defensively. "Beth left Richmond a year ago." He never stopped working, turning a mountain of hash browns, flipping eggs, and deftly pouring batter to make a half dozen perfectly round, golden brown pancakes. He never met Alex's eye, either, and though it might have been care for his customers' breakfasts, it seemed more like dissemblance.

When he left Verle's, Alex drove through the Fan, slowing at each figure on the street that looked the slightest bit familiar. He accomplished nothing except irritating the drivers behind him.

The second place on his list was the headquarters for Richmond's First Precinct, where he asked at the desk to see Jacob Grauman and found he was speaking to him. Grauman wasn't much more helpful than Verle had been. "If I hear from Beth, I'll tell her you want to talk to her," he said. That sounded to Alex like he knew something, which was a relief, suggesting he knew Beth was okay. And while he wasn't sure what Verle would do, Alex thought Grauman would pass on his message.

Next he stopped at the main branch of the Richmond Library, where Bert said Loser had often spent time. When Alex showed the clerk behind the desk a photo of Beth as a police cadet, he made a vague gesture at her face. "She looks familiar," he said, taking the picture and holding it at arm's length. "But it doesn't feel like I ever saw her in person."

That was because the picture had been splashed all over the papers several times. First when Beth had been accused of killing her husband and child and again when she was hailed as the Homeless Hero. Now it brought a frown and a scratch of the librarian's head. *How soon they forget,* Alex thought. He showed the picture to a few other staff members, but no one recalled seeing Beth recently. "She used to come in here a lot," one older woman told him. "She was always quiet and careful to abide by the rules." Her nose wrinkled as she added, "She didn't always smell so good though."

Leaving the library, he checked on his phone. He had time to visit the All-Aid before he was due in court. He drove back through the Fan, watching in case Beth had showed up during his absence. In front of the store were two men who looked familiar, and Alex approached them. "Hi," he said, unsure how to start the conversation. "I'm a friend of Beth Lousiere's, and I need to find her."

The taller one never stopped talking to himself, and it was doubtful he'd even heard. The other, a big guy in a motorized wheelchair, seemed mentally competent and willing to be social.

"You're the one brought the apples." He put a hand to his stomach as if wishing he had one now. "They was good, wasn't they, Penrod?"

Alex recalled a day at the farm in Beulah, when Beth had asked him to take a box of apples to the All-Aid Drug Store near the Fan. "Let the people standing outside have all they want," she'd said.

"I did bring apples," Alex said, hoping the fruit brought him some goodwill. "Now Beth's in Richmond, and I need to talk with her."

Instead of answering, the guy asked his own question. "If she wants to talk to you, won't she do it?"

He got the sense the man knew where Beth was, but even more strongly he felt the knowledge wouldn't be shared. Beth's friends would lie in the mistaken belief they were protecting her. He had to find a way to convince them she might want to see him. In fact, he thought ruefully, he had no way of knowing that himself. Why hadn't she let him know she was coming to Richmond?

Alex left a card with each man, asking them to pass it on to Beth. Nobody promised anything.

Back at the office, Alex looked at the clock. He was due in court in an hour. He re-read the notes he'd added to his list of people who might have seen Beth.

All-Aid homeless-No response: know more than they admit?

Jacob Grauman-admitted nothing.

Verle-ditto

Library-nothing-probably truthful

He felt frustrated, but there was a tiny sense of relief too. Some of these people had heard from Beth. From loyalty they wouldn't tell him what they knew, but at least she wasn't lying bloody in some alley. He had to hope she'd contact him eventually—or one of her friends would if she got in over her head.

After spending the night in the fenced back yard of an empty house, I visited a Goodwill store to buy clothes. My hop into the trash bin had ruined what had been my decent outfit, staining my pants and shirt with something tomato-based and leaving me reeking of gasoline. My Loser clothes were under the bed at Verle's, left behind in my hurry to get away from Flo. Searching the racks, I chose pants and a shirt, not colorful, stylish, or even attractive. Along with it I bought tie-up shoes in case I had to run again. At the last, I added a large purse to the pile. I seldom carried one, but it helped to create an average-woman look.

Once I had a middle-of-the-road outfit, I searched out the worst clothes I could find and an oversized tote bag. Tossing my stained clothes in the waste basket, I put on the neutral outfit and stuffed my new/old Loser clothes in the tote, which I intended to hide under the porch of an empty house nearby. No telling when I'd need to be Loser again. Adding sunglasses to my ensemble, I boarded the bus for the South Side.

Maureen lived on the outer edges of Manchester. The ten-story building, obviously constructed for efficiency rather than beauty, was cement-colored, with an identical, peanut-sized balcony on each unit flanked by windows hardly large enough to deserve the term. Bypassing the elevator, I climbed eighteen flights of stairs before making my way down the narrow hall to unit 931. The bell didn't work, but when I knocked, the door opened almost immediately. One glance inside suggested why: there wasn't much space to cover.

A little heavier than I remembered, Maureen Daley was dressed in pajama pants and a tired-looking T-shirt. Her auburn hair hung limply around her face, and I guessed that if she had a job, today wasn't a work day. Though slightly taller than I, she was barefoot, so our faces were nearly level. Her cheeks had plumped out, making her eyes look smaller and more intense. I remembered her as attractive, even pretty, but it was hard to see that now. She looked—*haunted* was the word that came to mind.

It took her a second to react. "Beth?" She glanced down the hallway. "I didn't hear the elevator doors."

"Stairs," I said, nodding in the opposite direction. "Don't like elevators."

"Beth!" Opening her arms, she pulled me into an enthusiastic embrace. "It's so good to see you!"

I tried to respond warmly, but we stood locked together for what seemed like hours. Finally I said to her shoulder, "Can we talk?"

She let go and backed out of the doorway. "Of course. Come in."

I stepped inside and she closed the door, sliding the deadbolt and security chain into place. It was a studio apartment, one large room with a kitchenette on the left, a work area beyond that, a loveseat next to the sliding glass door that led to the balcony, and a bed along the right-hand wall. A door next to it opened onto an efficiency-sized bathroom. A second door on the opposite side was closed, probably to hide a walk-in closet from view. The cheap, rickety furniture practically screamed the tenant was experiencing hard times.

"Sorry the place is a mess," she said from behind me.

That was an understatement. At the academy Maureen had always been neat and clean, even spiffy, and I'd pictured her home the same way. I'd been wrong. Items of clothing, newspapers, and trash were strewn all over the place: a half-full chip bag, several pop cans, and a stack of empty cupcake wrappers. The tiny desk was stacked with mail, most of it unopened. In the kitchen area, an open pizza box revealed one sad-looking leftover slice, and the counter and both sinks were stacked with dirty dishes. "Dishwasher's broken," she said as her gaze followed mine. "Have a seat."

Moving a jumbled pile of what might or might not have been clean laundry, I took the love seat. Maureen pulled the chair away from the desk, turned it, and sat. "It's so good to see you," she repeated, and I thought she meant it, though she seemed unsure what to say next. "I can't tell you how many times I've wondered how you were doing."

I dismissed her concern abruptly, recalling her part in my troubles. "I'm fine."

She huffed a sound of disbelief. "Living on the streets? Eating out of trash cans? I was really upset when I read that in the papers. Then you disappeared again, and I was afraid you'd done something drastic. Where'd you go?"

"Home."

"Home?" The chair wobbled precariously. "You mean West

Virginia?"

"Yeah."

"Oh." She put one hand over the other and massaged. "That's good to hear. What brings you back to Richmond?"

I gave her a brief account. She frowned at the mention of Carole Ann. "You think the cops are after you for that?"

Trying for optimism I replied, "I'm not sure, but my old partner Jacob is trying to clear me."

Her forehead furrowed. "I forgot about him. He was sick or something, right?"

"Yes, but he's doing okay now. He helped me find you, thought you might be able to help."

She snorted a laugh. "Fat chance! They wouldn't believe me if I said the Atlantic is salty!"

I leaned toward her. "What's been going on, Maureen?"

"Crap. Lots of crap." She gestured at our surroundings to indicate how bad things were. "I suppose your old buddy Jacob told you what happened to me."

"I know you aren't on the job anymore."

"Yeah." She leaned back in the chair and I saw the back shift under the weight. Rumpling her hair she said through tight lips, "It's been a nightmare."

"Want to tell me about it?"

Maureen flicked her fingers contemptuously. "Men can't be trusted. You of all people know that."

An interesting statement, coming from a woman who'd ducked out when I needed her. I waited.

"The guys at the Second figured out I was onto their skimming operation." She looked at me speculatively. "You didn't tell anyone, did you?"

I shook my head.

She smiled to take the sting out of the question. "I didn't think you would, but they knew somehow."

"Who's 'they'? Who figured it out?"

She chewed on a fingernail. "One was my partner, Bobby Davis. Cjaika and Hamilton, the other two, work together." She looked up, smiling grimly. "They're great guys, you know? Funny, tough, salt of the earth types. At least that's how they look to everybody else."

"But you think they're stealing."

"I don't think," she corrected. "I know. They pick up a little something at a crime scene before stuff gets confiscated and counted. They like cash, but they'll take drugs or jewelry too."

I frowned, and she sighed as if expecting to be doubted. "You were a cop, so you understand, even if you don't agree. We're out there putting our asses on the line every day for slave wages. They screw us on retirement and promotions, the politicians keep making more dumb laws, and the press puts every move we make under a microscope and decides we did it wrong no matter what."

She must have heard the outrage in her own voice, because she stopped, grimacing self-consciously. "See, it even gets me going. Some guys believe they deserve a few bucks here and there."

"That isn't right."

"I must have said something like that early on, so they knew I wouldn't play along." She bit her lip. "Maybe they didn't want to split four ways and figured I was too dumb to notice. Hard to say."

"But you did notice."

"Yeah. After all that stuff with you, I finally said something."

"To your partner?"

"Yeah." She crossed her arms, gripping her elbows. "One night we see these two guys walking down the street carrying a friggin' safe, if you can believe that. They said they were moving it, but it was three in the morning, and they weren't safe-owning types, if you know what I mean. Davis told me to go back to the car, call it in, and arrange for someone to come and pick up the safe. When I got back, it was still there, but the suspects were gone."

"What did he say happened?"

"Said a third guy came up behind him and knocked him down. They all took off." Maureen sniffed. "He didn't look like he'd been chasing anybody though. I figured they slipped him some money to let them go." She ran her hands through already tousled hair. "I'd seen it before, people we caught who never made it to the squad car. There was always an explanation, but it was never a very good one."

"You called him on it."

She nodded, eyes on the wall behind me. "I told him I couldn't let it go on anymore. I said I wouldn't tell on them, but it had to stop."

"And he said—"

"He got all huffy. Said he thought we'd been good working together." Her voice took on the tone I imagined had been in Davis' voice. "He was very hurt by my distrust."

"And from then on, you were the enemy."

She nodded. "If I arrested someone, I used too much force.

If I questioned anything, I was insubordinate. If I reacted to their nasty comments, I was volatile. Davis said it, and Cjaika and Hamilton backed him up. Finally they got this pimp to say I attacked him, that I lost control." She grimaced disgustedly. "D'Nard could make any cop go off, but I swear, Beth, I never laid a hand on him."

I reacted at the familiar name. "Who?"

A frown creased her forehead. "D'Nard Dobermeyer. Actually, he's Carole Ann Minier's man—or I guess I should say he was. I think he's also Hamilton's C.I., because they tend to look the other way when D'Nard commits a crime."

The man's angry face appeared in my mind. He was menacing enough by himself, but if he was a confidential informant for a police officer, that made things worse, for me as well as for Maureen.

She went back to her story. "About eight months ago, I was told to report to the department psycho."

"Dr. Blevins?"

"You've met her?" Maureen looked embarrassed. "Oh. Of course you did." She went on, "Then you know she's a snotty bitch who makes snap judgments then looks for evidence to support them. She asked if I thought I had emotional issues, and I said 'Hell, yes! If you reported your partner for cheating the system and everyone said you were lying, wouldn't you?'" Maureen's fists clenched. "She suggested anger management counseling."

I nodded, recalling Blevins' cold demeanor. She'd been so sure of herself in my case—and so wrong.

"What about Internal Affairs?" I asked. "Did you contact someone there?"

Before answering, Maureen rose and went to the sliding glass door that led to the balcony, kicking a damp-looking towel out of the way with her foot. She looked out at the city, her expression troubled. "I know I sound like some conspiracy theory nut, but yeah, I did call I.A. The first guy I talked to seemed willing to listen, but a day later I was visited by Detective Wilcott, who wasn't about to believe a word I said."

I tried to examine Maureen's story impartially. Crooked cops were a possibility. My personal experience had showed me our department psychiatrist could be mistaken. Still, Internal Affairs was charged with keeping cops honest. Someone should have investigated the charges.

Turning away from the window, she stood with slumped shoulders as if she anticipated my disbelief. "I found out Wilcott's married to Cjaika's sister." She waved a hand. "He probably gets a cut."

I looked down at my shoes, and she said in a softer tone. "I shouldn't have said that. I don't think the whole RPD is rotten." She sighed deeply. "It's just hard to buck the system." Counting her points on her fingers, she said, "Like you, I'm from out of state. I'm a woman, which makes a lot of male cops nervous. And the guys I accused are friends with everybody. No one wants to believe they'd do anything wrong."

Being both female and an outsider had been difficult for me too. I'd been lucky to get Jacob, who didn't see either of those things as a disadvantage in a partner. "So what happened?"

Her shoulders rose and dropped. "They won. It was decided that I was the problem, and they gave me the chance to resign or face charges and get fired."

"I'm sorry." I felt my resentment at Maureen fading. Her

refusal to help me hadn't brought the security she'd hoped for, only a delay in her downfall.

"The bust you asked me to photograph? The one that never happened?"

She chewed on the fingernail again before answering. "They were playing mind games, hoping I'd call I.A. and look like a loony-tune."

A move meant to discredit Maureen had ended up hurting me. I'd had no way to prove I was on an unofficial stakeout while my husband and baby were murdered.

Leaving the window, she returned and stood before me. "I should have helped you back then."

Yes, you should have, I thought. *It wouldn't have saved your job, but it might have saved my sanity.*

"I'm really, really sorry, Beth."

I could only nod, understanding but not able to approve her choice.

"And now you think you're a suspect again."

She looked so sad that I tried for optimism. "I'll be okay. If things get tough, I'll call my lawyer. He helped me last time."

"Yeah. That was lucky." She gave me a grim smile. "You're like a cat, Beth, always landing on your feet. I bet you can do it again." She looked at her apartment. "Wish I knew how to do that."

"You'll get past this, Maureen," I told her. "You've got options."

"You're right." With a change of mood that surprised me, she took my arm and pulled me to my feet. "This place is crummy, but you have to see the view." She led me to the sliding glass door, which opened with that gritty, grinding sound that signals dirt in the track. We stepped onto the balcony, which at first seemed as depressing as the apartment. Below was the back of the building, a sad-looking spread of concrete with trash bins and recycle boxes for decoration. Around us were other characterless buildings, with small patches of sun-burnt grass in a few tiny spots in between.

When I lifted my eyes above the ramshackle buildings in the immediate vicinity, however, I saw what she meant. The ugly disappeared and I saw the river and the north side of the city. It was lovely. We stood for a while, leaning against the railing and looking at it, and I thought of the two young women who'd gone to the police academy with such high hopes. How had we failed? It wouldn't have seemed possible to us then that we'd last such a short time on the job and both leave under a cloud of suspicion. *Life isn't fair,* Beth thought, and Loser whispered, *Nobody ever promised it would be.*

Maureen must have been thinking along the same lines, for she said, "Being a cop was all I ever wanted. Making things right for people."

I let go of my remaining anger at her. I, too, had wanted to make things right. Growing up in the foster care system, I'd seen a lot of wrong, but I'd also met people who tried to make things right. Like other public servants, cops were supposed to fight wrong, not participate in it. "Yeah," I said quietly.

She looked down at her hands, twisting them together. "I never believed for a second you killed your family. I agonized over it for days and finally decided I had to tell where you were that night." She looked up at me, meeting my eyes. "By the time I got the courage up you were gone, and nobody knew where." Her voice turned bitter. "I wanted to keep my job, but you see how that worked out."

"Yeah."

She swallowed hard before continuing. "Last year when you showed up in the news, I was glad, but I couldn't stop thinking I should have done more. Then I lost my job, and I thought, *This is how Beth felt. She was innocent, but she couldn't prove it.* That was partly my fault." She waved a hand toward the clutter behind us. "You see how well I'm dealing. Just can't get it together."

I didn't comment. Who was I to judge her? I'd been unable to get it together for some time myself.

"A while ago I found this article about how you'd got your life back. After I read it, I thought, *No, she didn't, not really*." Putting her fingers to her chest, Maureen said, "You won't be right until everybody knows you didn't kill your husband. I know, because it's how I feel. I won't be okay again until I prove it wasn't me who was the bad cop, you know?"

It was why I'd felt compelled to come back to Richmond. It was why I'd come to this building. Though not accused of murder, Maureen understood a little of what I'd been through.

She went on, "We're trained police officers. We know how to investigate crime. If I help you prove you didn't kill anyone, maybe you can help me turn my life around too." She combed her thick hair back from her face with both hands. "It's like that's where I screwed up, when I didn't help you. We were friends, but I didn't act like a friend."

I'd mostly thought of Maureen as a fellow cop, not as a friend. Still, I told myself, I needed all the help I could get, especially from someone who knew the South Side well.

"You want to help me prove I didn't kill Darrin?"

"Yes. If you'll help me with my case." Turning her back to

the city, she leaned against the railing. "I've already been all over Richmond asking questions."

"I know you talked to Aisha."

"You heard about that?" She shook her head. "I thought she'd help, but I figured out she's a big old liar."

"Where is she now?"

"Arlington, I think. I gave her a little money, and she said she was going to buy a train ticket. Some guy had beat her up pretty bad, and she wasn't sticking around for him to do it again."

It was a relief to know Aisha was alive. "How about Carole Ann Minier?"

Maureen popped her lips, a habit I recalled from our days at the academy. She did it when she was concentrating, and I recalled thinking it would become irritating to someone riding in a patrol car with her for hours at a time.

"Yeah, Carole Ann," she said. "I arrested her once and rousted her a few other times. She never held it against me, and she'd always chatter away whenever I ran into her. One time she told me about this guy she used to date who treated her real good. When I asked what happened to him she said he died. She said the two of them had been planning to go away together. I must have looked like I didn't believe her, because she dug out a picture, her and him at some bar."

My stomach lurched, but my eyes never left Maureen's face. "You recognized the guy."

"Yeah," she said softly. "I met your husband at graduation, remember? Dalton? Real good-looking."

"Darrin." It came out in a whisper.

"I'm sorry, Beth. I don't get why a man would—"

"You saw Carole Ann recently?" I interrupted, unable to bear platitudes about the sanctity of marriage.

"The article brought that picture to mind. I started wondering if she might have killed your husband."

"And?"

"I don't know." She shrugged. "The woman was like a freight train, rolling down the tracks full speed. Hard to say what she was capable of."

"My baby." Despite years of keeping things inside, the words were out before I could stop them.

Putting her arms around me again, Maureen administered the prescription most people think is needed when someone's in pain. For me, the second hug was as uncomfortable as the first.

"I know she didn't like kids," she said when she let me go. "She'd had a couple of abortions, said she didn't want to raise a bunch of brats."

The word hit me like a blow. Kara had been wanted and loved. Anger almost overwhelmed me, but I reminded myself that Carole Ann was beyond my hatred and her stupidity. She'd paid for her sins.

"The other possibility is the boyfriend." Maureen began pacing. "If he found out Carole Ann was serious about another man, he's capable of murder."

"D'Nard? But it's been three years."

"What if Carole Ann knew he did it and he thought she might tell me, or at least say something that helped me figure it out?"

After my experience in D'Nard's territory, I guessed he'd have found out sooner rather than later that his girlfriend was talking to an ex-cop. If he'd held her somewhere until she told him everything, then killed her in the same way he'd killed Darrin, it explained why she'd gone willingly, leaving her dinner uneaten and expecting to return to feed the cat.

Maureen watched me as I thought my way through it. Pushing her hair away from her face again, she said, "Want to see her place?" When I looked at her questioningly, she grinned. "I know where she kept the spare key." Rummaging through the messy desk, she located her own keys. "It'll help you get an idea of what she was like."

We were silent on the way downstairs, since anything we said would have echoed through the concrete and metal tube. At the bottom, huffing a little, Maureen opened the fire door and followed me through. She turned toward a rear entrance that led to the parking lot, but a cadaverous-looking man who'd been waiting for the elevator called out, "Ms. Daley!" His suit came from an earlier generation and might once have been owned by a larger man. It hung loosely on his frame, and the lapels were fuzzy with pills. I wasn't close enough to smell the mothballs, but I could imagine them.

"I was just coming to see you." He spoke as if his teeth were also hand-me-downs.

"Mr. Arbin, I'm on my way out. We'll talk later." She waved at me. "This is my friend, Beth Lousiere."

Arbin's left brow rose. "Perhaps your friend can loan you the money to pay your rent."

Maureen didn't bother to answer but continued outside, where she turned and flipped the now-invisible landlord off. "He knows I don't get paid till the fifth," she complained, "but every month he comes by to remind me the rent is due on the first. I think he gets off on it."

Maureen's car was no prize, an ancient Plymouth with serious damage to the right front fender. "Some guy ran a yield sign," she said, unlocking the driver's door. "He can sue me if he wants to, but he was in the wrong."

The car smelled of fast food, and I brushed a couple of fries off my seat before sitting down. Maureen turned the ignition, which ticked like it might be counting down the seconds to Armageddon. "I know a guy who can fix that," she said when the engine finally started. It sounded like Armageddon too.

It wasn't far to Carole Ann's apartment building, but it took us a while to find a parking spot. Maureen refused to pull into a lot that charged money, though I offered to pay, instead wedging the car between a pickup and a delivery van at the back of a small bakery. The space was barely large enough, so she bore left, blocking her door and the passenger door of the pickup. She crawled out my side, where there was just enough to slide out and sidle to the back of the van.

"We won't be here that long," she said, brushing dust from the vehicles off her black pajama pants. She gave me a couple of swats as well, like Big Sister cleaning up Little Sis for Sunday School.

Together we made our way to 14A, and, after checking to see that no one was watching, Maureen put a hand into the nearest wall sconce and retrieved the key. She led me inside, gesturing in a Vanna White sweep to indicate the place was mine to explore.

I looked at everything, though I was careful to touch nothing. The apartment was decorated in inexpensive but attractive style, with a butterfly motif that showed up in wall hangings, bric-a-brac, and bedcovers. There wasn't much to indicate Carole Ann's past, nothing to predict the violence that had ended her life. The clothes in the bedroom were cheap but gaudy, a poor girl's attempt at glamour. All in all it was just an apartment for one, better than some and cleaner than Maureen's.

Had Darrin come here? Had he enjoyed Carole Ann's company? What had she offered him that I—

I had to stop thinking about that. What mattered was who'd killed Darrin, Carole Ann, and my baby girl. I saw nothing here that even hinted at an answer to that question.

"Let's go."

Maureen opened the door for me with her shirt-tail, glancing back at the apartment to see that everything looked okay before wiping the outside doorknob clean. She polished the spare key the same way and replaced it as we left. I waited while she backed her car out of its skinny spot, and then I dropped into the passenger seat, feeling springs beneath the insufficient padding.

The temperature had risen to broiling level while we were gone, but of course the car's A/C didn't work. "Let's find a cool spot where we can talk," Maureen suggested. Across the street and down a block, a parking spot had opened up under a wide-spreading maple tree, and she maneuvered the car into it. We rolled the windows down and sat there, watching the traffic for a few minutes. The visit to Carole Ann's apartment had been more stressful than I'd imagined. Seeing her things, her almost empty refrigerator, her closet full of skimpy clothes, her many butterflies, had made her real to me. I didn't like the feeling that I was somehow to blame for her death, but I couldn't shake it either.

"So who do you think killed your family, Carole Ann or D'Nard?"

I let out a long breath. "It's hard to believe either of them could commit murder and leave no trace."

She was silent for a few seconds. "Maybe one of them did it, and then called the other one, and they covered it up together. After all, you were gone all night."

"That sounds pretty far-fetched."

"Yeah, I know, but it could happen." She jerked to attention, staring out the windshield. "Wait here." She was out the door before I could ask where she was going, and it slammed with an odd sound, indicating it no longer sat firmly in its frame.

Across the street, a patrol car waited in front of a convenience store. A uniformed man sat in the driver's seat, but a second man exited the store, a couple of drinks and a sack in his hands. He had a distinctive silver streak in his hair that added a dash of distinction to an otherwise ordinary face.

When he saw Maureen he stopped, and I saw his expression harden. Going over to the car, he handed the food to the other man before turning to face Maureen. He said something to her, and she answered. Whatever she said, he didn't like it. With a glance around to see who was watching, the cop grabbed Maureen by the shirt and dragged her around the side of the building, out of sight. The cop in the car didn't move.

What should I do? I wasn't sure. She'd told me to wait, but... My indecision ended when the cop came into sight again. He hadn't been gone long, and he seemed irritated but not overly so. He got into the car and said something to his partner, who handed him his drink and started the car. They drove off without looking back.

Getting out of Maureen's car, I crossed the street and went around the building. Maureen leaned against the wall, her face marked with a large scrape along the cheekbone. I hurried over, but she waved me back. "I'm okay."

"What happened?"

"I told him I was going to have proof against them soon, and he didn't like it. He shoved me against the wall to make his point."

I looked at her in horror. "Why would you tell him that?"

Maureen touched her cheek, which oozed tiny drops of blood. "You can't sit around and wait for things to happen, Beth. You have to push it a little, let your enemy make mistakes."

I went into the store and bought medicated wipes for her face. As Maureen cleaned the wound, which wasn't serious but had to sting, she said, "You see I'm not making this up. If I help you solve your husband's murder, will you help me get these guys?"

"If I can."

"Good." She eyed me speculatively. "There is another possibility in your husband's death."

"What's that?"

"Remember Manville? Went through the academy with us?"

I chuckled. "Last year he arrested me for sitting on someone's porch."

"You might recall I didn't have much use for the guy."

My smile turned real. "You said he was a jackass with all the jack removed."

"Exactly. Remember how he harassed you all the time, how

I always had to make him back off?"

I shrugged, agreeing with the first part but not necessarily the last. I'd never asked for her help.

"I always thought he was kind of creepy, and—" She shifted in the tattered car seat. "I should shut up."

"Come on, Maureen! What does Manville have to do with this?"

She turned to look at me, pulling one leg up into her lap. "Remember in junior high how the boys used to snap your bra strap and pull your hair?" Maureen smiled. "Guys like Manville never get past that kind of behavior, because they never grow up."

"So?"

"So he had a thing for you. That's why he gave you grief during training. It's like he was screaming, 'Look at me, Beth! Look at me!' all the time."

That didn't seem right. "I'm pretty sure Manville despised me."

Maureen gestured impatiently. "Trust me on this. I saw it back then, but you were so in love with Darwin you looked right past it."

"Darrin," I corrected absently as I tried to decide if I bought her argument.

"Whatever." She laid the back of her hand against her damaged cheek. "It made him mad when you pretty much ignored him. I figured once we graduated we wouldn't see him much, so I didn't make a big deal out of it."

I was still trying to process the idea that Manville had a thing for me. It hadn't shown in any way I could comprehend.

Maureen stared out the windshield at the street, where

the world moved by in pantomime. "After I got fired, I ran into him in a bar. He was pretty drunk, and he started giving me fake sympathy about how I got such a bad deal. Then he asked if I knew where you'd gone. It was like he couldn't decide if he hates you or loves you." She shook her head as if banishing the memory. "I'll tell you this much, the guy's a little over the edge where you're concerned."

"Maureen, are you saying that Manville—"

"No!" Her voice rose. "I'm not saying anything, because I can't prove it. But there are things about him you don't know."

"Then tell me."

"I can't!" She put her fists to her temples as if trying to keep her head from exploding. "But now that people know you're back in Richmond, things will start to happen."

"What things?"

She glanced at her watch. "Damn! We'll have to talk about it later."

Maureen was avoiding an answer. What did she know that I didn't? "Listen—"

She waved her hands, palms outward as if to shush me. "I need to step on it if I'm going to make work on time. It's a pathetic job at the movie theater, but I gotta pay the bills, right?"

I sensed she was ashamed, but who was I to judge? I doubted she dug through other people's trash.

"I'll drop you at the bus stop." Starting the car, she pulled into traffic. To my discomfort, she took me to the one where I'd narrowly escaped D'Nard on my first visit to the South Side. His threat that I was not to return came to mind. I checked my watch. I'd have to stand at the stop in broad daylight for ten, maybe twenty minutes if the bus was behind schedule. "Is this okay?"

Swallowing my fears, I said, "Sure."

"Great, because I really need to go. The job sucks, but it gives me time during the day to follow leads. I plan to do some digging in the morning."

"I can help."

She shook her head. "He'll spot you a mile away."

"Manville?" I guessed.

"Listen." She bit on her bottom lip. "I'll tell you everything tomorrow. If my idea works, things will be a lot clearer. If it doesn't, you can help me decide what to do."

I frowned. "Don't put yourself in danger, Maureen. Remember, Carole Ann is dead."

She put a hand on my arm. "I won't do anything crazy, but if I can make it up to you for not helping when I should have, I want to do it." Shooing me out of the car she ordered, "Come to my place around 10:00. If what I have in mind works out, there'll be an arrest real soon."

Chapter Eleven

I got out of Maureen's car and crossed to the bus stop, scanning the area nervously as she made a noisy exit. As I walked, I put the sunglasses back on and pulled the hat low on my forehead.

It was a good thing. When traffic cleared, I saw D'Nard and some of his friends a half block away, sitting or leaning on the steps of a building and surveying their turf, like princes of the realm. They all wore sunglasses and hats of some kind, some baseball caps turned at odd angles, some more individual specimens. D'Nard was dressed in a deep rose-colored wife beater with an unbuttoned short-sleeved shirt over it. On his head was a beret made of leather, a sacrifice to fashion, since late spring in Richmond is no time for non-breathing accessories.

I made myself move forward, though I wanted to turn and run. Taking a stand near the bus stop sign, I turned away as if watching for someone. When the bus came I stepped on, paid my fare, and took a seat on the side opposite D'Nard's coterie. After a few seconds the bus lurched ahead, and I glanced sideways apprehensively. D'Nard was standing, glaring at the bus as his friends looked at him questioningly. He took a step forward, but the vehicle was already picking up speed. I turned to watch as he pointed urgently at one of the men on the steps. The guy jumped up and took off down the street, and I guessed he was going to get something, most likely a car.

I got out at the next stop, having peered behind as the bus chugged along. I'd seen no sign of D'Nard in the vehicles behind us, but it would take his buddy a few minutes to get the car, pick up D'Nard, and begin pursuit. They knew where the bus would stop along the route, so I couldn't afford to stay on it. As soon as my feet hit the pavement, I hurried into one of the ubiquitous drug stores that occupy every city corner these days. I bought a different hat, a pair of black-framed reading glasses with almost no correction, and a t-shirt that said *Transformers.* I wasn't sure what that was, but its colors were bright and splashy, very different from the shirt I wore beneath it.

I walked back to the Fan with my head full of what ifs. What if D'Nard came along? I told myself that wasn't likely, given my circuitous route. When he found I wasn't on the bus any longer, he'd probably drive around for a while and then give up. At least that's what I hoped.

Other questions nagged at me as well. What if Maureen was stringing me along, hoping to get her job back by capturing Carole Ann's killer? What if she had the police waiting for me when I went to her place in the morning?

On the other hand, she didn't seem to be on good terms with the police. The fact that she wanted to help me was gratifying, even though it wasn't totally for my benefit. I wondered how much of what she'd said was true. Manville, for example, was a poor excuse for a cop and a lousy human being, but murder? I didn't think he was capable of it. And there was Kara—what kind of man could smother an infant? It was beyond my imagination, but someone had.

I recalled the vandalism Helen Franklin had described. If Maureen couldn't keep quiet about the evidence she was collecting, might her former partner or his buddies have broken into her place looking for it? Maureen needed to be more careful, but I sensed desperation had led her to a point where she couldn't be. Her world was dissolving, all her plans had gone wrong, and she was unable to be circumspect as she fought back with everything she had.

Once I was on familiar turf again, I retrieved my tote bag from under the porch and headed for the nearest bathroom to change clothes. The outfit I'd chosen for my homeless persona was shapeless, suggesting a small man as easily as a woman. With one of the wildly colorful hats skiers wear and the hood of my new jacket pulled up, I was as anonymous as I could get. Most people look away from the homeless anyway, embarrassed by their poverty.

Sitting down in the recessed doorway of an abandoned print shop, I dozed a little and thought a lot. The sun was hot, and I felt sweat pop out in the usual places, but I stayed in character, wrapped in layers of stifling camouflage. People passed, and I listened to their footsteps, some hurried, some not, some definite, some shuffling. I heard a couple talking as they passed. "...smacked her right across the face," the man said.

"He's disgusting," the woman commented. "She should leave him."

Maureen had explained Aisha's disappearance. I recalled Billy's evasive answers when I'd asked about her, the glint of something in his eyes that suggested knowledge he wasn't sharing. He beat her; she ran.

I rose from my spot, dusting the dirt from the seat of my pants, and stepped onto the sidewalk. I needed to let Jacob know there was one less death to investigate.

"Hey!"

I knew immediately that I was in trouble. The nasal twang and peremptory tone could only belong to one person. Pretending I didn't hear, I turned toward an alley, intending to run, but he called again, "You in the hoodie. Stop!"

I obeyed but didn't turn until he grabbed my shoulder and spun me around. "Well, well, well. If it ain't Ms. Lousiere." I glared up at Manville, who grinned like a malevolent Barney Fife. "We got the word to detain you for questioning, Loser." He accentuated the epithet, giving it added meaning. "Some woman got knifed exactly the same way your husband did." Taking his cuffs off his belt, he spun me around and pulled my hands into position more roughly than was necessary. "Can't wait to hear you explain this one."

I remained silent, dreading the cell that awaited me. Locked in, maybe for a long time. Maybe forever.

Two hours later, the detective who'd taken me from Manville's none-too-gentle care wiped his face with one hand, continued up the side of his head, and finished at the back of his thick neck. "Mrs. Lousiere, we can't help you if you won't talk to us."

You won't help me if I do, I thought. Nothing I said would make him rethink the scenario he'd concocted. I'd come to Richmond, located Carole Ann, and killed her, apparently believing I was exacting justice. Someone had seen me and another woman entering the building where Carole Ann had lived, and they believed I'd gone back to remove evidence that would implicate me in her murder. Manville would probably get a citation for his diligent work in apprehending me.

The detective, whose name was Marshall, had been at me for an hour, starting with a business-like attitude and switching to an "I'm your friend" approach when I remained silent. In the end he settled for wheedling, but all he'd gotten from me so far was thanks for the glass of water he'd provided.

"You told us back then that your husband had a girlfriend, but they ignored you." He tried to sound sympathetic. "That could be your defense—diminished capacity due to extreme distress."

When I didn't respond, he tried a new approach. "We know Jacob Grauman has been keeping you informed. If you tell us everything, I'll see he doesn't get into trouble."

That was the first body blow. I didn't care what happened to me—well, I was trying not to, but Jacob? What would they do to him? A reprimand? Worse?

Marshall realized he'd struck a nerve. "Grauman has a good record, but—" He was interrupted by a knock at the door, and a female officer stuck her head in. Marshall listened as she whispered her news. They both looked at me, and I saw disgust in Marshall's expression.

"Your lawyer is here, Mrs. Lousiere."

I was surprised, to say the least, but I saw movement behind the officer, a dark suit, a red tie, and an anxious face. Alex.

Once we were alone he asked reproachfully, "When were you going to call us, Beth?"

I shrugged. The answer, of course, was never. I was embarrassed, ashamed, and unwilling to admit I'd gotten into another scrape that required rescue.

"They've got nothing," he said, reading my mind. "The woman was stabbed twelve times, but she was dumped in the river. There isn't much evidence for the M.E. to work with." He touched my shoulder. "They could hold you for unlawful entry, but I've convinced them that won't stick either. A confession from you would have made it easy for them."

I looked directly at him for the first time. While I was dressed in rags and hardly recognizable as a woman, Alex was as neatly groomed as ever, his dark hair shiny and his youthful face serious. His eyes showed concern, and I guessed he was afraid I'd retreated into the old Loser, the one who spoke no more than thirty words a day. Loser wanted to return. Struggling against despair, I'd felt the old defense mechanisms kicking in: *hide, say nothing, avoid eye contact.* But with Alex's appearance, Beth had taken control. At least she was trying to. "I can go?"

"You might have to promise to stay in Richmond for a while." He grinned, and for a second it felt like things would be okay. "I'm thinking you plan to stay until this is settled anyway." His hand reached toward me again, but he pulled it back. "Bert and I are hoping you'll let us help."

When Alex asked if I'd be charged, Marshall said no. What he actually said was, "Not at this time."

"How'd you know?" I asked as soon as we were out of the detective's hearing.

"Eddie," Alex replied. "He's pretty worried about you."

It might have made me feel good to have people who cared, but instead I felt like more of a loser. I should have figured out a way to let Eddie know I was all right.

Alex and I left the station house together, relief making my knees wobbly. I'd been holding it together through sheer will, but it hadn't been easy. Sensing that, Alex said, "Wait here. I'll get the car."

Gratefully I sank onto a bench outside the front doors. A breath of fresh air and I'd be okay. "Thanks."

He squeezed my shoulder before walking away, looking

like he wanted to say something. He chose not to, and I let the sun start working on the chill inside me. It was hot, even searing, but I didn't care. I wasn't inside, under arrest, charged with murder.

"They let you go, huh?"

I turned to see Manville leaning against a car with his thumbs hooked in his belt. Lowering my head, I tried to pretend he wasn't there.

He approached, entering my personal space in a classic move designed to intimidate. I remained still, looking at his feet. "We're going to get you, Beth." He bent down and spoke into my ear as I crouched like a cornered possum. "You killed your husband, you killed your own kid, and now you killed that hooker. This time we're gonna find the evidence that puts you away."

I shook my head fiercely, cringing at the certainty in his voice.

"Deny it all you want," he said, taking a step closer. "I know all about you."

His tone revealed enjoyment at making me miserable, and I forced my rigid lips to form words. "You don't know me."

Even without seeing it, I heard the nasty smile in his voice. "Even your friends were afraid of you."

"Who?"

Alex's car pulled up at the curb. No doubt reading the distress in my body language, he exited the car and hurried toward us. "Are you okay, Beth?"

"Who are you?" Manville demanded.

"Mrs. Lousiere's attorney—and her friend," Alex replied stiffly. "If you're harassing her—"

"No harassment, Counselor, just a few things she needed to know." As Alex inserted himself between Manville and me, his sneer deepened. "If you're her friend, advise her to face up to what she did."

"I'd like to see your identification," Alex said. "Any further contact with my client will result in—"

"Forget it, Alex," I interrupted. "Let's just go."

He reached out a hand as if to assist me, but his presence was enough to restore my courage. Straightening, I stepped around Manville and got into the car. As Alex moved to the driver's side, Manville said in a voice just loud enough for me to hear, "She told me everything, Beth. I know how crazy you are."

I didn't respond. When words won't change a thing, I'm good at silence.

"Who was that?" Alex asked as we drove away. "And what's he after?"

"His name's Trey Manville, and he's the one who arrested me. As to what he's after, I'm not sure." Folding my arms, I leaned against the butter-soft headrest, telegraphing my unwillingness to discuss the matter further.

"Okay." Alex's voice revealed a hint of agitation at my reticence, but he left the subject of Manville unfinished. "I don't suppose they fed you, and I was in court most of the afternoon. Want to see what we can find for dinner?"

Holding up my bag, I pointed to a gas station coming up on the right. "If I can change into Beth first."

CHAPTER TWELVE

Once I was more appropriately dressed, Alex took me to one of his favorite places, a Thai restaurant where the wait-staff moved almost silently around the room, smiling and bowing as if thrilled to serve us. The food was exquisite, and I relaxed a little, letting Alex pick information out of me about the interrogation I'd endured and my history with Manville.

"Who'd have told the guy you're crazy?" he asked when I'd finished.

"Lots of people think it," I admitted, "but he said it was a friend of mine, a woman." I considered. "It had to be Aisha. Manville works in the Fan, and she started claiming to be my friend after all that crap about the Homeless Hero."

"From what I heard, you were a hero." Alex went on without giving me time to argue. "Aisha is the woman who went missing about the time Carole Ann Minier did?"

I nodded, impressed that he was up on local events. Setting my soup bowl aside, I took a sip of jasmine tea. "The only other woman he might have talked to about me is Maureen." I told him who she was, ending with, "I was at her place today, and she says she believes I'm innocent." I set the cup down. "Besides, Maureen despises Manville."

Alex met my gaze. "It doesn't sound like you like him much either."

I explained our time together at the academy, when Manville had frequently aired his opinion that I was too small to be an effective cop. "Who's gonna want to work with her?" he'd ask, not caring if I heard. "A cop prevents trouble by looking like he can handle whatever comes up. One look at her and the bad guys will start snickering."

Fear he might be right had made me work hard to learn more and think tougher than those blessed with an intimidating physical presence. I'd vowed to never be a drag on my partner, to hold up my end of things, and for the short time I'd been an officer, I had.

Now I recalled Maureen's claim that Manville had been attracted to me. Unable to work my mind around it, I rejected her conclusion. Manville was simply an ass.

A rush of hopelessness hit me. What madness had made me think coming to Richmond was a good idea? It wasn't like me to speak my feelings, but jasmine tea and Alex's presence encouraged it. "This is worse than I expected."

He regarded me solemnly for a few seconds. "You came back to find out who killed your husband."

When I nodded, his hands moved across the table toward me a few inches. "Beth, let me—let Bert and me help." The movement changed direction, and he adjusted his plate as he went on in a more businesslike tone. "We have resources, you know."

"Yeah." It was hard to admit I needed help. Still, a gimpy, desk-bound cop and a few street people didn't make much of an investigative team, even if I were willing to put them in jeopardy. From my bag I took the small notebook where I'd listed what I'd learned the last few days and pushed it across the table toward Alex.

He took several minutes to read through it as I chose from the sampler platter the waiter set between us. He ate distractedly, hardly noticing what he took, but I found I was able to enjoy the different tastes and textures. From time to time Alex asked a question, and he often paused as if to digest the information along with his spring roll. I saw him struggle to take it all in, like he'd come to a play in the second act. Who was D'Nard? Who was Penrod? He must be asking himself what he'd gotten into.

"Okay," he said when he finished reading. "Carole Ann Minier had a card that apparently came from your husband. She also has a boyfriend with a criminal background. Let's start there." I hadn't had time to add last night's encounter with D'Nard to the account, but that was for the best. I didn't want Alex worrying about my physical safety, nor would it be pleasant to relate that I'd had to hide out in a Dumpster. It was so very Loser-like.

Checking his watch, Alex gestured at the waiter for the check. "Where are you staying?"

The question stymied me for a moment, indicating Alex's cluelessness about Richmond's underworld. People make assumptions. They ask questions like, "What did you have for dinner?" They can't fathom that there might not have been anything at all, that maybe there hasn't been for a while. His question assumed I would sleep in a bed, in safety, in a room with lights, wi-fi, and running water.

After a pause, I came up with a fairly honest, socially correct answer. "With friends." It was true. I'd be spending the night on the streets of Richmond, with the people who understood me best. Thanks to Alex, at least tonight I wouldn't have to dodge police cars.

"You can stay at my place." He looked at his hands, and I thought he had an inkling. "I've got a futon."

That set me to wondering what Alex's home was like. He'd

mentioned an apartment somewhere on the east side. I pictured us entering a manly but tasteful living room strewn with things that interested him. There'd be books, of course. I might see a spoon or a few forks in the sink, but I guessed the kitchen wasn't used much. I found myself thinking I could introduce him to cooking, to the joys of putting ingredients together and experimenting to see what worked best. He'd insisted my pies were the best he'd ever eaten. What would he think of my pumpkin soup?

Stop it, Loser. "Really, I'm good."

He gave me a long look but didn't press. "Can we meet tomorrow and talk about this?" He pushed my notebook back across the table, and I put it into my bag. "I can pick you up."

"I have something to do in the morning. I'll text you when I'm done."

"Okay." He sounded doubtful, and honestly, I doubted myself. I didn't know what I'd do after Maureen told whatever it was she had to tell. Signing the bill, he added the tip. "Where do you want to go now?"

"You can drop me off on Monument," I told him. "I'm meeting my friends there."

I walked to the All-Aid after Alex dropped me off near the statue of Robert E. Lee and Traveler. I wanted to ask the guys if they'd ever seen Manville talking to Aisha. Even someone as dumb as Manville should have known better than to believe her easily-spun fiction.

Penrod was alone at the All-Aid, and he seemed stressed. His repeated phrase came faster than normal, with emphasis on the word moment: "Choose an awkward *mo*ment. Choose an awkward *moment*!" When he saw me his posture relaxed a little. "Loser! Verle's looking for you."

Unable to filter or prioritize, Penrod felt keenly any responsibility entrusted to him. Asking a favor of him raised his apprehension to almost unbearable levels. He compensated by amping up his verbal sedative, so much that it often scared those around him. Now that he'd delivered the message, he could go back to his normal stress level, still enough to make anybody a wreck.

"Verle?"

"Yeah. He's been here a lot of times." Taking a big breath, he finished, "He said to come see him."

"I will, but I have a question for you." I asked about Manville and Aisha, but Penrod shook his head. "No. I never saw him talk to her, except once when she threw a fit in the middle of the street." A tiny grin formed as he recalled the scene. "He told her 'Move your ass or I'll put it in a cell!'"

"But they never talked."

He shook his head vigorously. "You know Aisha's scared of anybody in a uniform."

I thanked him and started off, wondering if I should find out what Verle wanted. I had no desire to run into Flo again. As I walked away, Penrod pushed his stomach one more time and called softly, "I like your new clothes, Loser."

I approached the restaurant warily, making my way down the alley to the side door. There were at least three people in the kitchen, Verle, Carla, and a woman with a Barbie-type ponytail. I sat down between trash bins to wait, taking care to keep the better of my secondhand outfits from getting dirty.

"Beth?"

The voice woke me from a gentle doze and brought me to

my feet, flight instinct in full force. Flo blocked my escape route. I backed up to the fence, watching her warily. I could climb the bin, scramble across the top, jump to the ground, and disappear into the alley. If she'd already called the police, I was in for a second trip to the station in one day.

Flo wore peach-colored Capri pants paired with a top Marta would have called skimpy, flip-flops with peach-colored flowers, and a bracelet that looked like it weighed six pounds. Nails on both fingers and toes, as well as the band that held her champagne-colored hair, matched the outfit perfectly. Besides the question of how long before the police would arrive, I wondered how much time she invested in putting an outfit like that together: shopping, styling, and accessorizing.

"Listen," I began, but Flo put up a hand.

"I have to get something off my chest." She heaved said chest as she spoke. "Come inside, will you?" When I hesitated, at a loss, she added, "I owe you an apology."

Ten minutes later, I sat at the rickety table in the apartment at the back of the building, still a little lost. Flo sat across from me, her forearms resting on the aged oil-cloth covering. "—so when Verle found out what I did, he was really, really mad." She put a hand over her heart. "He never hollered at me before, but he said it was dumb for me to think what I thought. He said you're a friend, not a girlfriend." Her face flushed as she added, "He said he loves me and doesn't want another woman." Batting back tears, she added, "He never said that before. Not out loud."

It might have been the end of a sit-com episode. Flo's jealous action had brought her and Verle closer together, which apparently meant I was now Flo's friend too.

Flo rose, got herself some toilet paper from the bathroom,

and wiped her nose daintily. Dropping the wadded tissue into the trash, she changed the subject. "When the cops were here earlier, they asked if they could search the place."

My gaze flickered to the bed, where I'd hidden my knapsack. I'd probably lost my remaining cash and clean underwear.

"I moved your stuff." Flo brushed her cheek with a hand as if hiding embarrassment. "Honestly, I was gonna throw it in the trash bin. That's when Verle saw me and figured things out." She smiled nervously. "After he got done hollering about how stupid I was to get jealous, he put your bag in the janitor's closet. He's going to bring it back here when he gets a minute." She waved toward the door like a magician's assistant, and *Presto!* Verle appeared, my original bag in hand.

"Loser! Thank god you're okay." He joined us at the table, using up all the chairs available. "Did Flo—"

"We're good."

Verle nodded at me and beamed at his wife. "That's great."

"I was just telling Beth this place is safe now. She can stay here."

"The cops aren't looking for me anymore," I told them. "They questioned me and let me go."

"That's great." Glancing at Flo, Verle went on, "You're welcome to stay, either way. Nobody knows you're here but us." He waved at the hallway behind him. "There's an old laptop down in the kitchen we use for ordering. You can use it to look for people and stuff."

Use it to look for people? Verle knew why I was in Richmond, and I guessed who'd told him.

I gave him a direct look. "You've been talking to Jacob."

His smile was weak. "Well, yeah. He called me this afternoon, wanted to know if you were okay." I got the impression from his tone that he and Jacob had discussed me at length.

"I—thanks."

Flo pushed herself up from the table, adjusting the straps of her top. "We'll be out of here in half an hour." She slid her arm around Verle's shoulder. "We gotta get home."

Closing the door behind them, I slid the barrel-lock into place then checked the knob of the exterior door to make sure it was locked. Though I would sleep in the alley, it was good to feel unreachable for the moment. I needed quiet time in Verle's lumpy old rocker to try to knit the bits I knew together into a fabric of truth.

Chapter Thirteen

I had breakfast the next morning at Verle's Restaurant. For one thing, he was my friend and a darned good maker of pancakes. For another, meals I'd eaten there before had been charity, or close to it, food bought with odd jobs. It was gratifying to settle my bill like any other customer.

The girl who waited on me was a stranger, probably a college student. She was friendly without being chummy, and she refilled my coffee cup almost every time I took a sip. I could see Verle at work in the kitchen through the serving window, but he never looked out at the dining room. The place was clean and bright, and I saw Flo's hand in the new décor, cups, saucers, and teapots of all types set on shelves at various levels around the room.

My pancakes gone and the plate discreetly removed, I sat sipping coffee and watching the street. Traffic was already heavy, and when I saw a figure on the opposite side, I didn't realize at first who it was. A man was leaning against a patrol car, talking to an officer inside. His skinny backside was to me, but something about his posture was familiar. Billy.

I couldn't see who the cop was, but I had my suspicions. Aisha's sometime boyfriend looked pretty chummy with a guy who'd no doubt rousted him more than once. He gestured widely, listened, then nodded agreement. When the car's brake lights came on, signaling it had shifted into gear, Billy thumped the window frame with his fingertips in a manly farewell. The car continued across the lot and entered the traffic heading eastward, and as the driver turned to wait for an opening, I saw his face clearly. Manville. I looked back at Billy, who was walking north, a satisfied smile on his face. It might have been paranoia, but I thought the topic of conversation had been me.

"She said you're crazy," Manville had claimed, but he might have gotten Aisha's opinion second-hand, from Billy. Waiting a few minutes to be sure he was gone, I left the restaurant and started south. What did a chat between Billy and Manville mean for me? I couldn't think of anything good.

Just before 10:00, I arrived at Maureen's building and began the long climb to the ninth floor. The multiple, switchback staircases gave me time to think. That's not to say the ascent was pleasant; the stairwell was as drab, echo-y, and dirty as it had been the day before. As I passed the lower floors, I heard sounds of human habitation, a child asking repeatedly for something, a man mumbling a goodbye before he closed the door and walked down the hall, a TV with volume tuned up much too high. A couple of times I heard muted crashes, the kind apartment dwellers learn to ignore in order to co-exist. Several of the stairway doors were blocked open with heavy objects, a violation of fire code, but no doubt convenient for the tenants.

Manville's unusual interest in my case had two possible explanations. One was that he was a conscientious police officer who wanted to protect the public from a person he believed to be dangerous. The other was he had his own reasons for wanting me arrested. Knowing Manville, I couldn't believe the conscientious part. Were Maureen's suspicions correct? Did his pursuit of me stem from unrecognized lust? I wished I could talk with Billy again, but I'd burned that bridge. I should have given him a few bucks so he'd be on my side instead of Manville's.

A little out of breath, I arrived at Maureen's and knocked.

The door receded under my hand, and I peered inside, dread hitting my gut like a sucker punch. She'd been careful to lock up yesterday, and since she was expecting me, she wouldn't have gone anywhere.

The mess from yesterday was much worse. A lamp that had sat on the desk was on the floor. The desk chair lay on its side, half in and half out of its nesting place. The blinds at the left of the sliding glass door were twisted out of position, and the door itself stood open. A slight breeze ruffled the air, and the slats clicked in plastic response.

The bathroom door stood open. The bed was empty. Where was Maureen? Drawn to the tiny balcony, I felt my dread worsen. A single sandal lay near the doorway. I stepped through, went to the railing, and looked down. Dread turned to despair.

She lay on the concrete below, her arms splayed and one leg bent like a leg never should. A dark stain spread slowly behind her head, the only part of the scene in motion.

Two police officers arrived within minutes. Spurred by necessity, I'd found Maureen's phone, called 9-1-1, and, stuttering, reported that a woman was dead at this address. I watched from the apartment, standing away from the door, as they approached Maureen's body, pushing away the few curious locals who had gathered. One checked for signs of life and looked up at the other, shaking his head. Once death was established, they both turned toward the balcony, shielding their eyes from the glare.

One man remained with the body, phone in hand, while the other disappeared, no doubt on his way upstairs. By the time he got to the door, Loser was in almost complete control. I found myself counting the words as I told how I'd come to see

Maureen and found the door open. In response to a question, I said I'd left the scene as I'd found it except for using the phone. The guy didn't seem to recognize me, but when I gave my name, he reacted. "Ms. Lousiere, I'm going to have my partner take you to the station while I secure the room."

It wasn't an arrest, but it felt like one. I might have objected. I might have demanded I call my lawyer. Those weren't things Loser did. I went meekly, asking only that we take the stairs. He agreed, probably relieved that the madwoman was reacting so calmly.

My custodial companion was no doubt putting together a scenario in his mind. I'd come to see Maureen. We'd exchanged angry words then blows, as evidenced by the displaced furniture, and she'd gone over the balcony railing. The question would be whether she'd fallen in the struggle or been pushed. Since I was suspected of doing away with anyone who upset me, I guessed they'd lean toward the latter.

When we reached the ground, an ambulance was there, and the EMT's were doing what's required when they arrive too late to be life-savers. The cop dragged his partner aside and spoke quietly. The partner reacted with an interested glance at me, stiffening his posture to readiness, I supposed in case I attacked them. I might have asked why they thought I'd make a break for it when if I'd wanted to, I could have left the scene without alerting anyone.

The younger cop approached, one hand resting on the butt of his revolver. "Will you come with me, please?"

It wouldn't do to ask if I had a choice. Instead, I let him put me into the back seat of the squad car, drive me to the station, and escort me to a room every bit as cheerless and hopeless as others I'd waited in while somebody in the building decided how best to get a confession out of me.

It took a while before anyone came, and I traced the timeline in my head. A detective had to be assigned. He'd visit the scene and draw conclusions from his observations and conversations with the first responders, the neighbors, and anyone else with information. He'd hear that I'd visited Maureen the day before, maybe even learn she and I had gone out together. Today I'd been found in her apartment with her body on the ground below. He was almost certain to conclude he had the culprit.

But who *had* killed Maureen? From the wreckage in the apartment, it was clear she hadn't fallen nine stories by accident. I thought about what she'd said, names she'd mentioned. D'Nard was a guy who might throw a woman off a balcony. She'd seemed to think Manville was dangerous too.

What about Maureen's claims of police corruption in her precinct? Might Carole Ann have known something about it, something that had gotten her killed? If so Maureen might have been murdered in order to keep her quiet. A lot of what she'd said seemed like paranoia, except for the fact that she and Carole Ann were both dead. Whoever the killer was, I'd become a convenient patsy, waltzing into Richmond at precisely the right time.

At 1:00 p.m., according to a clock above my head that operated with an annoying buzz, a woman stepped into the room, a folder tucked under one arm. She wore a navy skirt with a matching jacket and a white blouse underneath. Suspended from the jacket's pocket was a badge identifying her as someone who could come and go in this place while I could not. "I'm Detective Zender," she said with a wooden smile. "I have some questions about what happened today."

I let her pick the story out of me, judging from her phrasing how much she knew about the situation. My reticence was part Loser, part knowing how such things work. She gave relevant facts, and I mostly nodded. I'd gone through training with Maureen Daley. I'd been at the apartment yesterday, and we'd left together. When she asked where we went, I paused. The other detective had said we'd been seen going into Carole Ann's apartment, but Alex had argued the description might have fit a lot of women. I said instead, "We got something to eat." Under further questioning, I grew vague. Maureen had chosen the restaurant and driven to it, so I didn't remember the name or location. Something Chinese, I said, a buffet.

Zender went back to her notes. Maureen had returned alone, but she'd made a notation on her phone for today at 10:00: *Beth.*

"What brought you two back together after all this time?"

I gave her a little truth as a test. "Maureen said she had information about my husband's murder."

"I see." Zender opened the thick folder and paged through. It was designed to make me cringe, and it worked. "I remember some of this, but I hadn't made detective at the time. No arrest was made?"

"No."

Coming to a sheaf of papers fastened together with one of those big metal clips, she slid the first page up and scanned the one after it. "But they liked you for it."

I guessed I was supposed to protest my innocence at that point. When I didn't say anything, she let the top sheet fall back into place. "Looks like sloppy police work to me."

I looked up from examining the tabletop, and she smiled.

"You were a cop, Beth. You know there are times when things don't get investigated the way they should." She tapped the report sharply. "Somebody screwed up here. You looked guilty, so they didn't look any farther. You got shafted."

Her supposed outrage came a little too soon to be believable. She hadn't known me long enough to take a liking to me, and I heard the off-note in her voice. Did these people all use the same ploy, offering sympathy to a suspect to make her open up and perhaps confess? Meeting her gaze for a second, I returned to studying the fake wood before me.

Zender realized she'd blown her chance to come off as my advocate, and I saw her lips twitch in irritation. The interrogation room was warm, either because they thought it made suspects uncomfortable or because the A/C had been installed by the lowest bidder. I was feeling the heat, but so was she. Standing, she slipped her jacket off and hung it on the chair she'd been sitting in.

Pacing her side of the room, she began again with the same questions: why had I gone to see Maureen, what had we said to each other, why had I come back that morning. Having answered them once, minimally but truthfully, I didn't see any point in repeating myself. Once when Zender turned away I looked up at her, wondering if there was any way she might be convinced to take a fresh look at my case. While it looked on the surface like I was incapable of controlling my rage, an objective investigator might wonder if someone wanted me blamed. He'd known I was coming. He must have waited until I started up the stairs then killed her. He'd left the door ajar so I'd go inside.

The problem was, I had no idea who would do this to me, or why.

"I didn't kill anyone."

The detective's expression changed, and her calm manner evaporated. I saw the sheen of sweat on her upper lip as she leaned over the table. Irrelevantly, the thought crossed my mind that she was menopausal. Hot flash—take off the jacket. In a few minutes, the sweat she'd generated would cause her to feel cold and she'd want it again.

Right now she was warm, anger fueling with her hormonal rush. "Listen, Beth. You've been a mess for three years. Isn't it time to tell the truth about this—about all of it?" When I remained silent, she went on, "We'll get you help. You'll go to a hospital, not to prison, and you could be out in a few years."

If Zender thought the idea of a few years in a hospital was a comfort, she was woefully misinformed. It was still confinement. It involved people sticking their noses into every aspect of my life. It meant sleeping inside, where the voices would drive me over the edge. I really would go mad.

Of course, she didn't know me. Mabel or Howard or Penrod could have told her more than all the papers in that folder of hers. It was true I'd been a mess, but I was coming back—at least I'd been working on it when things started to fall apart again. For a moment I wished I'd called Alex. He would have come right away. He wouldn't let this woman hold me without charging me. He would—

A knock on the door interrupted, and Zender went to answer. The thought of Alex had given me hope, but when the door opened, I saw Detective Marshall standing outside. His gaze flickered to me, making sure he had the right room before he spoke to Zender in low tones. I couldn't hear words, but I caught the surprise in her voice, followed by a hint of satisfaction. Finally, she stepped back to the table, picked up the folder, and said, "I'll be back in a few minutes. Use the time to think about your situation, Beth. Make it easy on us, and we'll make it easier for you."

I sat there for a while, doing as I'd been ordered since I had no other choice. Two detectives together was a bad sign. While neither had enough evidence against me for an arrest, together they might approach a judge to suggest I be locked up for public safety. Since it looked like I was running around Richmond killing everyone I was mad at, the judge was likely to agree. My lips began to quiver, but I pressed them together. No time for panic at the thought of being closed in a cell. I had to think.

Moving silently to the door, I tried the knob. It turned. I wasn't locked in. That meant, however, that Zender knew I couldn't just walk away. I tried to recall what was out there. I'd been so miserable on the way in that I hadn't paid much attention. Concentrating, I brought up a mental picture. The interrogation room was one of several along a hallway that ended at a blank wall. We'd passed a desk where an officer in uniform sat, no doubt responsible for monitoring who came and went.

The questions were how good was the guy at his job and how busy was he?

I spent a few seconds with the door open the tiniest crack, watching. The cop had things to do in addition to monitoring the six doorways. He answered the phone. He sorted papers into piles and stapled them. Every once in a while he shoveled something into his mouth from the drawer on his left. From the occasional flash of color, I guessed M&Ms.

Turning back to the room, I assessed what was available. On a small table in the corner was an empty manila folder. I took it up, retrieved some papers from a trash can beside the table, and put them inside to make it look full. As I bent over, I spotted a rubber band under the heating unit. Snatching it up, I pulled my hair back and secured it in a bun at the nape of my neck. Taking Zender's jacket from the chair, I slipped into it, pushing the too-long sleeves up on my forearms until they stuck.

Time was slipping away. Soon the two detectives would finish comparing notes and return. Peering out the door again to be sure no one else was out there, I straightened my spine, lifted my head, and relaxed my facial muscles. Taking a deep breath, I let it out slowly, remembering from a long-ago speech class that it made a person appear relaxed, at least temporarily.

My moment came when the desk phone rang. The cop turned to answer, and I exited the door, stepped to the center of the hallway so it wasn't obvious which room I'd come from, and moved toward him with a purposeful stride. I heard him confirm that the caller had reached the correct number as I walked past the desk, apparently focused on the information in the folder I carried. His glance took in the badge on the jacket, and he didn't look further. He might not have connected the confident woman passing his desk with the timid suspect hauled in earlier, or he might have missed the whole performance as he answered questions and reached for more M&Ms. Science has proven there really is no such thing as multi-tasking.

Past the desk, I kept moving, all the time looking for a way out. After a few wrong turns, I located the exit. Two uniformed men stood beside it, and I stopped to consider how best to get past them. Slipping off the jacket, I approached the guy on the right. "Do you happen to know Detective Zender?"

"Sure," he answered, his tone betraying what might have

been status envy.

"She left her jacket in the ladies' room." I held it out, and he took it. "Will you see she gets it back?"

"Sure." He seemed happy to be able to do a favor for a detective, however small it might be.

"Thanks." I smiled, keeping my eyes on his. "I have to be back at the First by 2:00 or I'll be on Billings' list." I said a silent thanks to Jacob for mentioning his current supervisor. "He's big on punctuality."

The guy on the left snuffled a laugh, and the other joined in. "Yeah, they got some stories over there."

Thanking them again, I left, working hard to look like I deserved freedom. My footsteps sounded like minor explosions on the sidewalk. Surely someone would glance out the window to find out who was making so much noise. They'd see their suspect escaping, and any second I'd hear Zender screaming for someone to stop me. There was nothing.

When I turned the first corner I picked up my pace, moving diagonally to get out of their line of sight. Down an alley, across another street, and through a parking lot, I made four blocks in less than a minute and then slowed, matching the pace of shoppers on the sidewalks. I headed toward Verle's, avoiding public transportation and places where there were surveillance cameras. It's difficult in a modern American city but not impossible if you're used to making yourself invisible.

I hoped Verle's contention the police wouldn't search his apartment twice was correct. Right now that crummy two-room space seemed like heaven to me.

I spent the rest of that day and all night wandering the

apartment like an ape in a cage. I avoided Verle and Flo, figuring they were better off if they could claim they hadn't known I was back there. That left me alone with my thoughts. I was used to that, but it didn't mean it wasn't lonely—and scary.

The idea of calling Bert and Alex kept coming to mind. They'd made it clear they wanted to help me, but how long would it be before they asked themselves why corpses showed up wherever I went?

Since I was unwilling to ask for help, I had to proceed on my own. I couldn't hide at the back of Verle's restaurant for the rest of my life. I couldn't return to West Virginia. With sharp-eyed Manville on the job, I couldn't even go back to being Loser. I toyed with the idea of going to another big city and taking on a similarly anonymous role. That wasn't what I wanted. I wanted my home on the mountain, where Eddie and Mabel waited and where Alex dropped in unexpectedly. I wanted the world to know I wasn't a homicidal maniac. I wanted Jacob's job to be safe, despite the fact he'd helped a wanted fugitive. I wanted Bert's faith in me rewarded. I imagined him chomping on an unlit cigar and drawling, "I always said she didn't do it."

But if I wasn't the murderer, who was? Resentful that the police didn't ask themselves that question, I listed the possibilities as I saw them. The pimp, D'Nard, might have killed Darrin in a jealous rage and Kara in some drug-induced frenzy. Three years later, if his spies told him Carole Ann and Maureen had been talking, he might have taken Carole Ann somewhere, made her tell him what Maureen was up to, and then killed them both. The problem was I didn't see him being smart enough to blame it on me.

Maureen had contended that crooked cops were after her. They might have killed her and Carole Ann, but they had no reason to kill my husband and daughter. If Davis and the other two cops were to blame for the recent deaths, then I was back to square one with solving the crimes I most cared about.

Maybe I was simply a convenient scapegoat. My husband had been carrying on with Carole Ann, whose pimp was apparently aware of, possibly in league with, corrupt police officers. If those cops thought Carole Ann and Maureen had joined forces, they wouldn't have liked it. If they'd learned I was back in Richmond—Billy came to mind as a possible source—word might have gotten around to Davis, Cjaika, or Hamilton. If they had Carole Ann locked up somewhere, they might have seen a chance to get rid of her and blame it on me.

Though it didn't explain everything, it was a start. My case and Maureen's weren't connected, but some of the same people showed up in both. It was up to me to find out who'd done what, and I had one advantage on the Richmond Police. I didn't think I was guilty.

CHAPTER FOURTEEN

"Mr. Bronson, there's an Officer Jacob Grauman calling for you."

Alex checked his watch. He had clients on the way and paperwork stacked to shoulder height on his desk, but he wasn't about to miss the chance to speak to Beth's former partner again. Snatching up the phone, he said, "Bronson."

Grauman spoke softly, as if he were trying not to be heard by anyone near him. "Mr. Bronson, if you know where Beth is, you need to tell her she has to come back in."

"Back in?" Alex took up a pen and pulled a notepad toward him. "She was arrested again?"

"And she escaped somehow." Grauman's low tone rose, but he shushed himself. "She's got to turn herself in. She can't just walk out of an interrogation room—"

"Go, Beth!" Alex said exultantly. "She's awesome, Grauman, you've got to admit that."

"Yeah, I guess." The cop seemed to be smiling despite the seriousness of the situation. Once he explained though, Alex understood his worry.

"They think she killed Maureen Daley too?"

"The theory is they got into a disagreement, and Maureen went over the balcony. It wouldn't necessarily be premeditated murder, but with all the other dead bodies in Beth's past, even accidental death adds to the belief she's got a violent temper and a tendency to over-react."

"Do you really think she should give herself up?"

Grauman's answer was almost a groan. "I don't know."

"If they have Beth in custody, will they look at other options, or will they just look for evidence to confirm she's guilty?"

Jacob made a noise that was neither affirmative nor negative. "I could push—I could make them—" Alex heard a sigh. "I thought it would look better if she came in of her own accord, but you're right. She might be safer with—"

"—with me. With Bert and me."

"I intend to forget you said that, Bronson."

"Good idea. I will tell you this much. Right now, neither of us knows where Beth is. If you prefer to continue thinking along that line, do so."

"I wish she'd contact me."

"It would be nice to know she's all right."

"Beth's smart." Grauman sounded as if he were trying to make himself feel better.

"And tough," Alex added. "Thanks for the call. We'll just have to hope tough and smart is enough."

Setting the phone down, Alex left his office and headed to Bert's. The hum of voices inside made him pause, but he heard tones of dismissal, soft sounds of chairs relieved of their burdens, and papers sliding into folders. The clients were leaving, and Alex stepped into a vacant room. Anxious to talk with Bert about how to help Beth, he didn't want to be delayed by polite pleasantries.

Ten minutes later, Bert had absorbed Alex's news and was leaning back in his chair, looking at the ceiling. "I'm distressed she didn't call us, this second time, but Beth has difficulty asking for help."

"That's an understatement."

"Her case always troubled me." Bert laced his fingers over his substantial middle. "Someone wanted Darrin Lousiere dead, but he or she also wanted Beth to go to prison for murder."

"You were convinced of her innocence?"

The look he got was as close to disapproval as Bert had ever given him. "I was. Darrin was one of those people you like but know enough not to trust—a born salesman—but he was also a careful man. He sold insurance, which I suppose makes one aware of life's pitfalls. As soon as they were married, he took out large policies on each of them and had wills drawn up."

"Here."

"Yes. He'd researched different firms, and he told me this one had a reputation for honesty and economy." Bert grinned. "I'm not sure which was more compelling."

"You met Beth at that time?"

"Yes. I liked her from the first. There was a vulnerability about her even then, a sense she thought she might be dreaming. Darrin was a striking man, and I don't think Beth ever believed in her own attractiveness." Touching the folder he'd pulled from the files Bert added, "I didn't know why then, but I learned most of it over time. Neglected by her father, taken into the foster care system, shunted from pillar to post for years. It skewed her view of herself."

"A handsome charm-bucket comes along, and she thinks it's true love."

Bert smiled thinly. "They never revealed the details of their emotional entanglement to me, but that was the sense I got. Beth felt lucky to have Darrin, and Darrin was pleased at her adoration."

"But that wasn't enough for him."

"According to Beth's testimony, no." Bert glanced out the window, where bright sunlight sparkled off a windshield in the parking lot. "Darrin apparently tried to end the affair with the woman he was involved with, and she threatened his family. Afraid of what she might do, he confessed to Beth."

"But there wasn't anything to support Beth's contention later."

Bert huffed disdainfully. "As I said, Darrin Lousiere was a very careful man."

Alex had read every account he could find of Beth's tragedy, trying to see where the police had gone wrong. In the end he'd admitted to himself their conclusions were justified—except for one thing: Beth herself. She wasn't capable of killing someone she loved, certainly not her own child. Bert agreed, and he wasn't half in love with Beth Lousiere. With an inward grimace, Alex edited out the word *half* in deference to complete honesty and dragged his mind back to what Bert was saying.

"—who this woman was, but I didn't have any luck. It seemed likely that either she'd killed Darrin herself or someone connected to her had, perhaps a jealous husband or lover." Bert rose and walked a few steps, as if he were speaking to a jury. "I leaned toward the lover for three reasons: the murder of the child, which seemed meant to punish Beth; the multiple stab wounds on Darrin's body, indicating rage; and the fact that the killer apparently wore Beth's clothing during the crimes."

"The news reports said there was no physical evidence of anyone else in their home."

"Two pieces of Beth's clothing, sweatpants and a sweatshirt, were found in the washing machine. A half bottle of bleach had been added, ruining any forensic evidence that might have been there."

Alex made a note to find out what Carole Ann Minier's height and weight had been, but sweats were pretty forgiving. Add socks, gloves, and a cap, and a person could be fairly sure he or she would leave nothing behind—especially if the police thought they'd already figured out what happened.

"To be honest," Bert said regretfully, "Beth wasn't much help to me." He raised a hand. "I don't mean to criticize. Though devastated by the murders, she held herself together at first. She claimed an alibi but needed permission to reveal it. Later, she said she'd been wrong."

"That was Maureen's big fail."

Bert nodded. "I see that now. When her foster mother arrived, I thought Beth would be all right. I didn't know until days afterward that the woman died suddenly. I spoke to Beth on the phone, and she seemed distant and"—He paused to find a word. "—empty." By the time I found out what had happened, Beth disappeared as if she'd dropped off the face of the earth." Bert's voice revealed his concern. "I even had the firm's private detective look for her, but he found nothing. She didn't use her credit cards, didn't leave any trace of her presence. Someone turned in her phone when they found it on the sidewalk, but she hadn't made a call in days."

"How long before you heard from her?"

"Three months. One day I opened my email, and there was a message: *I'm okay. Thanks for being my friend.* After that I heard from her every once in a while, but it was clear she didn't want to be found."

"She didn't trust anyone, like she doesn't trust us now to help her."

Bert frowned. "That's not it, Alex. Beth trusts you. She just doesn't believe she deserves our help."

"Of course she deserves—"

"Saying it doesn't make it true for her," he interrupted. "It will only be true when she believes it." He rubbed his chin thoughtfully. "I'm sure all this has thrown her—reliving the days of her tragedy, returning to the places where she was that other person, Loser."

"So how do we find her?"

"That list you made—let me see it." When Alex handed it over, he stared at it for a few seconds. "Try the restaurant again. She'll want a place to stay out of sight during the day. Verle provided that before."

"I tried talking to him. He didn't tell me a thing."

Bert smiled. "A tough guy, is he? In my experience, men like that often don't know what to do when you push past that tough exterior and hit them in the mushy center." Bert reached for the half-chewed cigar that sat on the corner of his desk and leaned back, his expression thoughtful. "If we can find her, I have an idea for keeping Beth hidden. See what you think."

By noon I was going stir crazy. At night I'd slipped out and slept on the ground, but at sunrise I went back inside. I opened the windows to relieve the feeling I was in prison, though I kept the heavy curtains in place. When Verle rapped gently at the door, I was pleased. I'd been feeling very much alone.

"I just had a chat with your friend Alex."

I stood up so fast I almost knocked over the lamp. "Alex? Where?"

One brow went up, along with one side of Verle's mouth.

"He wanted to sample my fine baked goods, I guess." Closing the door behind him, Verle pulled out a chair and sat down at the table. "When he gets done eating his slice—he had the apple—he says to Sandra, 'That pie was almost as good as Loser's. Can you send Verle out so I can tell him in person?' Sandra's eyes looked like them goofy-looking animals on the funny greeting cards when she told me."

He waited for me to respond, but I wasn't interested in Sandra. "How'd he know where I am?"

Chuckling, Verle pointed at me. "He predicted that would be your first question! 'Tell her Bert ratted her out,' he says." Rubbing his stubbly chin, Verle added, "At first I told him I got no idea where you are. He said would I please go to the back and see if anybody wanted to take a ride in the country."

"When?"

"Now, I guess. He said he'd wait in the alley behind your old house."

I made my way to Grace Street, feeling as if a big arrow overhead said, *Here she is! Arrest her!* I tried to act like a resident, stopping to admire flowerbeds as if planning my own.

Alex's black BMW sat at the curb. From all appearances, he'd pulled over to write a text, as a good citizen should. When he saw me, however, he closed the phone and leaned over to open the car door. I slid into the passenger seat, and he checked oncoming traffic before pulling away from the curb.

We traveled for a while in silence, me because it's natural and Alex because he was apparently chewing on something. He was usually pretty chatty, covering my lack of conversation with little stories and interesting patter. Today was different, and we reached the outskirts of Richmond in silence. He drove northwest, passing through Manakin-Sabot and beyond. When we'd left Greater Richmond, Alex abruptly pulled off the road, entering a small park where a few moms sat talking while their kids played on a colorful plastic climbing frame. The women sat in the shade, their movements slowed by the building humidity. The kids seemed unfazed by it, their voices reaching us across the green space as they laughed and called shrilly to each other.

Alex put the car in park but left the engine running. "Why didn't you call this time?"

I didn't have a good answer, and it would take more speech than I could manage to explain how unhappy I was about burdening the Suggs Law Firm once again. "Aren't there things you should be doing besides hanging out with suspected murderers?"

"You're no killer." He fiddled with the A/C controls. "Bert asked me to find you. He was worried."

Two of a kind, I thought. Where else in this day of made-for-TV lawyers did a person find a firm truly dedicated to its clients' welfare? "Neither of you should worry about me. Go back to the office and bill a bunch of hours. Get rich."

"I don't need more money than I have."

"What if you want to get married or travel or buy a time share in Ecuador?"

He kept his eyes on the kids, obviously embarrassed. "I'll be taking over the firm in a year, when Bert takes down his shingle."

I turned in the leather seat to regard him directly. "Bert's retiring?"

He nodded. "I didn't know it when I met him, but he was looking for a successor."

"How'd he find you?"

Alex shrugged as if stymied by the question. "I was about to finish law school, and he came to speak at an honors luncheon. It was my good luck to be seated beside him, and we got to talking." He licked his lips. "I can't say what he saw in me, but Bert is the kind of lawyer I want to be: independent, respected, and, frankly, very well off. When he invited me to become his partner, I was thrilled and a little surprised. He could have had his pick."

I smiled. "He did, Alex, and he chose you."

He waved that away. "Anyway, it's like I fell into a pot of honey. I enjoy what I do, I admire Bert more than anyone I've ever met, and he recently told me he's handing the firm over to me. He has no family—or as he jokes, none he recognizes." He kept a light tone. "It's not a 100 percent sweet deal. I'll be heading a firm I didn't build with clients who'll think I'm too young and inexperienced for the job. But I'm trying to learn the ropes, trying to earn my spot, so Bert's faith in me isn't misplaced."

It wasn't hard for me to see why Bert had chosen Alex. Their meeting might have been happenstance, but they shared a view of the world. Though neither had suffered a day of want in his life, both had compassion for those who did. Neither could fully understand my descent into pain and madness, but neither had ever urged me to "get a grip" or "straighten up and fly right." Unlike bottom-feeder types who promised easy money to gullible citizens, they were principled men who helped clients cope with complex legal issues. Alex wasn't Bert's son, but he was his rightful heir.

He was waiting for a reaction. "That's cool, Alex. It's very cool."

His shoulders relaxed a little, and he returned to my situation. "Okay. We're your attorneys. Either Bert or I should be there when you speak to the cops."

I tried for a joke. "I don't speak to them much."

For once he didn't smile in response. "They'll arrest you the minute they find you."

"Which means you shouldn't be anywhere close."

He cut the air between us with a hand. "Lawyers don't have to tell everything they know."

"Unless they're protecting a murderer." I tried to change the subject. "How'd Bert know where I was?"

"He guessed you'd go to ground in familiar territory."

Like a rabbit chased by dogs, I thought. "What if the police had followed you to Verle's? Do you think they'd believe you went there for the spaghetti boat special?"

Alex ran a hand through his hair. "Let's not worry about that right now. Just promise me that if you get arrested, you'll call me first thing—or Bert, if you don't want to deal with me."

I felt terrible at the implication in his words. "It isn't that, Alex."

"I know Bert helped when your husband and daughter were killed. It's only natural that you trust him—"

"It isn't about trust." I turned away, watching a kid climb the frame and stand like a victor at the top, pleased with himself. "I'm in another mess, and it isn't fair that you have to wade in and fix it. Or Bert either. I know you feel sorry for me, but you don't have to." It was the longest explanation I'd attempted in years, and it didn't explain anything.

I kept my face averted, but I could feel his gaze, steady and strong, like Alex himself. "I don't feel sorry for you, Beth. I feel something altogether different."

The silence stretched between us, and I felt stretched, too, like an elastic band pulled to its farthest point. If Alex meant he cared for me, he wasn't seeing things clearly. And if I cared for him, even a little, I saw no way it could end well. I was a societal dropout who'd soon be charged with murder. Alex was a sympathetic person, as good professionals are, but professionals must learn to maintain emotional distance from clients, especially clients damaged beyond repair.

"All right," I said, keeping my voice even. "I'll call you right away next time I get in trouble."

It took a moment, but he answered just as coolly, "Excellent, because I'm a pretty good lawyer."

Putting the car in gear, Alex backed out of the parking lot and re-entered the highway. "Where are we going?" I asked.

"You can't stay at Verle's forever. They thought of it once, and sooner or later, they'll think of it again."

I sighed. "I know." I thought of the half-ruined building where my car sat waiting. I might be able to stay there if Alex would agree to provide food. I didn't like the idea of him waiting on me or the thought of him seeing me as Loser, growing dirtier each day. My earlier idea returned: I should leave Richmond. If Alex would get me money from my account, I could start again somewhere new.

His idea was totally different. With a playful look he asked, "How do you feel about becoming a fashionista?"

"What?"

He tilted his head. "What do the police know about you? They know Beth Lousiere, who wears sensible shoes and plain clothes." It might have been a criticism, but it didn't seem to be. “They also know about Loser, who wears layers of crummy second-hand clothing.”

Shame that he’d seen me like that engulfed me for a moment. Even a bum has her pride.

“I propose we take a page from Poe—who was a Richmond guy, you know—and hide you in plain sight, like the purloined letter.” I gave him a look, but he went on before I could object. “Let’s say the Suggs Law Firm needs a new receptionist—which, incidentally, we do. Melanie is slated to go on maternity leave in a week. I asked her this morning if she might like to take off right away with full pay, and she said she’d jump at the chance. Her feet are killing her.”

“Alex—”

He raised a hand. “Hear me out. You become our receptionist. You answer the phone, take appointments, and make sure there’s coffee for clients. We’d planned to do without Melanie, but this is perfect. You’ll be in on the action without anyone knowing you’re there.”

I opened my mouth to object, but there was so much wrong with the idea that I didn’t know where to start. How did I explain how difficult it would be for me to do as he asked? In the first place, he was a man, and it had obviously escaped him that receptionists for modern, classy law firms dress stylishly, highlight their hair, and are never seen without a killer mani/pedi combination. I couldn’t imagine Loser picking up a phone and saying, “Suggs Law Firm, how may I help you?” Too weird.

“I can’t—”

Again, Alex interrupted. “You used to carry a gun and chase bad guys, Beth. You can handle this.”

He was so sure! I tried again to imagine working at the firm. The job required talking to strangers, but I'd gotten better at that thanks to Eddie's prodding. It wasn't like I had to bond with anyone on a deep emotional level.

Sensing his advantage, Alex added a little more persuasion. "Eddie showed me pictures of you back in high school drama club. Think of this as a role in a play."

Pretending to be someone else had been fun for Beth the teenager. "This goes beyond learning lines and blocking."

"I'll be there to help," Alex argued, "and Bert too of course." Turning on the blinker, he pulled up alongside a building. "I'm hoping some time here will help you get used to the idea."

I looked at the sign over the front door: *Lovable You Day Spa*. "What is this?"

"Let these people do their thing. When they get done, no one will suspect you're Loser, or even Beth."

I considered refusing to go inside, but what were my choices? Both of my personalities were sought by police, which meant I needed a new one. With a sigh, I surrendered myself to the idea of being someone new, someone who'd fit in at the Suggs Law Firm.

Alex left Beth in the capable hands of the spa staff, but he had misgivings. Would she despise him for turning her into someone she was not? Would she retreat into silence and stillness, as she had when they first met? Or would she walk away, leaving him again with no idea where she was? He almost turned around but forced himself to go on. He had to trust Beth, as she was trying to trust him.

The mall he and Christina had recently visited was a short distance away, and he drove there, still distracted. Though its created coolness was welcome, he felt nervous. Heading to the store where Christina had bought her clothes, he wondered if he could do this. They'd ask questions he couldn't answer, and he'd look like an idiot. Would Beth accept what he chose? He hadn't been this lost since his first hours in Afghanistan. This was a different sort of battle, and Alex was pretty certain he wasn't properly equipped.

"Can I help you?" The clerk was middle-aged and kindly-looking, like his Aunt Ruth.

"I need to buy clothes for a friend."

"I see. Do you know her sizes?"

"Um, no." He looked around helplessly. Racks and racks of pants, shirts, dresses, and jackets. Farther on, rows of shoes, and after that, underwear. He bit his lip. "Give me a minute, please, then come back."

The clerk melted away, her smile lingering like the Cheshire Cat's. Taking out his phone, he called the spa and explained the situation. The first woman didn't seem very interested. "I don't think we can give advice over the phone about clothes and stuff," she said bluntly.

"Can I speak to—" Alex searched his mind for the name of the manager with whom he'd arranged Beth's appointment. "—Willa?"

There was a wait. The clerk floated past once, saw that he wasn't ready yet, and disappeared again.

"This is Willa." He pictured the trim, neat woman who'd greeted them, so well-groomed one hardly noticed she wasn't beautiful.

"Hi, Willa. It's Alex, the guy who brought—"

"Oh, hi, Alex. She isn't near done yet."

"That's not why I called. I need to buy her new clothes, but I'm pretty clueless about sizes and stuff."

"Oh." The meaning in that one syllable told him what Willa and the others thought was going on. He was Richard Gere, Beth was Julia Roberts, and this was a real-life remake of *Pretty Woman*. Shrugging mentally, he asked, "Can you tell me her sizes?" Seeing the clerk approaching again, he beckoned her over. "Better yet, tell this woman, and we'll go from there."

The clerk took the phone and moved to the sales desk, where she located a pad and pen. She listened for a while, asking questions that embarrassed Alex enough that he turned and tried to pretend interest in the rack behind him. The fact that it contained bras didn't help.

Eventually the clerk handed back his phone. "I've written it all down," she said, waving a slip of paper. "Now we can start putting together an outfit. Are we thinking evening or daytime?"

He hesitated a moment before replying, "Let's do several of each. I want her to have choices."

Chapter Fifteen

When Alex ushered me into the softly-lit, mostly-white, reception area, greeted the girl at the desk with a cheerful "Here she is!" and left me standing there, I was horrified. The spa staff descended on me, approaching guardedly like witnesses to an auto accident. They'd expected me and apparently had been told some story to account for the shape I was in.

Terrible was the term the three women tossed around, speaking to each other, not to me, as they developed a schedule for my rebirth. I got right away that I was allowed no input. The experts would have their way with me. It began with a massage, performed by a girl named Janine who looked frail but had fingers like something from *I, Robot*. I'd never had a massage, but aside from having to get undressed, it was okay.

Once I was relaxed and softened, Janine turned me over to the hair stylist, Cassandra, who clucked and tsk-tsked as she ran her hands through my hair. "We're going to have to go short," she mused, her eyes never meeting mine in the mirror. "Yeah." She pulled the strands between her fingers. "Short."

I watched in apprehension as she took out a razor, put in a fresh blade, and began cutting. Tufts of hair fell to the floor, subtly changing my face. My cheekbones "popped" to use Cassandra's terminology, and my neck seemed to grow longer. When she'd finished cutting, she wrapped strands of my much-shorter hair in foil and brushed color onto them with a wide, flat brush. "Tones," she told me. "Varied tones will make you look like a whole different person."

That was encouraging, though I guessed she had no idea

that was what Alex intended. As we waited for the color to develop, Cassandra turned me over to Kim, who went to work on my fingernails while her assistant Su removed my shoes and socks. It was weird to have someone touching my feet, and I tried to keep still, but Su's smile said she was used to jumpy customers. When she asked Kim a question in a language I didn't understand, Kim handed her a bottle of nail polish. "He said red."

Alex had chosen the color for my digits? Just as Kim and Su finished with me, the timer rang. Cassandra took over again, lowering my head to the sink, where she rinsed, conditioned, and towel-dried. "You have quite a head of hair there," she said. "It's real nice to work with." Sitting me back up, she turned me toward the mirror so I could see the results, about three inches long on top and tousled, much shorter on the sides and pointy. The color varied from reddish blonde to strands of copper and sable. My face looked longer, my eyes bigger. I almost didn't recognize myself.

There wasn't time to dwell on that change, because the next step in my transformation loomed. Willa plucked away the facial hair she thought unnecessary, and then applied makeup, instructing as she worked so I could achieve the same look in days to come. I doubted that, but I paid attention, hoping some of it would sink in. I'd worn makeup in the past. How hard could it be to take it up again?

When they were finished, I indeed felt like a different person. They wouldn't let me put on the clothes I'd been wearing, and their smug looks told me another surprise was in the works. In my fluffy white robe and spa slippers, I sat in a corner to await Alex's return. I picked through the magazines, but they were all about movie stars' best and worst moments, reported with equal glee. I soon lost interest.

When I glanced up and caught my image in the mirror, I was surprised every time. Looking at this new person, I could almost forget Loser had ever existed, and Beth had never looked this good. I reminded myself it was all fake. Inside, I was still the same person. Uncertain, likely to screw up. A loser.

Alex's voice sounded in the foyer, and the receptionist came to the back, face averted so she could look at him as long as possible. "This is for the lady," she said, holding out two shopping bags. When I didn't take them, Janine did. "Your guy had us estimate your sizes," she said. "Let's see what he got."

I took the first bag, which came from Dillard's, and peered in apprehensively. There was underwear, and beneath it, a shoebox. My apprehension grew. Heels? I'd wobble like a calf on ice.

The other bag, also from Dillard's, contained a red dress, which I'd expected from the nail color. I held it up to my body. It was tasteful, beautiful, and...red. I was going to feel like a fire engine.

The spa staff oohed and aahed at it. I couldn't make myself look at Alex, who stood back, letting the women control the scene.

"Try it on," Cassandra urged. "I bet you'll look great."

With grave reservations, I did as ordered. As I put on the garments, memories surfaced, some good, some not so good. I hadn't worn a real bra for a long time, and I'd forgotten how confining they were. The feel of quality panties, however, was welcome against my skin. And I had to admit the dress required a decent bra to make it fall into place nicely.

I came out of the changing room to cheers and applause,

which would have sent me back in if I'd known where my old clothes were. Willa took me to the mirror and turned me so I got the full effect. I avoided Alex's gaze, reflected behind me, but I couldn't miss his appreciative smile. The woman in the mirror seemed to know what she was doing, unless you looked directly into her eyes. It made me wonder if others who appear to have the world on a string also quake inside like half-set pudding.

The women backed away, anticipating Alex's reaction. I turned to him, and for the first time in years felt the reaction any woman feels when a man's gaze tells her she's looking good. The girl who comes downstairs in her Prom formal, the bride who enters the church and catches her bridegroom's eye, or the wife who dresses up for a special dinner with her husband, all feel the same glow when they see the effort has been worthwhile.

Glancing at the spa staff, Alex cleared his throat and said, "The dress fits well."

Looking at his left shoulder I replied, "Yes. Thanks for getting it for me."

It was the lamest conversation imaginable, right up there with that long-ago Prom night when I'd thanked Jerry Dahlin for an over-large, slightly faded corsage, and he'd said I looked "real nice." After a moment, the women turned businesslike, a little disappointed. At least they had a story to tell over the next few days about the hot guy in the expensive suit who'd played Pygmalion to a shabby Galatea.

After an equally lame argument about who would pay, which Alex won, we left. Once we were in the car, I insisted he had to charge my account for everything: the clothes, the spa, even the tips. "You'll earn your new stuff," he informed me.

"We don't intend to pay our new receptionist a salary." He grinned. "That would mean paperwork, and a law firm's got enough of that already."

As we drove to the office, neither of us said much. I was fighting battles on several fronts. Yes, I looked the part, but could I play it? What if I couldn't make myself answer that first phone call tomorrow morning? Things Alex had said earlier replayed in my mind, and I didn't know whether to feel happy or scared. He claimed he cared about me, but he didn't really know me. How would he react if his pretty woman fell apart in front of everyone at the Suggs Law Firm and retreated to a corner, unable to speak?

Chapter Sixteen

Alex's plan was to wait until most of the building staff had gone home for the day, which meant we had a couple of hours to kill. He suggested we get something to eat, and I chose the drive-through at Taco Bell, unwilling to trust my new red heels until I'd had a chance to practice a little. After we got our food, he parked at the back of the lot in a surprisingly attractive spot under a big tree that shaded the car from the afternoon sun. No one else was back there, so I relaxed a little. It was kind of fun, sharing nachos while we discussed what I should do, could do, and would do, though I wasn't used to having to worry about whether I dripped cheese on my clothes.

At first Alex did most of the talking, assuring me again that I looked great, that I was capable of doing the receptionist job, and that it was the best way to proceed. "We can put our heads together," he said, "and Bert or I can reach out to others for information as we need to."

It was a workable idea, and glancing in the side mirror, I felt confident no one would recognize me. Red hair made my eyes seem more brown than green, and makeup made them look wider and slightly different in shape. Besides, who was going to look for Beth Lousiere at the front desk of the Suggs Law Firm? It was a bold plan, which is why it was likely to work.

I was ashamed to admit my biggest fear to Alex—the telephone. While he knew I preferred texting, he couldn't know the knot in my gut that formed at the prospect of answering calls all day.

He knew some of my phobias from observation, others from talking with Bert. Over the past year, I'd noticed them gently leading me back to doing ordinary tasks. I'd been encouraged to handle my household finances, I'd been consulted on investments made in my name, and I'd been cajoled into making a will so that Mabel and Eddie would be secure if I died. Alex no doubt saw overcoming my dread of the phone as another step in my recovery, but things like that always seem easier when you aren't the one with the problem.

Finishing my soft taco I wadded the wrapper. "I won't like it, but I'll try."

Alex took the last chip and dragged it through the cheese. "Good. Now, while you were off getting yourself into trouble, I was doing some digging."

"Really."

"You told me you talked to Maureen's former landlady."

"She was really nice."

Alex wiped his fingers on a napkin. "Here's the thing about nice people. They believe that if you haven't got anything good to say about someone, you don't say anything at all."

I nodded. Marta had held to that philosophy.

He shook the ice in his cup and took a sip. "We want to know the not-so-nice stuff, things that made Maureen less than likeable. That's why people get murdered."

"But Helen's even less likely to tell you anything bad now." Hand in hand with the rule of niceness was that one about not speaking ill of the dead.

"Right." Alex put our trash into the bag. "So I bypassed Ms. Nice and visited Mr. Franklin at his work place. He says if Maureen hadn't been his wife's friend, he'd have slapped a restraining order on her."

"That's interesting."

"He's interesting. He was all ready to tell me about Maureen until I said I was your lawyer. That set him off on threats to sue you for harassing his wife."

"Me? I—"

He raised a palm to quiet me. "I know, I know. The guy's looking for a way to make this pay."

"Jerk!"

Setting his cup in the holder, Alex started the car and put it into reverse. "I offered fifty dollars for a half hour of his time. That got his attention, and he said his wife has women's group from six until eight this evening."

I glanced at the dashboard clock. Quarter to six.

"You're going there?"

"You are. I told him my associate would be conducting the interview."

I stared at him as if he'd lost his mind, but he went on, "You knew Maureen, so you'll know what to ask." With a grin he added, "I told him my legal assistant's name is Della Street."

"As in Perry Mason's secretary?"

Alex waved a hand, dismissing my concern. "Trust me. He isn't the type who'll get it."

Reaching into the back seat, he took a shopping bag from several set neatly in a row. "This one has casual clothes in it." He winked. "I just had to see you in the red dress."

Peering into the bag, I chose black pants, a plain blue button-up blouse, and a light, loose jacket. Wobbling into the Taco Bell, I located the bathroom and made yet another transformation. Another change of clothes, another persona.

When I returned Alex said, "I'm going to let you take this one alone." I opened my mouth to object, but he went on, "I think Franklin will respond better to a pretty girl than a fancy-ass lawyer—his term, not mine." Raising his brows, he warned, "He did mention God twice and Jesus once in a relatively short conversation, so go for sweet young thing, not Jezebel." I made a rude sound and he laughed. "I get it, but we need to find out what the guy knows about Maureen."

"So I haven't been on the job for a day and I've already been promoted from receptionist to investigator?"

"The Suggs Law Firm has faith in you," Alex said cheerfully. "In fact, I have faith you'll remember the way to Franklin's house too."

We rode in silence for a while except when I said, "Turn up there," or "Take this exit." Alex had something on his mind, because he was uncharacteristically quiet. Usually I'm okay with silence, but the set of his jaw told me he'd be better off if he got whatever it was off his chest. "A penny for your thoughts."

He turned briefly to look at me. "Obvious, huh?"

I nodded, and he huffed a sigh. "I did something recently that—I don't know. It might have been wrong." He told me about a night when he'd gone to a bar, waited in the shadows, and beaten a man in order to convince him to allow his abused wife to get a divorce. He made it sound brutal, using words like *defenseless* and *attacked*, but I knew better. Alex was neither brutal nor unfair, but it was apparent that guilt plagued him. "I broke the law, Beth."

"Sometimes individual effort is the only way to make things right."

"But people can't go around exacting justice like vigilantes in an old western. Society doesn't work that way."

"Society doesn't know everything." I put up three fingers. "Ask yourself these questions. Were you sure the guy hurt his wife?"

"Yeah. The police had multiple reports but no convictions. She was too scared to press charges."

I touched the second finger. "Did she want to get away from him?"

"Yes. I think she's done lying to herself now."

Clasping all three fingers, I asked, "Was there any other way to convince him to let her go?"

Alex chuckled. "Okay, I get it. I did what I had to do. So why do I still feel guilty about smacking the guy around?"

"Take it from someone who knows about guilt. You can't put it down and walk away, no matter how many people tell you to. You can only learn to live with the extra weight."

He nodded slowly, digesting it. "I guess I can do that."

Alex stopped some distance back from the Franklin's property and got out of the car so I could go on alone. The thought of driving his car made my teeth clench, but he sat down by a tree and shooed me on my way.

I found Ken at the house Maureen had rented, shifting material around on the porch. He was a middle-sized man with a lot of bald and a tight, pinched face. I pictured the two of them at church, her face beaming with Christian love as her husband waited for Old Testament proscriptions, the *Thou shalt nots.*

Getting out of the car, I squared my shoulders and stepped forward, holding out my hand. "Mr. Franklin? I'm Miss Street."

He glanced at my hand before taking it, and I sensed I'd stepped wrong. I was probably supposed to curtsey or something.

"I told that fellow I don't have time for all this," he began. "I talked to the police, and now I'm supposed to repeat it all to some girl."

I took out the fifty-dollar bill Alex had provided and stuck it in the notepad I carried, leaving one end out as a tease. "I'll try not to take too much of your time."

"You work for that lawyer?" Disdain was apparent in the way he said the word.

Coming from a small town, I knew his type well. "Just until my boyfriend gets home from Afghanistan," I told him. "Then we'll be getting married."

"Afghanistan, huh?" He stood a little straighter. "Tell him thanks for his service."

"He'll appreciate that, sir." Past the preliminaries, I turned to the subject of Maureen. "I understand that your wife and Ms. Daley were old friends. I guess they had a lot in common."

His nose wrinkled like I'd lit a match under it. "They weren't alike at all, and that was the problem. My wife's a nice person, a good person. Maureen Daley wasn't." He waved angrily. "A real nut case, and I don't care if she is dead. It's the truth."

I gave him a moment to get his control back. "How did Ms. Daley come here?" I was interested in hearing how his view differed from the answer Helen had given.

Franklin rubbed the sandy stubble on his chin. "We bought the two houses, and somehow she heard about it. She called my wife and talked her into renting her this place." He cast a glance at the house. "It was in bad shape, but my wife has a hard time saying no. I guess Maureen had a tough time back in S.C, and my wife wanted to help."

"You agreed?"

He gave me a grim smile. "To tell you the truth, we needed the money. My hours on the job got cut in half, and I was hustling to make the payments."

"So Mau—Ms. Daley moved in."

"Yeah." Anger vibrated in his voice. "She was a royal pain from the first. She hung out in our kitchen every free minute. She'd invite herself for dinner, stay after while my wife did the dishes, and then suggest what we should watch on TV. The whole time, she'd go on about how it was great Helen was going to make something of herself in the big city."

I recalled Helen saying that once she met Ken, she'd wanted only to be a wife. "Was that true?"

Franklin shook his head. "My wife came here with big plans: college, law school, a career. But things like that always seem easier when you're looking at them from far away." He sounded way too satisfied with the death of Helen's dreams for my taste. "After a few classes, she found out that *A*'s in high school don't necessarily mean *A*'s in college. By the time Maureen got here, we were expecting our second and school wasn't an option anymore." He paused before delivering an uncharacteristically sensitive comment. "I think she had a hard time telling Maureen though. The girl kept going on about her having goals, and it was hard for my wife to think she'd let her old friend down."

"How did you two meet?" I asked, guessing it hadn't been in a college class.

"A friend of hers from school brought her to a church picnic. We started dating, and in a month I asked her to marry me." Franklin scratched at a spot on his neck. "She's figured out she doesn't want to be a lawyer. She wants to be a wife and a mother, and that means she stays at home, even if I have to work two jobs. Nobody can raise kids like their mother can." He shifted his feet. "I mean, I help out. I'm not some Neanderthal. But kids need a mom that's thinking about them all the time." He added defiantly, "Too many thinking about their career or a promotion."

I might have argued, but if I'd been a homemaker instead of a cop, my husband and daughter might still be alive. "Maureen disapproved of Helen's change of plans?"

"Big time." He gave a harsh laugh. "She started bullying her about going back to school every second I wasn't in the room. One night I followed her back here and told her to lay off." He paused, perhaps trying to read my reaction. "We been going to classes at church, and what they say makes sense. The man works and earns money. The woman sees the house and kids are taken care of. It's a fair system, and everybody knows what's expected. A lot of the mess we've got today is because people don't know what they're supposed to do."

I stopped him before he really got rolling on how to save the world. "How did Ms. Daley react?"

"She was pretty angry, but she stopped hanging around our house till all hours." He glanced across the driveway. "It was nice not having her underfoot all the time."

That was why Maureen had relocated. Helen had disappointed her and Ken had let her know she was unwelcome. It didn't explain her death, but I understood Maureen a little better.

"You had no contact after she moved into the city?"

"My wife worried some about that." His chin set. "Nothing

to fret about, I told her. That one will find somebody to latch onto."

I paid him then and left before he could say "my wife" one more time. If Franklin wasn't a Neanderthal, he hadn't made it much past medieval times. I wondered if he used Helen's name in the throes of passion, when she submitted herself to him as a good wife should.

CHAPTER SEVENTEEN

I filled Alex in on the conversation with Ken as we drove back into the city, ending with, "It sounds like Maureen didn't have any self-confidence when she first came to Richmond. I guess it's good that she had success at the academy and learned to see herself as competent."

Alex stepped on the brake abruptly, turning into the driveway of an oil-change shop that was closed for the night. Putting the gearshift into park, he turned to me. "But she didn't, Beth. Maureen was the kind of person who needed a hero, someone to pattern herself after. When Helen abandoned her dreams, you became that person."

Raising a finger to stop my argument, he went on. "I looked up the records for your academy class. Maureen was average in all categories, but you excelled. On the shooting range, you beat everyone. On paper tests, you were always at or near the top. Your instructors' notes make it clear you were their shining example." He waved a hand. "She needed a new Superwoman to emulate, and there you were, showing the boys how it's done."

Though it was true I'd done well, I rejected the idea that anyone might see me as Superwoman. I'd been good at some things, sure, but someone Maureen would strive to emulate? Loser stood directly in the way of that idea.

Alex put the car into gear, and we were on our way again. After a minute I asked, "Why would it matter anyway?"

"I don't know Maureen or what she was like with you, but...do you know why she was fired?"

"I know what she told me."

"Well, your buddy Jacob did some digging—"

"Wait. When did you speak to Jacob?"

"Yesterday. I was looking for you, remember? I knew you wouldn't contact us, so I started reaching out to the people who might have helped you." He gave me a sideways glance. "He's not happy that you broke off contact with him."

"Like he needs to put his job on the line for me."

Alex was watching the road, but he sounded a little sad as he said, "There are some who think you're worth it, Beth." After a beat, he took up the previous thread. "Maureen left the Richmond P.D. under threat of dismissal for unstable behavior and possible corruption. She agreed to resign. They agreed not to press charges."

"She told me her coworkers—some crooked cops—framed her."

He frowned. "Okay. Tell me her side of it."

I relayed what Maureen said had happened. He listened carefully, even having me repeat some of it. When he fell silent, I asked, "What did Jake say? Did she really get railroaded out of her job?"

"That's hard to say. We have to figure out who's lying, and what is he or she lying to protect?"

Just after 7:30, we entered the discreetly elegant offices of the Suggs Law Firm. Though most in the building and everyone else in the office was gone, Bert waited behind his mahogany desk, looking much the same as he'd looked when I'd last seen him a year ago. He pronounced the results of my makeover, "Charming, my dear. Completely charming."

Turning to his associate, Bert made a shooing motion. “Alex, you’ve done enough for one day. We will see you in the morning.”

Though obviously unwilling, Alex went. Once he’d closed the door softly behind him, Bert leaned back in his chair and asked, “So what do you think of our plan?” Before I could answer, he went on, “My idea, but Alex approved. He’s a smart young man, but I suppose you’ve noticed.”

He watched to see my reaction, so I shrugged, admitting Alex’s intelligence without indicating interest in him as a person. Bert nodded almost imperceptibly, as if he’d expected me to be obtuse. What followed was part interview, part interrogation. Bert asked question after question, clarifying things Alex had told him and taking notes on everything I could relate about the last few days. He delved into my contact with Jacob, my visit to the Franklins, my arrest, and what happened with Maureen, both in the past and recently. I found it fairly easy to talk to Bert. Like Alex and Jacob, he had my interests in mind, so I tried to answer his questions honestly and completely. As I watched him write things down, I reflected that though Bert was getting old, he hadn’t lost a tick of mental acuity. His queries were detailed, and I found that things got clearer in my own mind as I responded.

“We will hide you in plain sight,” he said, a light in his pale blue eyes revealing enjoyment of the challenge. “Seeing the way you look now, I predict success.” Escorting me to the reception area, he went over the job requirements, which were not rigorous. I would answer the phone, lead clients to the correct room, and keep the coffeepot full. When he’d assured me that I could do the job, Bert glanced at the door. “I thought you might want to spend your nights here as well.”

I looked up in surprise. Bert knew I couldn't sleep inside, but he pointed a finger upward. "At the end of the hall you'll find a doorway. Up one flight, and you'll be in the open, under the stars."

"Nice," I said, relieved I wouldn't be sleeping on the lawn. I've been surprised by sprinklers more than once.

"I've been known to spend nights on the couch in my younger days, but the roof seemed like a spot you'd approve of." Bert gestured. "There are blankets in the credenza, and my bathroom has a shower."

It was perfect. If I could manage the receptionist's job, I had a place where the police would never think to look for me. Even better, I was connected to Bert, Alex, and their resources. I had computer access, and in the evenings I could do research.

"I hope I don't disappoint you."

"Beth," Bert said gently, "you've come a very long way from those days of despair, and I believe you can function in any role you choose. You helped that boy Eddie find out who killed his momma. You took your friend Mabel in and made a home for her. You might not feel ready, might not want to be, but you have to trust me. You can do it, and it's the only way we'll find out who's trying to frame you for murder."

It was a relief to hear that he'd come to the same conclusion I had. "You think it's deliberate?"

"I do." Bert pushed his chair away from the desk. "But we'll talk about that in the morning. You need some alone time, I'd guess, and I have a tiresome but necessary meeting to attend."

After he'd gone, leaving behind a ring of keys that would get me in anywhere on the third floor, I found the stairway to the roof and explored. It had a parapet—if that's what they're called nowadays—that screened the roof from view and a flat surface studded with air-conditioning units, ventilation shafts, and an array of devices that covered the last twenty years of communication methods: a wi-fi hookup, two satellite dishes, and even an antiquated TV antenna, bent but still in place. Going back downstairs, I looked through the shopping bags Alex and I had carried into Bert's bathroom. At the bottom of one I found soft cotton pants and a baggy T-shirt, which I guessed were meant to serve as sleepwear. They felt so much softer than what I was used to that I made myself a promise. If I got through this with my freedom, I'd stop buying my clothes at dollar stores.

At full dark, I went back up to the roof, laid one of Bert's blankets down as a cushion, and looked up at the stars, dimmed by competing city lights but still visible. Unable to sleep for a while, I began to doubt myself again. A little nail polish and some highlights weren't enough to hide Loser from the world. It was possible a cop, maybe Zender or Marshall, would come to question Bert about my whereabouts. Could I maintain a Miss Friendly attitude with a detective staring into my eyes?

Typically, my night thoughts were counterproductive. I tried to recall Alex's assurances and Bert's faith in me, but Darrin's voice whispered in my head.

Loser! You've exposed two good men to embarrassment and trouble.

Stay away from Alex and Bert or they'll pay, like I paid. Like our daughter paid.

Loser!

Only one thing kept me on that roof: I had nowhere else to go. Even the streets weren't safe now, with every cop in Richmond on the lookout for me.

Alex left the office building, but he didn't head for home. Instead he called Jacob Grauman's cell. He thought the two of them were learning to trust each other, and it was helpful to have someone who knew about the workings of the R.P.D.

When he filled Jacob in on the story Maureen had told Beth, Grauman played devil's advocate, arguing there was no suspicion concerning the four cops and plenty of suspicion surrounding Maureen Daley. "She broke the pimp's arm, Bronson. Why would he lie about who did that?"

Alex couldn't come up with a reason, but he thought it was time he spoke to one or more of the four officers. He asked Grauman where he might find them off-duty.

"What time is it?" Jacob answered his own question. "Eight fifteen. A lot of cops go to Dunnigan's after shift. It's just off the Midlothian in the Canton Shopping Center. They might be there."

Twenty minutes later, Alex left his car and headed toward a strip of shops that included Dunnigan's Tavern, which had the inevitable shamrock on its sign. The outside had the anonymous look of a neighborhood bar uninterested in attracting new customers. He entered the darkened-glass door, squinting to see once it closed behind him. The place was long, skinny, and murky, and the patrons were obviously working folk, mostly men who'd put in a day of physical labor. Many wore uniform shirts, most wore baseball caps, and more than a few had a layer of dirt they had yet to shower away.

At a table in the corner where the bar ended sat a group he guessed were the men he'd come to see. There was something about them, possibly their erect bearing or maybe a sense that they were watchful and ready, even in moments of relaxation. Alex pretended to be looking for someone in the noisy crowd. Apparently disappointed, he stepped to the bar as if to wait.

The men hardly glanced at him before returning to their beers and conversation. There were six of them, and he guessed it would be hard for a woman to break into the group. Two were past middle age, but not by much. They looked fit, though one had a belly that was starting to gain on him. From Beth's description he guessed the one with the silver streak in his hair was Vince Cjaika. That meant the one with the belly was Bobby Davis, Maureen's old partner. The rest were younger, and they listened to the older men's stories like students attending to the master.

Instinct told Alex he'd have no luck approaching the group as a whole. He ordered a beer and sipped at it, formulating a plan. If the men were corrupt, approaching them directly could put him into a bad situation. He decided he'd wait and hope one of them left alone. When that happened, he'd follow and ask a few questions. Remembering the last time he'd met a man in a bar parking lot, he hoped the encounter didn't end the same way.

It took over an hour, but finally the guy with the silver streak slid his chair back with a scrape, rose, and laid some bills on the table. The others made the casual farewells common to those who'll see each other the next day and the day after that. Tossing a bill on the bar, Alex exited ahead of the man, out the door into the night.

The man stopped for a moment on the sidewalk and punched the button on his key fob before heading for his car. The resulting chirp led Alex in the right direction, so he was there when the owner of the vehicle arrived. When the guy realized Alex was waiting for him, he tensed but didn't seem particularly afraid. "Yeah?"

Alex handed him a business card. "I'm working for a woman named Beth Lousiere, who's suspected of killing Maureen Daley. I was wondering if you could answer some questions."

The man frowned. "Who told you where to find me?"

"What's going on, Vince?" Alex turned to find three men behind him. He was now trapped between the cars.

"Guy wants to talk about Maureen." Emphasis on the name revealed how Cjaika felt about her.

Davis took a step forward. "What's your interest, buddy?"

"I'm trying to help my client prove she didn't murder her."

One of the younger men snickered. "Good luck with that. I hear she eats out of garbage cans and shit."

Alex had a hard time keeping his hands from forming into fists. What did these guys know about Beth and what she'd lived through? Reminding himself of his purpose, he said, "She didn't kill Ms. Daley."

"Well, we can't help you," Cjaika said.

"Will you take my card in case you think of something?"

"Sure." Cjaika took the card and flipped it onto the passenger seat. "But we got nothing to say about Maureen." He opened the car door, pushing it out all the way so Alex had to step back. He turned to go, and the others backed away just enough to let him through. They watched him go to his car and get in before dispersing to their own vehicles.

Alex turned on the engine and cranked up the A/C, waiting a few moments to let his flush of anger fade. He reminded himself that these guys had no reason to help Beth, and if they were dirty, they had every reason to hope she remained the prime suspect. It was his desire to clear her that made him take a step he'd known in his heart was possibly useless and even dangerous.

His phone vibrated in his pocket, and he pulled it out. "Bronson."

"Drive around the back of the building." It was Vince Cjaika.

"On my way." Putting the car in gear, Alex backed out of his parking space, his mind racing. He could be heading into an ambush. While the four men were unlikely to jump him in the middle of the lot, they might be waiting for him out of sight. Still, he'd come for information, and he doubted they'd murder him just for asking questions. As a precaution, he took out a tire iron he kept under the driver's seat. Not much defense against a police revolver, but he worked with what he had.

The low, square building backed up to another one just like it, leaving a narrow alley lined with rear-entry doors, each labeled with the name of the business as an aid to deliverymen. About halfway down a car waited, engine running. Alex saw no sign of anyone other than the driver. Pulling up beside it, he rolled down his window.

Cjaika sat tall in the driver's seat. Despite the streak in his hair, his face was unlined, his eyes wide and clear. He studied Alex for a few seconds. "I'm listening, Counselor."

"Can you tell me anything that might help me clear my client?"

The cop shook his head. "I doubt it. But I can tell you what kind of person Daley was."

"That would help."

Cjaika twisted uncomfortably in his seat. "The thing is,

we're supposed to keep quiet about this."

Alex felt a glimmer of understanding. "The department made her a deal."

"It's never good when a cop gets fired for dereliction of duty," Cjaika said. "Every arrest she ever made gets put under a microscope. Every criminal she put into the system files an appeal. It was best for everybody if Maureen resigned. They told her if she did, there'd be no charges and no publicity."

"I see." Alex ran Cjaika's words through his mind, comparing them with Beth's account. Someone was lying. Had this man decided the best way to get rid of him was to feed him a story? Or had Maureen been the liar? "What did Daley do that got her into trouble?"

Cjaika let out a long breath. "Davis and me been friends for years. Our captain likes to put a young cop with an older cop, which is a good idea, so I got Hamilton, who's in his third year now, and Davis got Daley. She was okay at first, a little in-your-face about being a girl, but I guess they gotta do that."

Alex almost smiled at the unconscious revelation in the man's tone. "They" would have felt the built-in prejudice of the male officers from Day One. According to Beth, Maureen wouldn't have liked that at all.

"The first time Davis said anything to me about her was three or four months into their partnership. He thought Daley was taking money in exchange for letting suspects off the hook."

"Like Carole Ann Minier?"

He shrugged. "Petty criminals. Davis said they'd make an arrest, she'd make up some reason for him to leave the two of them alone, and when he returned, she'd claim she let her or him go, saying they promised to leave town or get help. The first few times he thought it was a girl thing, like she felt sorry for them, but after a while, it reeked."

"That's interesting," Alex said. "Maureen told my client you guys were the ones taking bribes."

Cjaika snuffed derisively. "She tried that with I.A. too, but we're clean. Davis and me been on the job for over twenty years, and we ain't got a thing on our records. When the shit Maureen was pulling got laid out in front of them, they knew who to believe and who to get rid of."

"My client saw Maureen after an altercation with you a few days ago. She was pretty roughed up."

The dash light showed the man's surprise. "Roughed up? I never touched the—I never touched her." He set his jaw, took a deep breath, and said, "Here's the thing. She was doin' stuff to us, and to Davis too. We kept getting pranked, and at first we thought it was kids. An emergency call that wasn't real. Damage to our car when we came out from having lunch. Stupid stuff, but one day Hamilton saw her sneaking away, and we found a rotten orange shoved up the tailpipe. That's when we knew it was her."

"So what did you do?"

He shrugged. "We started taking turns staying in the car. It really pissed us off, you know?"

"So you shoved her around a little to get the message across."

Cjaika shook his head vigorously. "No, I didn't! I talked to her, that's all. I said she'd better cool it or she was gonna get hauled in for malicious mischief." After a pause, he added, "I lied a little, told her we had evidence it was her doing all this crap. I figured that would make her pay attention."

"What did she say to that?"

"It was weird. She said something like, 'Go ahead and arrest me. I don't care what happens anymore." Cjaika put both hands out the window in a gesture of honesty. "I never touched her though, I swear. If she got bloody, it was from somebody besides me." Pointing a finger at Alex, he added, "And if somebody killed her, it's because she tried to pull crap on him like she pulled on us."

Chapter Eighteen

Alex showed up bright and early Friday morning with coffee, rolls, and enough enthusiasm to make me feel downright cranky. I came down from the roof to find him unlocking the office door. If he was surprised to see me there, he didn't mention it. Instead he smiled, which made me even crankier. I hadn't slept much, and the thought of putting on that little red dress and smiling for the public wasn't helping my mood.

"I figured you could use some coffee to help you get started making coffee," he said, handing me a large cup of Starbucks regular. "I'll be in all day if you need anything."

In response to his cheerfulness and a welcome jolt of caffeine, I tried for positive thoughts. *You can do this,* I told myself. *It's not rocket science.* If I could smile and make banal conversation at Eddie's parent-teacher conferences, I could do the same here. Loser didn't believe it, so Beth took control. Sipping at the hot coffee I assured him, "I'm fine."

"Good, because I have news." Leading the way to the break room, Alex showed me where the supplies were while he told me about his conversation with Vince Cjaika. He ended with, "We need to re-examine everything Maureen told you. She had some sort of agenda I don't understand."

I didn't understand either. Maureen hadn't been looking for corruption; she was corrupt. She hadn't been railroaded out of her job; she'd been fired for cause. How had I missed it? Because we'd been through the academy together, I'd assumed she was like me. I'd believed what she told me. That had been a mistake. Looking at things she'd said, I realized that she'd played me too. My dislike of Dr. Blevins, my desire to be a cop who made things better for people—Maureen had tapped into my emotions, leading me to believe her through supposedly shared experiences.

Alex was looking at me speculatively. "We'll figure this out, Beth."

I couldn't bring myself to agree. Instead I said, "I'd better get ready for my first day at work."

"Right," he said lightly. "Don't want the boss to arrive to find you sipping coffee in your jammies."

In Bert's little bathroom, I attempted to reconstruct the look the spa had created the day before. They'd given—well, sold—me a cosmetics kit, and I made a stab at it. Alex had provided the basics of hygiene, toothbrush and paste, comb and brush, and even a nail file, something I hadn't used in years. My manicure looked good, so I left it alone and brushed my teeth, fluffed the hair into a semblance of its former glory, and put on the clothes. When I emerged, Alex whistled in approval, but Loser whispered he was only trying to give me confidence.

Looking at my reflection in the mirrored wall of the reception area, I admitted it was unlikely anyone would see me at the front desk and think "suspect in a homicide." I looked more like a bit player in a career-girl chick-flick, which I guess was the idea. At nine o'clock, I unlocked the entry door and returned to my ergonomically designed chair to wait for the first clients of the day, listed by the now-absent Melanie in easy-to-read block letters on the planner.

The morning passed quickly. I mastered the phone system, which was clearly labeled and user friendly. "Suggs Law Firm. Good morning," I said each time it buzzed. The first time I stuttered over it, but by the fourth call, it felt almost normal. If my tone was a little fake, it was no worse than other greetings delivered with mock enthusiasm: "Hi, I'm Tyrone, and I'll be your server," or "Mainstay Insurance. We care for your family as much as you do."

Calls came in, and I directed them to the appropriate employee: to the parapros, to Alex, or rarely, to Bert himself. I answered questions about office hours, gave directions to the building, and promised to deliver messages to those who didn't answer their phones. No fan of voice mail, Bert required a personal response to each call received during business hours. I did refuse, politely, of course, to give legal advice, interpret Virginia law, or speculate on pending Virginia State Supreme Court decisions.

From my seat at the entry I served as gatekeeper, making sure clients had appointments and brought the requested paperwork Melanie had dutifully noted on the day planner. I checked clients' documents against the master list, hoping I recognized the difference between a quit-claim deed and a grant of trust. I didn't make anyone angry, didn't generate more than polite small talk, but I also didn't feel the knot at the back of my neck lessen for one second all morning long.

The last client of the morning came to see Alex. I led the man to the office where he sat working, papers spread over the desk as he consulted notes and filled in blanks. He looked different in the office setting, still handsome and capable, but somehow more serious. He did, however, wink at me when the client bent to adjust his chair. "Thank you, Eliza."

He'd chosen the name, and he thought it was pretty clever, playing at being a modern-day Henry Higgins. Actually, my father had called me Liza, one of the many nicknames for my given name, Elizabeth. When Marta took me into her home I'd chosen Beth, since I'd concluded by that time that Liza generated neither interest nor affection. Still, I didn't mind it when Alex said the name and grinned over our shared secret.

I ate lunch with the parapros, two women who chatted amiably about their kids and husbands. I found a bag in the fridge with my name on it, written in Alex's bold strokes, but if either of them wondered why the boss had brought me lunch, neither mentioned it.

The afternoon turned spooky when I answered the phone and heard Detective Zender's voice. After identifying herself, she said, "I'd like to speak to Mr. Suggs." Her tone made it a demand.

"One moment, please." I resisted the urge to try to disguise my voice, letting my bright tone create a difference between Bert's receptionist and the woman she'd questioned two days ago.

When I told him about the call Bert replied calmly, "Put her through." I managed to push the right button, but I couldn't resist going to his office doorway to listen in. Bert's personal assistant, a woman named Virginia, had given me nervous glances all morning, like I might spontaneously combust. She probably knew who I was, having met me a few times, but guessed she was not supposed to acknowledge it. As I stopped near her desk, fluttery movements signaled her discomfort. Luckily, Bert saw me hovering and gestured for me to enter. To my relief and Virginia's as well, I moved out of her personal space and onto the tasteful Persian rug in front of his desk.

"No, Detective," he was saying. "Mrs. Lousiere has not called this office." He listened for a while before saying, "I can promise you that if she calls, I will relay your message immediately. However, I can't guarantee she will respond as you wish." His eyes met mine, and there was a mischievous light in them. "My client makes her own decisions."

He listened again. "Has it occurred to you that someone might be attempting to direct your suspicions at Mrs. Lousiere in order to hide his own guilt?" I could almost hear Zender's question, and Bert said, "I would never try to do your job for you, Detective, but I understand that the first victim was associated with a man of unsavory reputation."

After a moment he said, "No, that doesn't explain Ms. Daley's murder, unless she stumbled onto the identity of the killer and tried to deal with him alone."

There was argument from Zender, and Bert rolled his eyes at me. "Why would Mrs. Lousiere leave the home she's established and the peaceful life she's created in West Virginia to return to Richmond and begin killing people? It makes no sense!"

Whatever Zender said disgusted him further, and he shook his head. "Detective, I've told you that if Mrs. Lousiere telephones anyone in this office, we will relay your demand that she turn herself in. I believe you are mistaken in your approach to the matter. Beth did not kill her husband and child three years ago, and she hasn't killed anyone else either. Someone wants to destroy her life, and you have become that person's unwitting confederate. Good day, madam."

He put the phone down with a gentleness that signaled an effort to avoid smacking it into place. "Any day of the week, I prefer a dumb flatfoot with no preconceived opinions over a smart cop who thinks she has it all figured out."

I shrugged. "Can't blame them. People keep dying when I'm in the vicinity."

Bert didn't argue. "I hope I've planted a seed in Zender's

mind. If she's smart, she'll think it through and see that someone is working to implicate you."

"The question is why?" I asked. "Who wants me to go to prison?"

Reaching for the day's cigar, Bert set it at one side of his mouth. "That is indeed the question." Rolling the cigar to the opposite side, he said, "It's happened not once, but twice, indicating a pathological need. I'd guess the reason is not something the rest of us would understand." He looked at me as if gauging my ability to handle a concept. "Darrin might have died due to anger, but the death of your little girl was meant to punish you."

I swallowed the lump that always rose in my throat at the thought of Kara. "That was three years ago. You think this person is still after me?"

He nodded. "What the killer wanted to happen didn't happen."

"Because you stepped in."

Bert nodded graciously "I was happy to help. But then, without conscious intent, you removed yourself from the killer's reach. Beth Lousiere became Loser, and nobody knew where you were, not even me." There was no accusation in his tone, but I knew that time had been tough on Bert.

It was difficult to accept that someone had deliberately framed me for Darrin's murder, but Bert's theory made sense. The plan had succeeded, despite my tormenter's failure to see me convicted of the crimes. I was destroyed, though it was a private, not public destruction. Apparently that wasn't enough, because I was back in the crosshairs of two new murder investigations.

I tuned in to Bert, who'd gone on. "When you emerged as the Homeless Hero, the killer must have been pleased to know where you were, but you left the city almost immediately." Bert kneaded one hand then the other. "At least that time I knew where you were." From the attention he gave his knuckles, I guessed they hurt. Or maybe he was remembering the pain I'd caused him.

"So I'm missing for a year, but something brought me to the killer's mind again."

Bert pointed a finger at me. "Exactly. The article that claimed you were living somewhere in comfort and peace must have brought back all his anger. He brought you to Richmond by kidnapping the woman who might have evidence to exonerate you and also someone he thought was your friend."

"Figuring that one or the other would do the trick."

Alex appeared in the doorway. "Are we having a war council?"

"Come in, Alex." Bert recapped Zender's call.

When he finished Alex commented, "Anyone who knows Beth wouldn't expect her to call."

"Luckily for us, the detectives don't seem to have taken the time to study her." Bert's tone revealed disapproval of those who failed to do their homework.

I squirmed a little at the thought of anyone studying me, but it was obvious someone had. Not the cops, but the killer. He or she wanted me arrested for murder, and Maureen Daley and Carole Ann Minier had paid the price for it.

As Bert and Alex talked, I thought about why someone would murder Darrin and Kara to implicate me. It was painful to consider, the sort of thing I usually pushed into a corner of my mind and walled in. It took a huge amount of effort to keep that wall from crashing down and re-exposing the searing pain of those deaths. Every time I peeped behind it, I saw Darrin's pale corpse and felt Kara's tiny, cold body in my arms. I'd spent a long time hiding from those memories, but it was time to face them.

Bert was no slave driver, and on Fridays everyone went home at 3:00 p.m. To Alex, the weekend was a problem, since he couldn't accept that I didn't need to eat three times a day. As he left at 3:15, he leaned over the desk and said quietly, "I'll be back around six with dinner."

"That's okay," I lied. "Bert's taking care of my meals." I'd told the same lie in reverse to Bert, figuring somewhere in the building I'd find a vending machine that would do.

Alex straightened, automatically sliding his tie into place beneath his jacket. "Oh. Well, I'll stop by tomorrow."

"Alex," I said firmly. "Take the weekend off. Do something fun. Call your girlfriend."

His expression told me there was one, and a trace of guilt in his eyes said he'd been neglecting her. I wasn't prepared for the little stab of jealousy I felt.

"Okay." He set the briefcase on the desk, opened it, and took out a no-plan, no-frills phone. "My number's already in there. Call if you need anything."

Taking the phone, I set it on the desk. "Thanks, Alex. You really are a good guy."

His smile seemed forced, but he managed a flippant answer. "Glad you noticed."

Once everyone had gone, I let myself give in to despair. The

Loser Effect had been eating at me since Zender's call, and I'd had to force myself to speak and smile. My failure to see Maureen's mental instability brought rolling waves of guilt. *You listened to a crazy woman's fantasies and left your family alone—left them to die.*

When the office phone rang, the noise brought me out of my fog. I found myself sitting on the floor in a corner, knees drawn up tight against my chest. It rang again, and I raised my face, struggling to pull myself together. I didn't have to answer it. The machine would pick up after a couple more rings. I couldn't bring my murdered husband back, couldn't prove I didn't kill Maureen Daley, couldn't even answer the phone, the only thing Bert asked of me.

"You've reached the Suggs Law Firm," Melanie's recorded voice said. "No one is here to take your call. Please leave a message after the tone including your name, the day and time, the person with whom you wish to speak, and a brief explanation of your reason for contacting us. Thank you, and we will return your call as soon as possible."

The machine beeped, and a familiar voice said, "Um, it's Friday, 3:55, and my name is Jacob Grauman—"

I was there in a heartbeat. "Jacob? Jacob, it's me!"

"Beth! I was going to leave a message for Bronson." He paused. "What are you doing there?"

"You're talking to Eliza, the new receptionist at the firm."

Jacob chuckled. "Suggs is a wily old coot."

I smiled for the first time in hours. "He is that."

Jacob's tone became businesslike. "All right. Officially, I'm speaking to the receptionist to report what I've learned about Maureen Daley to Mr. Suggs' associate, Alex Bronson. Since he isn't in the office, I'll convey that information, and you may apprise him of it when you see him."

"I can do that, Officer Grauman."

"Daley was financially insolvent. She'd juggled credit cards for years, but she was about to go under."

I recalled the meeting in the foyer with Maureen's landlord. "I know she was behind in her rent."

"She was about to be evicted. To make things worse, she got fired from her job a week ago. She'd been helping herself to the money in the till, and they caught her on video. They planned to press charges."

"She told me she had to get ready for work the day I was there."

"Well, she lied. Does that surprise you?"

"With what I know now? Not a bit." I filled him in on Alex's conversation with Officer Cjaika.

Jacob made an I-should-have-known grunt when I finished. "That's why nobody would talk about Daley's departure from the RPD."

"Do you think Cjaika is telling the truth?"

"It's hard to decide what to believe, but Vince is known as a straight-up kind of guy."

"While Maureen sounds like someone in a downward spiral."

"Yeah." Jacob cleared his throat. "There's one more thing, and it's just gossip. According to some of the guys I talked to, Trey Manville and Maureen Daley were an item for a while."

I felt something shift inside me, and despair took a back seat to curiosity. I wanted to know how the pieces fit together. "Says who?"

"Manville. I guess he was more than willing to give details to anyone who'd listen."

Maureen and Manville: I'd caught her in another lie. Had she been the one who told him I was nuts?

"Beth—I mean, Ms. Receptionist?"

"Yeah?"

"I know you're trying to protect my job, but if there's anything I can do, promise you'll contact me."

"I will, Jacob. And thank you."

At six, I heard the ping of elevator doors and hurried to Bert's private bathroom. I was closing the door when Alex called softly, "Beth? I've got chicken." He also had mashed potatoes, coleslaw, baked beans and biscuits with honey. As he unloaded the bag, he said dryly, "I was afraid Bert would forget. He's old, you know."

"I should have known you two would compare notes." I sighed. "Since you brought all this, I propose you help me eat it."

A few minutes later we'd spread our meal out on the table in the break room. Alex sat opposite me, taking lids off various items and smiling appreciatively. The man liked to eat. As we worked, I told him about Jacob's call, including the rumor about Maureen and Manville.

"What if he went to her place and they got into an argument?" Alex whisked some biscuit crumbs into the waste basket with one hand. "She went over the balcony railing, maybe by accident, but he sees it as an opportunity to implicate you."

"Why? Because I outshot him on the pistol range back at

the academy? Manville's a jerk, but I can't see him going to all this trouble to frame me for murder."

"It's obvious he's got some personality problems. What if they're bigger than we realize?"

I recalled Maureen's contention that Manville had the hots for me. While I couldn't trust what she'd told me, I also realized the guy was fixated on me for some reason. "I guess it could happen."

He heard the doubt in my voice. "The other possibility is D'Nard. He finds out Maureen is sniffing around, trying to figure out who killed Carole Ann. He goes to her place to scare her off. They fight, she dies, and he runs."

"Then who killed Darrin?"

He thought about that. "My money's still on Carole Ann. Um—I mean, there was some anger there."

I lowered my face, staring at my food. "He told me he'd ended it with her."

"She probably intended to kill all three of you." Surveying the bucket, he chose a thigh. "Too bad the police focused on you and didn't investigate other possibilities."

Bad Luck Girl, that's me, I thought. What I said was, "Why would D'Nard kill Carole Ann that way?"

"To implicate you?" It was a question, not an explanation. Neither of us had much faith that a pimp from Bellemeade with an eighth grade education could dream up a copy-cat crime. How would D'Nard have known I was in Richmond? Why would he keep Carole Ann somewhere for a week before killing her? How would he have come up with the idea of blaming me? It was a reach. Still, some criminals had cunning even without much intelligence. D'Nard might be one of them.

Tossing his chicken bones aside, Alex let out a long breath. "What about the homeless woman?"

It took me a second to comprehend. "You mean Aisha?"

Alex shrugged. "Is there any way she might be involved in this?" When I frowned he reminded me, "She went missing about the same time Carole Ann did, but she hasn't shown up, dead or alive."

I considered the idea. "Aisha didn't know me or Darrin, and she isn't capable of plotting a murder or framing me. She's crooked as a river, but she's no killer."

"One of them is smarter than we think," he insisted. He took a wing, looked it over, dropped it back in the bucket, and chose a drumstick, but his phone played a little tune, and he set the meat down to answer. "Hello, Bert."

Alex listened for a few seconds and then grinned at me. "Yes, as a matter of fact, we are. Okay." He spoke to me. "Bert wants to talk to both of us, so I'll put this on speaker."

"I wanted to let you know that I just left the Franklin home."

Alex looked surprised. "I thought Mr. Franklin didn't want to speak to a fancy-ass lawyer."

"I am not without persuasive power, young man," Bert said with a chuckle. "Actually, since money worked before, I offered two hundred for an hour with the two of them."

"Why?"

"Two reasons, really. First, I wondered if they'd ever seen Maureen Daley with a man."

"You were thinking lesbian."

"The thought had crossed my mind, given her fixation on female friends, but they laughed at the idea. Well," Bert amended, "Mr. Franklin laughed. Mrs. Franklin looked at her lap and blushed. It seems Maureen had an active sex life, always with men. In fact, she left behind medical papers indicating she'd had an abortion. He was quite incensed, and I endured a brief lecture on the right to life."

"I remember now Maureen saying she didn't want kids."

"Okay," Alex said, "we know Maureen slept with boys. What's the other reason you went there?"

"Well, it bothered me that we got such a different picture of Ms. Daley from him than we did from the wife. I wondered if putting the two together might clarify things."

"Meaning Mister Franklin would make Mrs. Franklin take off her rose-colored glasses," Alex said.

"Helen Franklin must have known Maureen was mentally unstable, but she began kindly rather than candidly. I told her it was commendable, but with murder involved, she needed to be honest."

"What did you find out?"

With a sigh, he admitted, "It wasn't easy. She claimed Maureen was simply mixed up due to her unhappy childhood." Bert's tone changed as he shared his interrogation methods. "I watched Mr. as she talked. If he frowned, I asked her the same question a different way. He began putting in comments, and eventually, Mrs. admitted the truth."

"Which was?"

"Maureen made her nervous. In their school days, she wore clothes similar to Mrs. Franklin's and even asked for things she'd outgrown. Knowing there wasn't much money in the Daley household, Mrs. Franklin gave her things, but she said it always felt odd."

My mind conjured a day at the academy when Maureen had raved about how much she liked the sweater I was wearing. When I'd gone to get it at the end of the day, I couldn't find it. A few days later, Maureen had worn one exactly like mine. "I found it at a little shop near my house," she'd crowed. "Same color and everything." I'd never found the one I lost.

While I relived a scene from the past, Bert had continued Helen's revelations. I tuned back in to his voice. "...admitted to feeling relief when she graduated and moved here. She'd forgotten Maureen until she called wanting to rent their second house."

"If Maureen made her uncomfortable, why'd she agree?"

"I asked her that," Bert replied. "She figured Maureen had outgrown her hero worship, and as I said, she felt sorry for her. They'd been neighbors all their lives, she knew the girl had very little money, so Mrs. Franklin thought she should help out."

Alex threw the whistle-clean bone into the take-out box, wiped his fingers again, wadded the napkin, and reached for another drumstick. "I suspect her gut told her all along it was a bad idea, but as we know, Helen is a nice person."

"She soon learned she should not have ignored her instincts," Bert said. "Maureen was very angry with her for getting pregnant and giving up on college. She felt Mrs. Franklin had wasted her talents, becoming what she called 'a baby factory.'"

At Bert's use of the term, I recalled Maureen saying exactly that in regard to her own mother. 'She was a pretty talented artist,' she'd told me, 'but she gave it up when she got married and went to being a baby factory.' She'd added angrily, 'A woman should be more than that.'

Alex said, "Bert, I applaud your skills as an interviewer. You've clarified our picture of Ms. Daley."

"Years of practice, lad, years of practice." He cleared his throat. "Things did get a little uncomfortable when Mr. ordered Mrs. to tell me about an event from years back."

"What was that?"

"Apparently a young man Mrs. Franklin—then a Miss, of course—dated a few times made some comments about Ms. Daley. A month or so after their relationship ended he said to her, 'That little neighbor of yours is something else.' He proceeded to explain in some detail how Maureen had thrown herself at him and how, um, satisfying the result was. Mrs. Franklin was left with the distinct impression that Maureen took up with this person because he'd once been her boyfriend."

"Creepy." Alex was looking at me in an odd way. "But eventually Maureen accepted that Helen is an adult who gets to make her own choices, right? Stopped harassing her about the babies and all."

"She did," Bert said. "Over time they didn't talk as often, but when they did, Maureen often mentioned Beth. She admired you very much, it seems, and as you know, she led the Franklins to believe you two were close friends who did everything together."

I felt the hair on the back of my neck stand up. How had I missed that Maureen was so needy? Like Helen, I'd been caught up in my own life, too much to realize she didn't have one.

Alex seemed to sense that I needed time to process. "Bert, we'll talk about this when we get together."

"There's one more thing," Bert said. "When I rose to leave,

Mr. Franklin walked me to my car, which was a little odd after all his negative comments about lawyers. He wanted to tell me something he was uncomfortable telling Beth, since she's female and might have an attack of the vapors."

I grimaced at the phone, and Alex grinned. "I'll catch her if she faints as you retell it."

"Then here it is. When Ms. Daley first arrived in Richmond, Mr. Franklin helped her move her things into the house. She told him candidly that she believed pregnant women weren't attractive, so if he needed a substitute, even temporarily, she was available."

I'd gone cold, and it had nothing to do with the A/C in the office. "Anything else?" My voice sounded like I'd swallowed an ice cube.

Bert chuckled dryly. "I believe I've shocked us all enough for one evening. Alex, a word." Alex turned off the speaker and listened. I guessed Bert was warning him I might take all this badly.

"I will," he promised. He ended the call and replaced the phone in his pocket. I had pushed my plate away, and he began putting lids on the containers. Putting the leftovers into the bag, he tossed the remaining trash into the box. He took a marker from a cup on a nearby shelf, wrote *ALEX* on the bag in big letters, and put it into the small refrigerator in the corner. I bagged up the trash. Our actions were unconscious, since both of us were focused on what Bert had told us and how it changed things.

Uncharacteristically, I spoke first. "If Helen was her friend, why would she want to sleep with Ken?'"

I spoke more to myself than to Alex, but he answered

anyway. “Because he was Helen’s husband.” Meeting my eyes he added, “She wanted so much to be like her that she tried to step into her life.”

“You’re saying that might be what happened to me.”

His eyes revealed how sad he was to say it. “I think we have to consider it.”

Images began to roll through my head, and I felt panic rising. “You need to go.”

Alex looked surprised. “What?”

“You can’t hang around here.” I cast about for a reason he’d accept. “Someone will get suspicious.”

“I guess you’re right.” He tried again. “I’ll bring breakfast in the morning.”

“No!” It came out harsher than I intended. Softening my tone, I asked, “Do you normally come to the office on Saturday?”

“Not usually, but—” He was at a loss, but he came up with, “You need to eat.”

I crossed my arms. “Alex, how many takeout cartons have we put in the fridge over the last two days?”

“That’s not breakfast.”

“Do you think Loser cared what she ate back then?”

“No.” His voice was soft. I didn’t often remind him I was Loser, but it was time to do it. He liked Beth, and I could feel his liking turning to something more serious. Loser had to stop that from happening.

I rose, went to the door, and held it open for him. “Go. Enjoy your weekend. I’ll be here when you come in Monday morning.”

He seemed uncertain. “Promise?”

"Promise," I said, holding up a hand. "Where else do I have to go?"

As sure as I'd been that I wanted him gone, the minute I heard the elevator doors slide closed, I felt like I'd lost my last friend. I fought the urge to rush after him, to tell him—

Tell him what? Loser whispered. *That you're attracted to him? That you depend on his strength and character? That you don't mind his goofy jokes and addiction to fast food? What then? He's an up-and-coming lawyer with a bright future. Should he tie himself to a woman who isn't sure she can face tomorrow, much less the day after?*

In a gesture somewhere between shutting Alex out of my mind and calling him back, I went to the window in Bert's office, standing to one side in order to remain hidden. I couldn't see the front doors, but as I waited, Alex came around the building and headed to his car. As ex-servicemen often do, he had a relaxed but erect posture. He seemed focused on his thoughts, which I guessed concerned me and my weird ways. I saw the tail-lights of his car flash as the doors unlocked for him, and he got in and started the engine. The lights flashed again and remained on to illuminate the way home.

A flash of movement caught my eye and stopped my silly musings. A man on the sidewalk below watched the BMW pull away. He must have been standing in the shadows until Alex left, but he stepped under the streetlight, where it was easy to see him.

After a few seconds he looked up at the window, a smug expression on his face. Manville had figured out where I was.

Pressing down my rising panic, I made myself think. He couldn't be certain I was here, though it was clear he'd followed Alex, watched him enter the building with enough take-out for six people, and saw him leave empty-handed. Still, he'd have to convince someone above him in rank I was here, and they'd have to do the paperwork that allowed them to search the office. It would take time, which meant I could still protect Bert and Alex if I got away.

Hurrying to the bathroom, I changed to jeans and a t-shirt and tied the arms of the flannel hoodie Alex had bought for me around my waist. The rest of the clothing and toiletries I stuffed into the shopping bags they'd come in. Finished, I examined the room closely to assure nothing remained to suggest my presence. I even wiped out the shower stall and sink to remove hair that wasn't gray.

Next I went to the refrigerator and looked inside. The amount of food there was perhaps excessive, but who was to say Alex didn't always keep leftovers for when he had to work through lunch? I supposed my DNA was on some of the items, but I didn't think they'd go that far.

Opening the garbage, I took my items out and put them in a different bag. I left Alex's in the wastebasket, indicating he'd brought his dinner to the office and eaten alone. He'd catch on and make up a story about work he'd needed to get done, even on a Friday night.

Doing a turn through all the places I'd been, I made sure there was no sign of me left behind. Then I went down to the second floor, where I located a janitor's closet with a high shelf stacked with toilet paper. Taking the rolls down, I stuffed the shopping bags at the back, replacing the rolls to hide them from view. The trash I put in a receptacle near the front door, where anyone might have disposed of it.

Having done what I could to erase my stay at the Suggs Law Firm, I made my way back up the stairs and past the third floor.

Bert had given me the code for the security system, so I could have gone out by the entry doors, but that would leave a record. There had to be another way out of the building, and I figured the roof was the place to start.

Moving to the side of the building away from where I'd seen Manville, I looked over the edge. Below was a courtyard shared by this building and the one next to it. There were lovely flowerbeds, shrubs, and tasteful statuary, but nothing that could help me. The nearest tree was some distance away, and there was no way I could reach even its longest branches. At the back of the building was a concrete slab that didn't look the least bit inviting. If I had to jump, I'd opt for the grassy side. Crouching, I moved a few feet down and peered over the edge to see if Manville was still in the same place. He was on the phone, waving his free hand and shifting his feet in agitation. He'd chosen his viewpoint well, because he could see two full sides of the building. I'd have to go down the courtyard side—somehow.

I went back for a second look, taking in the too-far-removed trees, the sheer wall below me, and the decorative stones lining the ground beside the building. Finding nothing, I turned to the rooftop to see if anything there could assist me. The cables were all too flimsy. The equipment was all fastened in place. There was nothing—

Wait! Stones along the building edge. Drainage! A flat-roofed structure like this had to have drainpipes, and it was old enough that they were probably attached to the exterior.

I was right. At the corner of the building was a metal pipe, its sections nested together and fastened in place by metal straps. Leaning over, I shook it to test its sturdiness. It felt pretty good—at least that's what I told myself as I sat down on the roof edge and put a foot on the nearest strap.

Facing outward was wrong, since I couldn't spider-walk down the side of the building. I needed to turn myself around, which meant putting my right toe where my left heel now was, holding myself in place with my right hand so I could swing my body around to grab the roof edge. Logic told me there were multiple spots in that maneuver where I might make a mistake that would mean plunging three stories and landing on gravel. Before I could think too long about how dangerous it was, I did it. Raising my left foot, I put my right toe on the metal strap, lifted my rear off the roof, and swung my chest toward the wall. Letting go with one hand, I grabbed the roof edge. Once I had a firm hold, I twisted my left foot between my torso and the other leg, scrabbling to find a hold before I lost purchase due to the rapid weight shift.

All four points of contact held, but just barely. Keeping as much of my weight on my arms as possible, I paused for a few seconds to steady myself, my chin almost resting on the low wall. When I heard the groan of the metal straps under my feet, I knew it was time to move. Still gripping the edge, I lowered my body to arms' length, searching with my right foot for the next strap. When I found it, I let go with one hand and grasped the pipe. Slowly, I lowered the other foot, cringing when the strap protested and gave a little. Keeping my body upright and close to the wall, I moved steadily down, stopping as briefly as possible on braces meant only to support the pipe itself.

It's difficult to be quiet when you're climbing down a metal pipe. It scrapes. It squeaks. It crumples. Every new noise multiplied my fears that Manville would hear me and come to investigate. When my foot finally touched the stones, they rattled against each other like castanets. I froze, my hands still clutching the pipe, but my street instincts kicked in. *Don't just stand there, Loser! Run!"*

In seconds I was in the trees at the back of the courtyard, crouching behind the largest one. It was just in time, since a patrol car pulled up, followed by an unmarked with a flashing light on its dash. Turning in a slow circle to assure that the back side of the block was clear, I left.

Chapter Nineteen

Alex left his car in the office parking lot for the third time that day. Keeping his lips together, he let his jaw hang loose, a trick he'd learned for court appearances. Never let them see you grind your teeth. He needed to appear unworried and slightly confused at being called back to the office so late at night, but in truth, he was very worried and not at all confused. Someone had figured out where Beth was hiding, and it was probably his fault.

When the police had called to tell Bert a fugitive from justice was hiding in their offices, they'd conceded that as a prominent Richmond attorney and respected citizen, he could not have known. Still, they asked, ever so politely, if he would allow a search, knowing the possible murderer would have her day in court and the chance to prove her innocence.

Assuring the detectives he would see to their concerns immediately, Bert had contacted Alex, who sped to the building, to find it surrounded by police cars. He called Bert and told him the situation. As he approached the building, he found his jaw had tightened again. With a determined effort, he relaxed it. He had to appear helpful, though he had no intention of helping.

Nearing the line of cars, he saw the cop who'd arrested Beth leaning against a fender. Dressed in civilian clothes, he looked pleased with himself. "Mr. Lawyer," he crooned. "Back so soon?"

Guessing he'd caused this little disaster, Alex said, "Manville, isn't it? Beth's spoken of you."

"I'll bet she has." He ran his tongue over his teeth. "You don't know what she's capable of."

"And you do?"

"I do."

Alex knew this could descend to a testosterone-level contest, but he was curious. "If you have something like evidence, I'd like to hear it."

Manville snuffed a laugh. "How about someone who heard her say she'd like to get rid of her husband?"

"And who would that be?"

Manville was one of those people who seldom met another person's gaze, but he watched Alex's face as he said, "Maureen Daley."

"Maureen told you this?"

"Yeah." Manville wrinkled his nose. "Me and her was talkin' for a while there, but it didn't last." He folded his arms. "She told me Beth said that, just a week before he got dead."

"What about the baby? Why would Beth kill her own child?"

"Beth didn't really want the kid. He wanted her to have it, but it was a pain, always crying and stuff."

"Sir?" a voice interrupted. "The detectives are waiting for you."

Alex nodded at the young cop who'd approached to escort him, saying to Manville as he passed, "Look at Beth as a person and Maureen Daley as a person. Which of them is more believable?" Manville's cheek twitched, but he didn't answer.

The officer led Alex to where two detectives stood. Marshall, whom Alex had met when Beth was arrested the first time, stepped forward while a woman with dull hair stood back, smoking a cigarette. "Mr. Bronson, this is Detective Zender."

Zender dropped the cigarette butt onto the ground and stepped on it—hard. Alex had the sense she wished it were his neck. "Is Beth Lousiere in your office, Mr. Bronson?"

He knew enough not to answer a direct question. "Why would you think that, Detective?"

A look passed between them, signaling they'd expected him to equivocate. Zender crossed her arms over her chest, but it wasn't from cold. The night was humid, and Alex could feel sweat running down his spine. He imagined Zender's anger at the trick Beth had played, escaping custody by using her jacket. Re-capturing her was no doubt Zender's personal goal of the week.

Marshall spoke, his tone friendly though there was a chill underneath. "Would you mind taking us inside for a look around, Mr. Bronson?"

"Do you have a warrant?"

Again looks were exchanged. "No, sir," Zender answered, "we don't, but here's what can happen. We can stand out here for hours while we wake up a judge, tell him about your after-hours visit this evening with a large bag of take-out food. When we tell him an officer of the RPD saw two figures in the window of your offices, one a female who didn't leave with you, in fact, didn't leave at all, we'll see what he says." She glanced at the building. "Or we can get this over with."

"A woman? Someone either has poor eyesight or a huge imagination."

Both Zender and Marshall rolled their eyes, but if he gave in too easily, it would only have made them more suspicious.

"I'll call Mr. Suggs again. If he gives permission, I'll be glad to take you inside." He and Bert had already decided Alex would delay as long as possible, and then agree to a search. Bert had phoned the office switchboard and left a message: *Eliza, you need to re-file those papers we discussed as soon as possible.*

"She's clever," he'd assured Alex. "She'll figure out what to do."

As he unlocked the door and stood back to allow the police in, Alex hoped that was true. If Beth was inside, she'd be arrested and charged. As for what would happen to him and Bert, Alex didn't let himself worry about that, but he guessed it wouldn't be good for business.

Officers fanned out as they entered the building, some to the ground floor, others to the staircase, where they took poses Alex had seen in movies, cautious but aggressive stances with guns drawn and anchored. *She isn't a terrorist!* he wanted to shout.

The thought of her being chased down, handcuffed, and led away made him sick to his stomach, but he doggedly followed the detectives up the stairs. He wouldn't let her face this without a friend, even one powerless to prevent it.

The vestibule was empty, the desk where Beth had spent the day neat and vacant, but that was to be expected. After Alex unlocked the door, one of the officers moved swiftly to the left as another went right. A third cop remained in the doorway, ready to block any attempted escape.

Marshall nodded at Alex, who opened the door to his own office. Marshall went inside but soon returned, shaking his head. Zender indicated the next door, and Alex opened the office shared by the paras.

There was no sign of Beth there, so they moved on. The

conference room was next: nothing. The break room was empty, though Alex smelled fried chicken. Zender tilted the garbage can and peered into it. "One plate, one cup. You had a pretty big bag of food, we heard."

He tried to look innocent, but inside he was cheering Beth's presence of mind. "I confess, Detectives. I have a weakness for the Colonel's cooking."

Ten minutes later it was over. They'd searched the third floor thoroughly and found no sign of Beth. Officers looked through the rest of the building, opening bathroom doors and poking into closets, but it was mostly to burn off energy. No one at the Suggs Law Firm had access to the securities firm, the travel agency, or the other businesses. A cop went up to the roof and came back to report, "She's not up there." His tone was light, and Zender flashed him a look of anger. For him, the search was another job in the day's work. For her, Alex guessed, it was a reflection on her reputation. She'd failed to find the woman who'd escaped while in her custody.

For Marshall, too, the night's work brought frustration. They'd gambled on catching Beth, insulted the integrity of a prominent law firm, combed through a building without a warrant, and come up with zilch. Both detectives were way beyond grumpy.

"If you're done," Alex said, "I'd like to get back home. My girlfriend is supposed to call from Detroit."

As they both nodded grimly, he tried to keep his satisfaction from showing. Beth was still free, and she had the burner phone he'd given her. She'd call.

She didn't call, but Christina did. He'd just entered his apartment, dumped his keys, wallet, and phone on the island, and started for the refrigerator when the ring tone she'd programmed into his phone for herself sounded. For a second Alex considered not answering. He wasn't in the mood. With a sigh, he picked up the phone.

"Hey."

"Hi, Alex. How are things in the big city?"

"Good. How is Detroit?"

"Distressed, but there are some good things." Her voice took on an odd tone. "In fact, there are some possibilities here."

"Yeah?" He couldn't generate much interest in the bankrupt city's assets and liabilities. He wondered where Beth would spend the night.

"Um, Alex, they want me to stay here."

That got his attention. "Stay? Why? I mean, for a while or what?"

"Like stay. There are all kinds of things that need to be done. Management sees great opportunity, and it's a chance for me to do something good, both for Detroit and for my career."

"I see." Times of distress offered businesses the chance to succeed if they could provide something essential to alleviate problems. Detroit was looking to repair its tarnished image, and Christina would tackle the problem with enthusiasm and intelligence. "You'd be my choice for the job."

"Thanks." After a beat she said, "They'd welcome a good lawyer."

He ran a hand through his hair. "I wouldn't leave Richmond, Chris. Bert's been good to me."

"I knew that." She sounded as if she meant it. "I just thought I'd ask." When Alex didn't say anything, she added, "Maybe you could fly up for a weekend. I'll take you around and show you. It's such a contrast, there's great stuff and sad places. It's quite a challenge."

"I'd like to see it."

There was an awkward pause. They both knew what this was, but neither was willing to say goodbye for good. Alex thought it should hurt more, being dumped for a corporate job, but he felt only vague regret. He liked Christina. He admired her. He didn't love her, and he didn't think she loved him.

Finally, she said, "Listen, I've got an early morning tomorrow, so I'll let you go."

"Okay. We'll talk again soon. It's my turn to call." Would he do it, or was it better to let the relationship die? He'd decide that later, once he knew Beth was safe. As he set the phone back on the counter, his thoughts had already left Christina in Detroit. *Where is Beth?*

Having no other choice, I returned to the Fan. It took most of the night to get there, since I moved like a cockroach, zig-zagging, scurrying, and freezing at the slightest hint of human presence. My days as Loser served me well as I drifted from alley to hedge to parked cars. Once I sat motionless beside a stone porch for an hour while a young couple spoke of love's hindrances: jobs, school, and unfeeling parents. Another time I waited while a drunk urinated into the bushes where I crouched. When he finished and staggered away, both of us were relieved.

Seeing the All-Aid up ahead, I felt like I'd reached Nirvana, but of course that wasn't true. There was no one there at this hour, and even if there had been, there was nothing they could do to help. I sat down between the trash bins to wait. Howard had worked for the railroad before he became disabled, and I hoped he could tell me how to catch an anonymous ride out of Richmond.

I dozed until the lid of the trash bin closed with a mighty, metallic slam. I jumped, but the clerk who'd tossed a bag of garbage in was already retreating, his red tunic dimly visible in the gray of dawn.

The humidity of the night before had become fog, and the streets at my front and side were invisible except when headlights defined their location for a few seconds. Some distance down, a traffic light blinked dimly, but other than that, the world shrank to the bin walls and the security light at the back of the drug store that illuminated a small square of blocks.

I wondered about the time but chided myself. Loser had operated on the earth's rhythms, awake when it was light, asleep when it was dark. I should begin returning to that frame of mind, forgetting I'd had a somewhat normal life for a while.

Eddie and Mabel came to mind. What would they do when I didn't return to Beulah? Maybe Bert and Alex would arrange for them to receive an income from my account. But who would go to parent-teacher conferences for Ed during his senior year?

My stomach let me know I was hungry, and this time I chided both myself and Alex. Beth had taken to eating three meals a day because that's what people do. Alex had provided more food than I was used to. Loser could have gone at least another day without eating, but Beth's stomach wanted breakfast. Loser won the argument, but that didn't end the complaints.

When light began to penetrate the fog, I made a guess at the time and pulled out the phone Alex had given me. From another pocket I took the number Jacob had provided and punched it in. Sasha answered, and I asked for Jacob, hoping he hadn't already left for work.

"Are you all right, Beth?" Sasha asked after she'd called for Jacob to come to the phone. "You don't sound right."

How do I answer that? Sitting between two trash bins, trying to keep from being overheard, hunted by police, and haunted by the idea that someone who said she was my friend had murdered my husband and my child. *My throat feels like it's closing after each word I force myself to speak, and I want to throw this phone as far as possible.* "I'm okay," I told her.

I heard the scratch of the phone being exchanged, and Jacob said, "Beth?"

"I had to leave, but I need you to do something for me."

"Of course."

"When you get to work, can you find Maureen Daley's file and take a look at her picture?"

"Yeah, but wait a minute. I think I can do it from here if that helps."

"Great." There was an extended silence, and I imagined him booting up his computer and accessing the information. "Okay, here's the department site." His tone was distracted as he tried to talk and work at the same time. "D-A-L-E-Y. Oops, that's active members. Have to find the file for former employees...Here it is. Okay, once again, D-A-L-E-Y. Here it is. You want me to look at her photo?"

"Yes." I could hardly contain my impatience. Jacob was the only person who could confirm what I suspected.

"Oh."

"Jacob!"

"Sorry. I—I see why you wanted me to do this."

“Is it her?”

“Yes, Beth. Maureen Daley is the woman I saw with Darrin that night in the restaurant.”

I think I managed to thank him for his help, but he was still talking as I closed the phone.

At midmorning the sun appeared briefly, burning the fog to nothing. In a not-so-great side effect, the heat it generated cooked the garbage on both sides of me. I detected bananas and peaches, among other things. Mixed together and half rotted, none of them smelled nice.

By noon my hiding spot was stifling. I’d positioned myself where I could see the building wall that was shaded all morning, and it was a relief when Penrod rolled around the corner into sight, his shoulder against the bricks and his mouth moving.

“Psst!” It’s a stupid sound, but it does get a person’s attention. “Psst! Penrod!”

He looked up suspiciously, and I stood so he could see it was me. Recognition lit his face. There was a pause as he considered how to get from the building to the trash bins, at least fifty feet of open space with nothing to hold onto. Bravely he launched himself away from the wall, staggering toward me. Ten feet away, he was already reaching, and his face relaxed a little when he touched something solid. Sensing my need for secrecy, he turned his back and leaned against the bin. “Are you okay, Loser?”

“The police are looking for me.”

“They been here a bunch of times. Howard and me don’t tell them anything, but Billy talked to them. Bubba and Aisha too.”

“Aisha’s back?”

"Yeah." He didn't sound pleased. "She came yesterday, acting like she never left. Howard asked if the police knew she wasn't missing anymore, but she said she don't talk to cops."

That sounded like the Aisha I knew. "Where's she been?"

I could see Penrod's tense back, the chords in his neck stretched taut. I was asking a lot of this damaged man, and he struggled to sort pertinent information out of the jumble in his mind. "With a friend," he answered. "She said she was staying with a friend."

"And why did she come back?"

"There wasn't money for Taco Bell anymore." Obviously proud to be able to remember and report, Penrod smiled a little.

"Do you know where she's sleeping?"

"Not with Billy. His car got towed." Flapping his hands in a gesture that implied Billy's reaction, he went on, "She used to have a spot at the cemetery she liked."

Cemeteries are good spots for sleeping, as long as you aren't haunted by the dead. They're often fenced, there's usually a curfew, and they aren't patrolled with any regularity. "It's a long way," Penrod said, sensing my indecision. "But she says it's cooler down by the river."

"Hey, you! Get away from the trash!" Between Penrod's legs I glimpsed the clerk I'd seen earlier, standing in the doorway at the back of the store with a cigarette in one hand and a lighter in the other.

Penrod bent at the waist as if he'd been punched in the stomach, and without a backward look, launched himself toward the drug store, reaching until he again touched its comforting surface.

I struggled to decide what to do. I'd meant to leave Richmond when night fell. It would be difficult without resources, but it had seemed my only choice. Penrod's report raised another possibility, more dangerous, but offering hope. Aisha and Maureen were connected somehow. Aisha knew things that I wanted to know too.

In the end I decided to delay my departure for a day. If Howard showed up, I could ask him how to get on a train without purchasing a ticket. It was even possible Aisha, though not as much a regular as some, might wander by and save me the trouble of looking for her.

Neither of those things happened, and I spent all day roasting between metal trash bins that absorbed sunlight better than solar panels. The smell grew worse, and I got so bored I began picking out individual odors and trying to guess their origins. Coffee grounds—that was easy, the staff break room. Perfume—a damaged or dropped bottle. Cinnamon—someone's leftover mini-buns. More intriguing was the smell of licorice. Candy? Cough drops? A bottle of absinthe? Those are the kinds of things a loser thinks about during a long day of waiting.

At one point I saw a black BMW pass slowly along the street. Its tinted windows didn't allow a view of the driver, but I would have sworn it was Alex's car. Would he stop and ask Penrod where I was? If he did, would Penrod realize he was a friend? Not likely. Penrod didn't look like a guy who could tell you anything that made sense, and Alex didn't look like a friend of Loser's. I thought of the phone he'd given me, buried in my pocket. I could call to tell him I was okay, but what would I say? *Sorry I've messed up your life again. Please go about your business and forget you ever knew me.* It was the message I should have sent, but I didn't.

The heat of the day built to broiling, and moisture thickened in the air. Overhead clouds rolled in off the ocean and blocked out the sun, layering in precise divisions of white, cream, iron, gray, and on the bottom, black. They brought no relief in the temperature, and from time to time they grumbled threats as they hung there. It would rain, the thunder promised. It was simply a question of when.

Chapter Twenty

The advantage to the heavy clouds was an early evening. Four o'clock seemed like eight, and by five, with shadows to creep through, I left my hiding place and started for the cemetery. I'd never seen Aisha's spot, but Bubba had once described it to us. "She got this little building with pillars on the corners and a roof that keeps the rain out, mostly." That meant a mausoleum. I pictured Aisha laying her things out on the grass around the tomb and humming, the way she did when she was happy.

The cemetery gate was already closed, but being more decorative than functional, it was easy to climb. Once inside, I zig-zagged the grounds, looking for mausoleums large enough for Aisha to hide behind. The growing darkness slowed my way, but at least it wasn't likely I'd be seen. I did worry a little about tripping over tombstones or falling into an open grave.

When my search paid off, Aisha and I almost scared each other to death. I rounded the corner of a large, rectangular mausoleum and came face-to-face with her as she started around the other way. We each let out sounds of surprise, mine a grunt, hers a little shriek.

"Aisha, it's me."

She leaned forward, squinting, and I caught a whiff of beer. Aisha must have been pretty once. She had decent bone structure and a symmetrical face with prominent eyes and full lips. Life and too much booze had left her looking ravaged, and though she was four years younger than I, she looked at least a decade older. Her eyes were blank, and their size exaggerated the lack of intelligence in their depths. Her skin was blotched and bumpy, her hands dry and caked with dirt. I had a moment of revulsion, not for Aisha, but at the thought this was how I'd looked as Loser. With Beth buried deep inside, survival had been for Loser a constant concern, and conversely, no concern at all.

"Loser," Aisha said, as if at a loss to explain my appearance.

"We need to talk." My eyes had adjusted to the darkness, and I saw the shift of her eyes. Sensing she might run, I took her arm firmly.

"Ow! That hurts!" She tried to pull away, but I held tight. If she took off, I could easily lose her in the dark cemetery, where tombstones provided lots of hiding places.

"I know you knew Maureen Daley, and Carole Ann Minier too."

She stopped struggling. "What do you mean I knew them?"

"Carole Ann's dead. Stabbed in the back a dozen times."

"Oh." The groan revealed genuine surprise. "She said she was gonna let her go."

Things began clicking into place in my mind. "Sit down. You're going to tell me everything you know."

It wasn't as simple as that, of course. Aisha was not the type of person who did the right thing because it was the right thing. Neither was she the type who did the right thing when faced with no other options. Watching her eyes, I saw her recover from the shock of Carole Ann's murder and start figuring how it could benefit her. She would lie. Aisha lied about everything, often simply because she could. But she knew the truth, and she was already calculating what she could get in exchange for it.

I started the bargaining process. "I have money."

She sniffed audibly. "I heard." Her eyes met mine,

challenge obvious. "I ain't seen it, though."

I took a folded stack of twenty-dollar bills out of my pocket. "I'll give you one of these for each answer." I heard her take breath to agree, but I went on, "If you lie to me once, even a little bit, I'll drag you by the hair to the nearest police station. The cops know you were in on Carole Ann's murder." I could lie, too, when I had to. Her eyes widened, and I added, "And with Maureen dead too, they'll think you killed them both."

"I didn't—"

"I want the truth. Twenty dollars an answer, or you get arrested. Your choice."

In a tone that sounded like a bratty little kid she asked, "What do you want to know?"

I held a twenty out between thumb and forefinger. The security light on the access road illuminated it, making it silvery and tempting. "How did you meet Maureen?"

Aisha sighed. "She come to the Fan after some reporter wrote a story about you."

"Because you said we were friends."

Pressing her lips together, she looked pointedly at my hand. I got the message: One answer at a time. Handing her the bill, I peeled another off the pile, cautioning myself to frame my questions carefully.

"How did you meet Carole Ann?"

The answer to this one took some thought, which meant Aisha knew she'd done something illegal. Because she felt compelled to justify her actions, her explanation shortened my list of questions.

"Maureen come looking for me 'cause that article said how I knew you real well." She grinned, and I saw a gap in her teeth where some man in her past had knocked out a molar. "He asked for it, Loser. I mean, he gave me forty bucks, and he bought me lunch too."

I recalled Billy saying she'd got twenty. Aisha wasn't quite as dumb as she acted.

"Anyway," she went on, "Maureen asked me stuff about you, and I didn't know the answers. After a while, she looked at me real mean and said I was wasting her time."

"She knew you'd lied."

She shrugged. "The next day she come back, said she needed my help." She pushed a lock of lanky hair out of her eyes. "Me and Billy had a fight, and I was—I needed to get away for a while, you know?"

I recalled the blood on the clothing in her bag. "He slapped you around."

Another shrug. "Maureen said she'd give me money, a lot of it." She paused, and I almost took another twenty off the stack, but she'd become caught up in her story. "She said Carole Ann used to screw your husband, so if we locked her up somewhere, we could get you to pay us to tell where she was."

As I listened, I tried to figure out what Maureen's actual plan had been. I doubted she'd told Aisha anything close to the truth. I guessed she'd originally intended to kidnap Aisha, hoping the disappearance of a close friend would draw me back to Richmond. Once she figured out Aisha had no friends, least of all me, she'd formed a new plan. Knowing Carole Ann from her days as a cop, she'd decided to tempt me with the possibility of evidence to prove my innocence. Since she needed Carole Ann alive until I actually arrived, and she couldn't monitor her alone, Maureen had looked for an assistant neither overly moral nor terribly bright. Aisha's dislike for me and the fact she'd do almost anything for money made her perfect for the job.

I peeled off a third twenty. "How did Maureen kidnap Carole Ann?"

Aisha turned coy. "I don't know, 'cause I wasn't there. She just asked me to watch her—"

"Okay. You weren't in on the kidnapping. Tell me what you know."

"Well, Maureen called and told her she had a job where they could make a bunch of money if she came to this place right away. Carole Ann went for it. She was pretty dumb."

The pot calling the kettle black. I nodded in apparent agreement.

"When she got in the car, Maureen pulled a gun and brought her to me. I was the keeper. I fed her and made sure she didn't get away. Maureen snuck into her place and left this card from your old man—"

"Wait. Maureen had the card?"

Aisha missed that I'd asked another question. "Yeah. She left it in the nightstand drawer, so the cops would connect him and Carole Ann." Her voice changed. "She had to make it obvious, 'cause they're all as dumb as rocks."

I recalled the words on the card: *I'm sorry. You're the only woman I really love. D.*

"Where did Maureen get this card?"

"She didn't say." Aisha's tone revealed no interest in how or why. "She laughed, though, 'cause she said everybody would think your old man liked a strung-out whore better than you."

The doubts I'd felt at the idea of my husband having an

affair with a prostitute hadn't been the wishful thinking of a betrayed wife. Darrin had probably never met Carole Ann.

Not that the truth was any more palatable. At first she'd settled for admiring my success as a cop and stealing articles of my clothing. When the opportunity arose, Maureen had swooped in and slept with my weak, self-pitying husband.

I waited, but Aisha rolled her eyes meaningfully. I handed over a bill. "Where'd you keep Carole Ann?"

"Maureen found this empty house and we fixed up a room to keep her in. She gave me money for food and bought me a phone. It was like I was on guard duty. I went to all different places so nobody saw I always got take-out for two people."

"What did this have to do with me?"

"Maureen wanted to know if you came to Richmond. She was pretty sure you would."

"And how did she know when I got here?"

"Well, Billy told me after he saw you at the bar, and I called Maureen right away. That's when she come and got the girl." There was honesty in her eyes for once as she added, "I thought she was going to take her to you, honest."

"You couldn't know what she had planned." My sympathy for Aisha only lasted a few seconds as an image of Carole Ann's ordeal formed in my mind. "Where is this place you kept her?"

Back to her mercenary self, Aisha held out a hand and I fed the piggy. Tucking the bill into her hat, she said, "2655 Marple Court."

"Where is that?"

"A couple blocks from the Boulevard Bridge."

"Which direction?"

Her hands moved as she reminded herself which was her

dominant one. "Um, left."

I was almost finished with her. "Why did you stay away after Carole Ann was gone?"

She grimaced as if that was obvious. "I wanted Billy to miss me."

"Does he know you're back?"

The smile that spread across her face spoke volumes. "We're all good now." It was almost a purr.

I turned to go, but Aisha asked, "Are you gonna go to that house?"

"Was Maureen actually there?"

"Well, sure." It might have been "Duh!" from her tone. "First her and me got the place ready. Then she brought the girl and shut her up in the room. Then she came and took her away." Aisha scratched an itch in her armpit. "She said I should stay there till she come back, but she never did. Pretty soon I ran out of money and I started missing Billy. I didn't know she was dead." Her voice took on a fearful tone. "Did you kill Maureen, Loser? I mean, I don't care if you did. She wasn't nothing to me, and I bet you had to do it, 'cause she really, really hated you. She kept saying you had to pay."

"I haven't killed anyone."

Aisha processed that. "I guess she was wrong." In a stronger tone she added, "I wonder why she thought you had to pay, then, 'cause she said she'd see you did, no matter what."

Figuring her dread of cops made it unlikely Aisha would report my whereabouts, I left her in her creepy resting place. My first stop was a convenience store where I picked up a small flashlight, some candy bars, and a bottle of water. Hearing the rumbles of thunder again outside, I added one of those packaged ponchos to my purchases, a little disgusted that Beth thought she needed protection from the rain. Loser would have ignored it as she ignored cold, heat, and wind. Like happiness and a full stomach, weather was a temporary condition that, left alone, went away by itself.

The long hike to the cemetery had at least brought me close to the river. I crossed Maymont Park, quiet except for a group of teens so intent on impressing each other they never noticed me. It was a good thing, because I was in too much of a hurry to hide.

Darrin's confession came back to me as if it were yesterday, but I was clearer-headed now. The painful memory was worn to a nub, still sore but not disabling. Listening to our conversations play in my head, I found spots that at the time hadn't mattered to me. He'd refused to reveal the woman's name, which should have told me it was someone I knew. The affair had gone on for a couple of months before he realized, he'd claimed, that his marriage meant more to him than she did.

"I'm sorry. You're the only woman I really love. D. Could that have been written to me? I couldn't let myself think it. If Darrin really had realized I was important to him, he'd been too late.

Darrin's lover had made threats. She would hurt him, she'd said, and his family as well. I recalled his words: "I didn't see it until it was too late. She's dangerous."

That sounded like the Maureen I'd come to know in the past few days. She'd focused first on Helen, trying to be like her. When Helen let her down, she'd cut her out of her life. Recalling the account of vandals trashing the house, I guessed it had actually been Maureen, signaling her displeasure with the Franklins.

Disappointed in Helen, Maureen had turned her focus to me. People had predicted I'd move quickly through the ranks of the police force, as she wanted so badly to do. Instead I'd gotten pregnant and even considered leaving the job in order to raise Kara and other children I might have. She'd wanted me to fight for a place in a man's world, and in her view I'd failed to do that, just as Helen and her own mother had.

How thrilled she must have been to have tempted Darrin away from me, to snare the man I loved! I wondered if she might have tired of us if Darrin hadn't rejected her. That must have set her on the path to punishing both of us. All of us.

The first drops of rain came then, the fat kind that promised this was no light shower. I retreated to the shelter of a tree, pulled my hoodie on, and covered it with the poncho. Dragging the hood as far over my face as it would go, I walked on. As the rain intensified, my shoes became soaked and my pant legs sodden. Soon I was slogging along through an inch of water, the only pedestrian on the streets of Richmond, it seemed. Cars passed from time to time, and I faded into the shadows, watching the splash of their tires until I was sure the driver didn't step on the brakes. I didn't need a Good Samaritan stopping to offer a ride, and I didn't want a patrolman wondering why I was walking in such foul weather.

When I came to the Boulevard Bridge, rain fell so hard it felt like I was under a waterfall. The crossing taxed my acting abilities, since the pedestrian walkway provided no shelter when a vehicle came along. Unable to hide, I bent my elbows and took up a brisk, purposeful stride, hoping passing motorists would assume I was a fitness nut. It was a stretch at nine o'clock at night in pouring rain, but I counted on the disinterest of my fellow humans.

Miserably I plodded onward, feeling like there was almost as much water above me as below. Operating in Loser mode, I blocked out my physical discomfort and tried to make sense of what I'd learned. It was hard to keep emotion out of it and concentrate on the facts. With a face to put into the image, I was tortured anew by thoughts of the night my family was murdered. I flashed back to a day when we'd left the academy together and passed the wife of one of our classmates, waiting in the car with her infant son. I'd stopped to admire the baby, but Maureen had not. When I caught up, she'd said plainly she despised babies. "Little leeches," she'd said. "Always wanting something."

When she'd released her rage on me and Darrin, Maureen had included our child too. Darrin and Kara lost their lives. I lost everything I cared about.

She must have wondered where I'd gone after the murders, but by then she was having problems with her job, her finances, and her private life. She'd been fired from the department, losing the role she considered her identity. She'd moved to a depressing apartment where she couldn't afford the rent. She drove a beater car, lived on Cheetos and soda, and no doubt nursed her anger at the world, at the Richmond police department, and at me. I guessed most of all, me.

"Hey, watch it!" a voice called, and I realized I'd exited the bridge and walked into the street. Hurrying to the other side, I turned west, looking for the place Aisha had described.

Westover Hills flanked the east and west sides of State Route 161, where the Boulevard Bridge, also known as the Nickel Bridge because that was the original toll, crossed the

James. Most of the homes were long-established, a mix of styles and ages with large lots. I wondered how Maureen had found a place to keep Carole Ann where no one would hear or see what was going on. I plodded through rain-drenched streets, the businesses closed, the house lights dim in the rain. With no one to ask the way to Marple Court, I wandered for some time, keeping the river on my left and walking south until I saw a sign that indicated I'd found it.

Marple Court, almost within view of the river, was a development that hadn't fully developed. It had no doubt been some designer's dream, three cul-de-sac circles of homes for young marrieds that would sell like hotcakes. They were so much alike that I wondered how a person would know his place from the rest. A lawn ornament, maybe, or a unique mailbox. It didn't matter, because foreclosure hit before the houses were completed, probably sending the mastermind and the builders running to bankruptcy court. A sign at the turnoff said a certain Richmond bank was willing to deal on the property. Half-finished houses generally aren't high on the list of things banks want to hold onto.

The house numbered 2655 was about a third of the way around the second circle, identical to the rest. I walked around to the back, looking for evidence to support Aisha's story, and there it was. The entry door had been pried open, using a bar of some sort that left the frame slightly caved in. The door appeared closed from a distance, but a firm push sent it crashing against the inside wall. I waited, listening for sounds from inside. After nothing for two full minutes, I stepped onto the raised doorsill and went in.

It was dark, but light showed ahead of me. The small mud area at the back was about six feet wide, but within a few squishy steps I entered a large room open to the roof. The space was divided by half-walls, both vertical and horizontal. A frame that would have become a bar separated the kitchen area at one side, and opposite me, a four-foot extension wall shielded the double front doors from the living area. Large, wide windows at the front let in light from street lamps installed for home owners who had not yet shown up.

Second floor windows cast light on an open staircase and a loft, where floor joists waited for underlayment. In the kitchen, black holes gaped where pipes and hoses would have run, and next to a hallway to my right, pieces of plywood lay flat in a corner, waiting for a day when they'd be useful.

Seeing no sign of habitation, I went right, past the kitchen, and tried a door at the side of the house. It led to an empty garage that hollowly echoed the sounds the door made. Retreating, I turned to my right and went down the hallway, leaving wet footprints on the bare wood. Here darkness again engulfed me, since the windows faced away from the street. There were several doors along the passage, all without handles, and I opened the first, a closet without shelves or hardware. Across from it was a bathroom, judging from the holes in the floor and wall. It was empty, and I went on.

Farther down were two more doors. I put my ear against the one on the left and listened. It was quiet inside, the empty kind of quiet I sensed in the rest of the house. When my shoulder brushed it, though, I heard metallic scrapes. Running a hand along the door, I found three simple hooks along the edge, one near the top, one in the middle, and one a foot from the floor. Figuring no one outside could see it from here, I turned on my flashlight and aimed it at the frame. In the door casing were matching eye screws, a simple but effective method of closing someone inside the room.

Keeping the flashlight beam aimed low, I scanned what would have become a bedroom. Boards had been nailed over its single window, a haphazard job but firm enough when I pulled at them. The smell of human waste permeated the room, and I saw a bucket in one corner that must have been Carole Ann's toilet. In the opposite corner were remains of meals, a crust of bun and some limp fries.

It was a sad sight. Carole Ann Minier had spent the last week of her life imprisoned here, and she'd probably never understood why. I pictured her lying down to try to sleep, her tears wetting the unforgiving particle-board floor. I hoped Maureen had been kind enough to let her believe at the last that she'd be set free. I hoped she'd never seen the knife in Maureen's hand.

Pushing pity for Carole Ann to the back of my mind, I left the room. I needed proof that Maureen had been here, something I could take to the police. Across the hall was a room of similar size. Here the sweet odor of pot hung in the air, strong enough to make me cough. The only window was covered with something dark and saggy, maybe a blanket. I turned on my flashlight again. The place was mostly empty, but scattered items indicated recent occupation. In one corner a jumbled mass suggested blankets or a sleeping bag, and in another a stack of light-colored objects resolved on closer inspection into disposable dishes and fast-food bags.

Aisha's leavings. I pictured her sitting in this room, toking and listening unmoved to Carole Ann's cries for help, mercy, and freedom. She claimed she hadn't known Maureen planned murder, but she must have suspected. Or was Aisha too self-centered to think past free food, a little excitement, and the promise of money?

Over the drum of rain, I heard something, maybe a vehicle. Turning off my light, I listened. There was nothing. Crossing the room, I tugged the blanket off the nails that held it over the window and peered out at a sideways view of the street. Rain fell in sheets, blurring the lights out front and blearing the window with continuous rivulets of water. A dark shape caught my eye, and I thought something moved behind it. Was there a car? Had someone gotten out of it?

I watched for some time but saw nothing more. I told myself it was unlikely there was anyone out there. The shape I'd seen could have been a hedge, an untrimmed branch pummeled by the rain. I almost believed it until a sound in the hallway turned me cold. It wasn't much, a carefully placed foot too wet to be silent. As I went to a defensive crouch, a second squish followed. Someone was in the house.

A policeman, even a neighborhood watchman, would call out. This person was silent, stalking me without revealing his presence. I wanted out, but where could I go? The window was screened, so an exit there would make noise. All I could do was hope whoever it was didn't come into this room. Still holding the blanket I'd taken from the window, I backed up next to the door. In the dark, the eye of anyone who came in would be drawn to the window's light. If I was quiet, I might slip out behind him.

Concentrating on silence, I heard the drip of water as it left my sodden clothes. I could still my breathing, but who can stop the rain?

The door flew open, smashing into the wall behind it, and I flattened my back against the wall, ready to head out the door the moment the intruder took a step into the room.

He didn't. The beam of a flashlight appeared, swept the room, and stopped on me like an unwelcome spotlight. "I tol' you I'd find you, bitch." D'Nard Dobermeyer's square frame filled the doorway. In his other hand was the baseball bat.

Chapter Twenty-one

By evening, Alex Bronson was tired, frustrated, and dispirited. He'd spent all of Saturday searching for Beth and fielding hysterical calls from Eddie, who threatened to start hitchhiking to Richmond. He'd managed to convince the kid there was nothing he could do to help, since Beth couldn't be found. Eddie had blustered that he'd manage somehow, but he wasn't dumb, just young. Alex was almost as frantic as Eddie, though he pretended otherwise to calm the boy's fears.

"Tell you what, Ed," he'd proposed after the fourth call of the day. "If I haven't found her by Monday, I'll get you a bus ticket." Eddie had reluctantly agreed to that, though Alex knew Beth wouldn't approve. The kid had finals to prepare for.

How do I find someone who doesn't want to be found? he asked himself as he turned onto Broad and made another pass through the area. He couldn't call the police and report that the suspect he'd been sheltering was now missing. Beth's street friends were unwilling, in some cases unable, to share what they knew. Bert, Verle, and Jacob had made their best guesses about where she might go, but his search had turned up nothing. Beth had dissolved into Loser, and Loser knew how to disappear.

Not knowing what else to do, he drove around the Fan again. Night was coming on, and he pictured Beth huddled in some alley, fearful of discovery and retreating into the silence she'd found comforting in the past. She'd done okay in the office, and he felt a tiny bit responsible for her success. Then the arrival of the police sent her running again. Remembering the smug look on Manville's ferrety face, Alex wanted to find the cop and punch him.

He passed the All-Aid, slowing to check the side of the building opposite the entry, where Loser and her friends congregated. The guy who muttered all the time was there. With him was a wild-looking guy in rubber boots, a dirty, knee-length coat, and a bandana that had once been yellow. The wild man talked non-stop, though he got no response. The tall man leaned against the building, touched his lips with his fingers, and repeated the words that apparently soothed his nerves.

Alex turned and pulled into a parking space on the other side of the drug store, trying to recall everything Beth had ever told him about her friends. What would convince them to help him? He closed his eyes, letting things she'd said come back. She didn't share much about her Loser days, but in telling what she knew of the murders, she'd mentioned several people.

Penrod suggested Billy might know where Aisha went.

I asked Howard when the reporter came to talk to Aisha.

Billy and Aisha are sort of a couple.

Bubba showed me where Aisha's stuff was stashed. Bubba knows everything, and he loves to tell.

Howard, the one who remembered the apples, had introduced himself, and he'd referred to Penrod, the mumbler, by name. The guy in the boots didn't seem like the type a woman would choose for a boyfriend, though Alex didn't claim to understand the dynamics of relationships on the streets. He thought he recalled Beth saying it was a miracle Bubba was so good at gathering secrets, because his seldom-zipped boots made his approach noisy.

The guy he wanted was Bubba. Could there be two like that in Richmond? Alex exited the car and waited, leaning against it and hoping Bubba might come his way.

The sky had been threatening rain, and the threat became imminent as the wind tossed garbage across the parking lot and threw dirt in his face. He leaned against the fender, debating. If he approached both men with his questions, the mutterer might warn Bubba to silence. But if he waited, Bubba might leave and go in the opposite direction. He walked around to where the two men stood.

"Can one of you help me load a box in my car?" he asked. "It's going to rain, and I need to hurry."

The mutterer turned away, but the other man stood a little straighter. "What's the rate?" he asked.

"I've got a five-dollar bill."

"Okay," he responded cheerfully. "Where's it at?"

Once they were away from Penrod, Alex asked, "Are you Bubba?"

His mushy face collapsed into a frown. "Yeah. Where's the box?"

"There isn't a box. I want to talk to you about Loser."

His fleshy lips turned flat. "Don't know her," he said.

"Then how do you know Loser is a woman?"

That confused him, and Alex felt a stab of pity. It was a battle of wits, and Bubba wasn't fully armed. "Listen," he told the ragged man, "I'm Loser's friend, and I need to find her." After a brief interior debate about whether monetary reward or emotional appeal would be more effective, he went with the latter. "She might be in danger."

"Loser's pretty smart," Bubba answered after some consideration. "She hides real good."

He nodded. "That's true. She was hiding at my place, but

the cops came and she had to run."

"Yeah?" Bubba raised a dirty hand, pointing at the sky. "When the President's a alien, you gotta watch out for who he sends to get you."

Alex had no idea where to go with that. "I can help her hide, but I don't know where she went." Bubba paused, and he guessed this was the time for money. "I'll give you the five for helping Loser out."

His face brightening, Bubba asked, "You promise you ain't gonna turn her over to the aliens?"

Raising a hand, Alex vowed, "Promise." With the other hand, he held out the five.

Taking the money and stuffing it into his pants pocket, Bubba said, "She went to talk to Aisha."

"The woman who's been missing?"

"She came back yesterday. I seen Penrod talking to the trash bin, so I sneaked up and seen Loser hiding in there. He told Loser she prob'ly was at the cemetery. A while ago Loser took off, and I bet that's where she went."

The guy was more observant than some trained soldiers Alex had known. "Which cemetery?"

Bubba's face broke into a huge smile. "For another five dollars and a ride in that car, I'll show you."

With a sigh, Alex pulled out his wallet. In this battle of wits, Bubba had all the weaponry he needed.

D'Nard was the last person I'd expected to meet in the house where Carole Ann had been held prisoner. I needed to get his attention and reason with him, but that's difficult with a man who wants you dead and is willing to act on it.

"I didn't kill Carole Ann."

"Yeah?" His tone was casual. "I don't think you got time to explain 'fore I beat you to death with this."

He came at me then, the bat raised. His arm swung in a long arc, like he was hitting one into the stands. I managed to duck out of the way, and his momentum carried him forward, twisting in the direction he'd swung. I jumped at him, spreading the blanket over his head, and pulled it tight, pinioning his arms and using his unbalanced stance to swing him around. Compelled to drop something in order to free himself, D'Nard let go of the flashlight. I kicked it into a corner, almost pulled off my feet as he fought to free himself, roaring with fury.

I didn't have the physical strength to subdue a man of D'Nard's size, so I had to run. As he twisted this way and that, straining to free himself, I let go of the blanket, raised my foot to his backside, and pushed with all my strength in the direction he was leaning. He staggered toward the window, crashing into the wall with an explosive curse, and I shot out of the room and scrambled toward the back door. I'd seen no lights between these houses and the ones in the next circle. Darkness would hide me.

Vaulting off the doorstep, I crossed the back yard, sliding in the wet grass. The rain had slowed, and the area was open, with nothing to hide behind. The trees forming a dividing line between this property and the next were skinny little birches, planted in a single row. There weren't even shrubs between them to shield me from view.

A lot of noise and a wildly jiggling light behind me indicated D'Nard had recovered his flashlight and was coming after me. I ran, imagining I felt his breath on my neck, though logic told me he wasn't that close. What would he do if he caught me? That was easy to answer, but other questions arose. Was he alone? If not, was I running away from them or into their arms?

I crossed several back yards before stopping to reconnoiter in the shadow of a house. Behind me I heard an engine start, and my worst fears were realized. What I'd seen earlier had indeed been a car, probably the one belonging to D'Nard's buddy Richie. As they'd done before, D'Nard would pursue me on foot while his friend used the vehicle to cut me off. It was strange that they'd found me here, but the more important question was how to get away from them. I looked around, desperate for that answer.

The light of D'Nard's flashlight became brighter as he neared where I crouched. At the same time, the car entered the cul-de-sac. As it crept along in the dark, I heard D'Nard's voice, the words unclear but the tone angry. He was on the phone, possibly with the driver of the car. They were closing in from two sides. Since there was a house on my third side, I had only one direction to go. As soon as the car passed my hiding spot, I sprinted across the lawn, keeping out of the spill of street lights as much as possible. Behind me, D'Nard's voice rose. He'd seen me, and he called for Richie to turn around and pick him up.

Passing the sign that offered the development to a wise investor, I ran north, toward the river. I had to get out of D'Nard's territory, where he had all the advantages. On the other side of the river, I knew the safe places. D'Nard and his friend would be the interlopers.

I wasn't sure exactly where I was, but I could hear the river before me. As I rounded a corner, the buildings cleared and I saw something I recognized, the Robert E. Lee Memorial Bridge, just a few blocks away. In my headlong run I'd gone west rather than east and ended up at the less familiar bridge. That might be good, since D'Nard would assume I'd taken the shorter way back to the Fan.

It wasn't good to be too optimistic. I'd seen him using his phone, and he might have called in more friends to search for me. If he posted a man at the south end of both bridges, they could intercept me. Even if I got there ahead of them, crossing the bridge—either bridge—was dangerous. I'd be in plain sight the whole time.

Traveling too fast and thinking of things other than what was ahead of me, I ran into an impediment and almost knocked myself to the ground. After the few seconds of recovery such incidents require—*What happened? Am I all right?*—I looked to see what I'd run into. It wasn't human, thank goodness, but a sign: *Walkway to Belle Isle.*

Smack in the middle of the James River, Belle Isle was an interesting combination of nature preserve and historical site. The river was rocky and fast there, but the city maintained pedestrian walkways from either bank. On the north side, walkers descended a structure suspended from the bridge above. From the south bank, a more traditional walkway reached the island's southwest end. There were lots of trees on the fifty-four-acre site, and it was possible I might cross the James undetected.

Now that I'd stopped running headlong into the night, I realized the rain had ended. To the west, the clouds were thinning. Listening to the silence I feared was temporary, I made my decision. I'd cross the river via Belle Isle, but I'd have to hurry. If the clouds broke and the moon shone through while I was on the walkway, I'd be clearly visible from above, like a spider in the sink. Forcing my weary legs to move, I started across, using the railing to pull myself along. It was slick from the rain, and the water boiled beneath me, fed by the storm into an angry roil. After what felt like forever, I reached the stairs and descended to the landing. The clouds were breaking fast. I'd have to hurry to reach the trees.

Clouds that had minutes ago seemed impenetrable now parted faster than I would have thought possible, and the island appeared before me, bathed in moonlight. Hearing a sound from above, I glanced up at the Lee Bridge. A figure stood at the south end, hunched against the railing as he peered downward. D'Nard had indeed put a guard on the bridge. Richie saw me a split second after I saw him, did a double take, and craned his neck for a moment before raising a hand to his ear. On the phone, no doubt telling D'Nard where I was.

I hurried into the trees, feeling like a bug under a microscope. The Lee Bridge cut across the island, so Richie, still visible overhead, would locate me if I left the cover of the trees. If I headed back the way I'd come, he'd intercept me at the walkway. If I tried for the opposite bank, he'd get there before I did. I'd heard that a person could boulder-hop to the north shore at times, but I doubted that was a good idea at night after a heavy rain. I was trapped on the island. D'Nard had all night to hunt me down, and a spotter to tell him which direction I was headed.

Hunched in the trees, I pictured the island in my mind. I'd been to Belle Isle once before, when Darrin and I were dating. We'd come down the wobbly but scenic walkway from the north and walked the road that ringed the island, enjoying the views of Richmond, the babble of the rapids, and each other's company. In my head I turned the route we'd taken around, since I'd entered from the south this time. The interior was hilly and rocky, I recalled, and there was a big gravel pit on the northeast side. I preferred not to go inland, being unfamiliar with the trails and the rough terrain. I also needed to avoid the gravel pit area. No sense escaping D'Nard only to stumble off its edge to my death.

To the west was the north walkway, but I'd be visible from above, especially when I got to the large, open area that had been a prison camp during the Civil War. I thought briefly about the thousands of Union soldiers who'd been held in horrific conditions: not enough tents, no shade, no shelter from sun or cold, not enough food or medical care. They'd no doubt dreamed of escape as they froze, starved, or succumbed to disease. At least if D'Nard caught me, his baseball bat would make my end quicker than theirs had been.

I might reach the north walkway without being seen if I stayed on the main road and circled east. If I avoided the turnoff to the gravel pit and kept to the trees, I'd be sheltered from view until I was almost to the walkway. The problem there was that once I stepped into the open, Richie would see me. With D'Nard at my back, I'd be trapped between them.

Unless someone came to my aid. A picture came to mind, Alex driving up in his Beemer and telling Richie in an authoritative voice to move along. He'd made me promise to ask for help, and I needed help now. I needed him.

Digging the phone out of my pants pocket, I hit the number he'd programmed in. Alex answered immediately, not a sleepy "Who is it?" or a businesslike, "Bronson." It was, "Beth, where are you?"

"Belle Isle," I answered. "D'Nard and at least one of his friends are here. I'm going to try to make the north walkway near Tredegar Street."

"I'll be there in five minutes," he said. "I'm at the cemetery.

I was looking for you or Aisha."

Something inside me, some tiny flame of hope, kindled at the thought that Alex had been both determined to find me and smart enough to get close. "I only saw two guys," I told him. "D'Nard is on the island, hunting me, another guy's on the bridge, watching and telling him where I am."

"Okay," he said. "Get close to the walkway and then wait somewhere out of sight. I'll deal with D'Nard."

The call ended, and I had a feeling of loss, as if a lifeline were jerked away as I neared it. Squaring my shoulders, I took a breath and pulled myself together. Alex would be there, at the walkway.

I paralleled the trail, moving quietly except for the occasional sucking sound as my tennis shoes pulled loose from the wet ground. Water dripped off the trees, plunking onto my plastic poncho with a sound slightly different from other drips around me, a hollow, man-made tick unlike the flow of water leaf to leaf, leaf to branch, leaf to ground. Though it was darker in the trees, the moon provided enough light that I could avoid crashing into trunks or getting slapped by outspread branches.

It felt good to move away from the watcher above. When I turned back once to look through a gap in the foliage, he was just a tiny figure in the distance. I began to feel...not optimistic, but hopeful. Alex was on his way, and my ordeal was almost over. That was Beth's thought. The other voice in my head argued, *Really? When did Loser ever get a break?*

A fork in the road brought me to a stop as I tried to orient myself. I thought a smaller path leading east led to an abandoned power plant. The main path turned north, following the arc of the island to the spot where Alex would be waiting. At this point the cover provided by foliage thinned to almost nothing, and I hunched down, considering. Trees on the opposite side of the road offered better protection, and Richie must have lost track of me by now. I'd only be in the open for a few seconds. As soon as I stepped onto the road, however, I heard a shout from the bridge. A second shout sounded like a question. The answer came from Richie: "Ahead of you!"

D'Nard was somewhere between me and the walkway. How had he passed me? How had they guessed I'd take the longer route? Crazy thoughts ran through my head: They had night vision goggles. They'd planted a tracking device in my clothing—

My clothing! Lunging back into the trees, I ripped off the poncho I'd bought and turned it around. On its back were two wide stripes of fluorescent material, a safety feature for traveling in the rain. A dead giveaway, picking up any hint of light to help my pursuers find me. While I'd struggled through the trees, D'Nard had circled around in front. He blocked the way north, and Richie, still on the bridge, would see me if I went in another direction.

Hanging the poncho on a tree branch, I began putting as much distance as possible between me and the place I'd been spotted. Alex had advised staying out of sight, but I'd failed at that. All I could think of to do now was hide until morning, when the park opened and D'Nard would have to give up. With that as my new objective, I headed down the lane that led to the power plant. I recalled that it was big and complex. There had to be places of concealment.

In seconds a *Crack!* sounded behind me, close enough to jar my teeth. "I hear you runnin', bitch!" D'Nard's footsteps pounded behind me, purposeful but not hurried. Every few seconds, he smacked a tree trunk with his bat, dead wood striking live. A warning, a challenge, a threat. I imagined the moment when the bat would connect with my skull.

Crack! Crack! Muttered names I'd been called before. *Crack!*

His action had the desired effect. I was almost unable to think as I waited for the next blow and the next. I ran on, unconcerned about the noise I made. I fought my way along the narrow trail, slapping into drenched branches, slipping on wet rocks, and caroming off slimy tree trunks. Then I was in the open, and I stopped abruptly. Before me was the ruined plant, its shape square and stark against the lighter backdrop of the river.

I took off again, my breath coming in sobbing gasps. I stumbled. I fell once, rolled a few feet, and pushed myself up and went on. The building became like home base. If I could reach it, I'd be safe. I would win. A foolish thought, I knew, but it was something to hold onto.

Crack! D'Nard came on. I could hear his words now as they echoed across the water and back. "You ain't gonna get away, bitch!"

His threat spurred me on, and I sprinted across the open space to a concrete walkway. It was a mistake to look back, but I did. D'Nard had left the trees, and he came on, shoulders forward, as inevitable as death. Grabbing the metal rail, I pulled myself around a corner at almost full speed and ran along the building's face, looking for a way in. The walls blocked the moonlight, so I was forced to feel my way along the brick surface. When my fingers found an open space, I ducked inside. It was some relief to no longer feel D'Nard's hard gaze on my back, but I knew he was right behind me.

I moved through the old building, sometimes able to see

the way ahead depending on how much light the angle of the walls or the glass-less windows allowed in. At other times it was almost black, and I traced the rough plaster walls with my fingers. The building was a shell, and the moonlight revealed no hiding places, only graffiti and garbage. Turning a corner, my foot hit a discarded bottle that clattered against the wall and spun back into my way. Kicking it aside I scrambled on, desperate. Hope had faded; my optimism was gone.

Coming to a set of concrete steps, I ascended and found a corridor lined with doors. I tried to be quiet, but behind me, D'Nard had no such intention. His bat now struck against metal: railings, joints, and a wheel fixed along the walkway, some sort of control mechanism for machinery long gone. I tracked his progress by the ring of the different sounds. Twenty, maybe thirty feet behind me.

I realized too late that a ruined building offers little in the way of concealment. Decades of disuse and casual misuse had left only empty rooms, empty spaces. With his flashlight and his ball bat, D'Nard would find me. I thought of Alex, waiting at the walkway. What would he do when I didn't arrive? Come looking for me? Loser pictured the outcome of that. My lifeless body used as bait. Alex would rush in, bend down beside me, and D'Nard would step from the trees with his bat raised...

Stop that! Beth ordered.

Pushing Loser's fears away I went on, searching for safety. Like a trapped bird, I flitted from one spot to another, unable to trust any of them to protect me for long. A strange line of compartments appeared out of the gloom in front of me, each a few feet high and perhaps a foot and a half wide. I had no idea what they'd been used for, but if I climbed in and slid back as far as possible, D'Nard might go by without seeing me.

However, if he shone his light into each one as he passed, I'd be trapped. It was a big chance, but how long could I keep running?

As I weighed the possibility, a hand touched mine. Gasping in horror, I turned, expecting D'Nard. Instead I saw a dim figure of about my height. "This way," it whispered and hurried off.

What did I have to lose? I followed him—or her—along the corridor, outside the building, and across a catwalk of some kind. A metal access ladder disappeared into the darkness below, and my companion scampered down it with ease. I followed, slower due to my shaking, weary leg muscles.

When we reached the bottom we were close to the river, and the rush that had been a backdrop became a roar. Waiting to see that I reached the ground, my guide moved off, darting nimbly over the rocks. I followed, not half as nimble but more than willing. Behind us I heard the sounds of D'Nard's frustration. He'd been certain of catching me, but now he was beginning to think I'd escaped. His curses grew louder, the sound of the bat on solid surfaces more frequent.

It didn't take long to reach our destination, a dark space under an old construction I couldn't identify. The place had been lined with sticks criss-crossed against each other to form a patchwork ceiling. Under their shelter were a few pieces of furniture, a chair with one broken leg propped on an empty crate and the shell of a metal lawn settee. On it a second person sat, but in the gloomy light I had trouble seeing more than a dark shape.

"Who's that?" A grating voice asked.

"She was running," my guide answered. "A man was after her."

A squatted figure in the corner rose, an old woman.

"Why'd you bring her here?"

The other, a boy of maybe ten, answered, "He was gonna hurt her."

"So you brung him after us?" She stepped forward, hand raised, and he hunched to receive the blow. "You got no bidness bringing her here."

"Your son meant to help," I began, but the woman snorted a laugh.

"Ain't no son of mine," she said harshly. "He run away from home 'cause his old man was usin' him for his whore." The youth's head sank, and the woman continued, "He stays long as he makes himself useful. You cain't believe what people throw away around here, but my eyes ain't what they was."

The boy had been foraging for tourist leftovers when he saw me and heard D'Nard's threats.

"We maybe help if you can pay!" The woman's voice rose, and I resisted the urge to shush her. We hadn't come so far that D'Nard wouldn't hear a loud voice.

"I can pay," I assured her. Digging in my pocket, I pulled out one of the twenties and held it out. Her eyesight was indeed poor, for she took the bill outside and held it up to one eye. "There's more," I said when she'd satisfied herself it was real. "I need to stay here until my friend can come for me."

"How much?" she demanded.

"Another twenty. I'll call him right now, and when he gets here, I'll give it to you."

She nodded, a sly smile indicating she thought she'd made a good bargain. Returning to her couch, she sat, feeling for the arm and supporting her weight with one hand as she dropped onto the seat.

I reached into my pocket to get my phone, but there was nothing there. I searched the other pockets, patting them in a frantic hope I'd put it somewhere else. Nothing. In my headlong flight, I'd lost it.

The boy realized my situation. "He won't be able to find you."

I nodded, unable to speak.

"You said you'd go!" the woman screeched. "You said twenty dollars when he came!"

I was thinking of strangling her to keep her quiet, but instead I said, "I'll give you more money."

Her nose twitched, and I thought of Hansel and Gretel. "We ain't fightin' one a' your men off while you wait for the other 'un."

"No. I'm asking the boy here—What's your name?"

He looked confused for a moment, as if it had been a while since anyone bothered to ask. "David."

"I'm asking David to go to the north walkway—Do you know it?" When he nodded I went on, "My friend will be there. He's a white man, tall and well-dressed. Tell him Beth needs him, and bring him here. Can you do that?"

David's expression turned doubtful. "Is he gonna believe me?"

I thought about that for a second. "Give him this." Taking off my toque, I handed it to him.

He took the hat and hurried off, leaving me alone with his less-than-friendly companion. She turned ingratiating, assuring me, "It won't be long. The boy knows this place like you know your underwear drawer."

I sat on the chair, which wobbled a little but held me. I

would have preferred quiet, but my companion wasn't in the mood for that. "You ain't dressed like somebody got a roll of cash in her pocket."

"Long story," I said softly, hoping she'd get the hint and lower her own volume. "I was on the streets once, like you."

She snorted again. "Not like me, no! I don't think so. You might have had a rough spell, but you ain't been turned out of your home. You ain't goin' blind. You ain't hongry!"

I drew breath to try to calm her, but a voice above us called out, "I hear you down there. Whoever's got the woman, I'll give you fifty dollars if you let me have her."

I saw the light in the woman's eyes and knew I had to go. As I rose, she grabbed my jacket, screeching, "She's down here! I got her! She's down here!"

Sliding out of the hoodie, I left it in her hands and ducked out of the shelter, heading in the direction opposite the sound of D'Nard's voice. I had no idea where I was, but anywhere was better than there.

Behind me I heard his questions and the woman's shouted answers. Imagining her pointing, I quickened my pace. The boy might bring Alex to the shack, but I'd be long gone.

Chapter Twenty-two

Alex parked his car and hurried to the walkway entrance, zipping up the windbreaker he'd retrieved from the back seat. In his pocket was a flashlight taken from the glove box. In his hand was the phone. He'd called Beth twice since she'd called him, but there'd been no answer.

At the entrance to the walkway he saw a man leaning against the framework. He might have been out for a moonlight walk, but Alex doubted it. He might have been D'Nard Dobermeyer, but Alex doubted that too. He looked like a guy doing what he'd been told. "Evening," Alex said as he approached.

The answer was a grunt as the man looked him over with a hostile glare. Young and angry-looking, he seemed like the type who used body language and facial expression to intimidate those around them. In Alex's experience, such men often had nothing to fall back on when those things failed.

"Are you with D'Nard?"

The man eyed him warily. "Who's asking?"

Alex balanced his weight on the balls of his feet, letting his hands hang loosely at his sides. "I'm a friend of the lady D'Nard has been harassing. I'm here to make him stop."

The man's face twitched in a one-sided grin. "Yeah?"

"Yes."

"Let me tell you something, bro. You don't want to mess with D'Nard, and 'sides that, you'd have to mess with me to get to D'Nard, and you don't want to do that neither."

"Really." Taking a half-step forward, Alex cuffed the man

on the ear. Before he could react, he planted a fist into his gut up to his wrist. The man bent double, gagged, and fell to his knees. As he fought to get breath back into his lungs, Alex said into the man's undamaged ear, "If I were you, I'd go home and let me and D'Nard work this out. You willing to do that?"

The man nodded, still gasping.

"I'm going to call the police now. If you're here when they arrive, that's your business. If you're gone, I won't mention I saw you." With that he started down the walkway, trusting cowardice, pain, and the threat of arrest to remove the minor player in this drama while he sought the major one.

Alex had never been down the Belle Island walkway, and he could see why some called it frightening. Suspended above the river, it shifted slightly under his feet as he descended. At the bottom he paused, unsure which way to go, but to his surprise, a boy appeared out of the dark woods. The kid seemed to know he'd be there, because he said, "Alex?"

"Yes."

"I'm supposed to take you to Beth." He held up a hat Alex recognized.

"Where is she?"

The boy hesitated. "At our place. It's kinda hard to find if you don't know where to look."

"Have you seen anyone else tonight?"

"You mean the guy after her? Yeah." The kid's grubby face revealed pride. "I helped her get away."

"If that's true, I'm grateful."

The boy's thin shoulders rose and fell. "She said she'd pay if I came to get you."

Alex nodded understanding. "Tell you what. I'll match what

she's paying if you hurry."

The shack was situated under a concrete structure of some kind, and I scrambled up the bank to the top. Here the river was below me, and the piled sticks that comprised the shack looked like no more than river detritus, washed in by floods and lodged there by haphazard chance. From here I could see the structure I'd climbed was the dam that had once fed the power plant.

I looked around, trying to decide which direction to take. Traveling along the rain-swollen river would make footing treacherous, and I'd be in the open. I guessed D'Nard would expect me to turn inland and try to reach the road. Instead, I decided to return to the plant. Those cubby holes I'd seen seemed inviting compared to the prospect of running through the woods in the dark. The idea of hiding pleased Loser, and Beth tried not to worry about where D'Nard was or what might happen to Alex if the two of them met.

I'd forgotten the woman. As I climbed onto the ladder David had led me down a few minutes earlier, it shifted, making a squeak. It wasn't very loud, and I paused a second before taking the next step. The ladder squeaked again, and I heard her shout, "Somebody on the ladder! She going up! She going up!"

Abandoning stealth, I hurried up the rest of the way. Her shouts became even louder. "Where's my money? Where's my fifty dollars?" Her speech turned to gabble, the angry utterances of one so beaten by life she no longer expected fair play. More softly but still audibly, she muttered, "He said—" and several times, "fifty dollars." As I huddled against the building wall, she made a last comment, "That's what he said. It's what he said."

"I been lookin' for you." D'Nard stood a few feet away, the baseball bat held casually at his side.

It was almost enough to make me give up. All my running had come to nothing. *Loser loses again*.

"We got some things to talk about," D'Nard said, and something in his tone surprised me. "It might make a difference in how I do this." There was more to this than revenge.

"What do you want?"

"Some answers." He shifted his feet. "Maybe just one answer."

Despite my fear, I was curious. "How did you find me at the house on Marple?"

"Got to know a guy named Billy." One side of his mouth quirked in a grin. "You wasn't very nice to him, were you?"

Aisha had said Maureen gave her a phone, but I hadn't paid attention. It was a bad habit I had—focusing on one thing and missing others that might have been useful. Listening better might have saved me from the beating D'Nard intended to give me.

"Aisha told Billy where I was going, and Billy called you."

D'Nard shrugged. "I dint ask him how he knew."

"Listen to me!" I made my voice commanding. "The cop who broke your arm, Maureen Daley, is behind all this."

"She was for sure one messed up bitch," D'Nard agreed, "but she dead. You prolly killed her too, like you killed Carole Ann." His next statement surprised me, but it shouldn't have. "I liked that girl. I really did, but if you tell me where the money is, I'll let you go."

Money?

I must have mouthed the word, because D'Nard smiled,

and the moon reflected a diamond chip embedded in his front tooth. "You dint think I knew about that, did ya?" He set the head of the bat onto the floor and leaned on it. "Carole Ann tol' me we was gonna get a lot of money outa that Maureen, but you come along an' killed 'em both."

I paused as comprehension dawned. D'Nard was no lover set on exacting vengeance for his lost love. He was a businessman, something I'd known all along but hadn't factored in. Money explained much more clearly why he'd gone to such lengths to find me. I could admit I'd tortured and killed Carole Ann, and D'Nard would probably just ask again where the money was.

I tried the truth, fairly sure it wouldn't work. "There isn't any money. Maureen—"

He picked up the bat again, taking a few practice swings. "Don't lie, bitch. I know that cop take money. Saw her myself, stuck a wad of bills in her bra 'fore the rest of 'em got to countin' it." Rubbing his forearm, he added, "Bitch broke my arm, tol' me to keep me quiet."

Cjaika had told the truth. Maureen was the one who'd taken money and let bad guys slide. To set me up for Darrin's murder, she'd turned the story around. Later, she'd used the same story to try to save her job. She'd had a talent for blaming others for the things she did. Or had she begun to believe her own lies?

Blaming others for the things she did. Suddenly I knew it all.

I shouldn't have expected D'Nard to listen, but I tried again. "You're right. Maureen stole money, but they caught her at it and she got fired. Things got worse and worse for her, and she got weirder and weirder. She wanted people to think I—" I stopped. How could I explain the complexity of Maureen's hatred for me? I recalled her insistence that I come to her apartment at 10:00. *If what I have in mind works out, there will be an arrest real soon.* I thought about her surprise at seeing me, her hesitation at first and abrupt shifts in focus. I'd had to look at the view. I'd had to see Carole Ann's apartment. I'd been a witness to her encounter with Officer Cjaika, but what had I seen? He'd been angry. They'd moved out of sight for a while, and he'd returned to the patrol car. I'd found Maureen roughed up, but Cjaika denied laying a hand on her.

She'd done it to herself.

"Maureen killed Carole Ann to frame me," I told D'Nard. "When that didn't work, she killed herself, knowing I'd be blamed for it."

I couldn't see his face, but his tone was dismissive. "Killed herself! That's just crazy."

"Exactly," I said, as reasonably as I could. "Maureen was crazy. She wanted to be like me, and when that didn't work out, she tried to destroy me." I watched his face. Could D'Nard grasp a concept I could hardly comprehend myself?

He shifted, and a shaft of light from the doorway illuminated his face. His jaw moved forward like a bulldozer blade. "The money. Tell me where it is or I'm goin' beat it out of you."

He swung the bat with a quickness that caught me off guard, catching me on the shoulder, and I cried out in pain. I ducked aside, scraping along the wall toward the stairs on my right. I heard the next blow coming, a whoosh of air near my ear, but I crouched and the bat hit the brick wall with a force that must have stung his hands. Before he could recover, I was up the stairs and onto the upper level.

When I exited the stairwell, moonlight revealed I was atop the massive old structure with nowhere to go. The river gurgled below me, the rain-washed air surrounded me, and D'Nard was coming up the stairs behind me. I started along a catwalk that edged the building, passing massive iron gears now rusted to the wheels they once turned. About thirty feet down a second catwalk crossed to the opposite side, its end shrouded in darkness. I turned onto it. It might lead only to another edge, in which case I'd face D'Nard and his bat again, but I had nowhere else to go.

When I reached the end of the walkway, a staircase exactly like the one I'd come up awaited. Breathing a sigh of relief, I descended to the second floor again and hurried along a corridor lined with empty rooms. At the end of it were the stairs that led back to the ground floor.

In only seconds I heard D'Nard coming down the stairs behind me. Gasping air as quietly as I could, I tried to decide what to do. Logic dictated I continue downward, leave the building, and disappear into the trees. The problem with that was my pursuer would know it too. I feared he'd catch up with me before I could get out of sight. I decided to try deception rather than flight. Pulling off a shoe, I tossed it onto the landing at the top of the steps and ducked into the nearest room, my back against the wall.

D'Nard came to a stop at the end of the corridor, still muttering threats. He had to choose: search each room he passed or assume my shoe on the landing meant I'd hurried down the stairs so fast I left it behind. I stood there, shoulder throbbing, and willed him to make the latter conclusion.

He did. Lumbering past me, he stopped on the landing, picked up the shoe, and looked over the railing. "Where you go, bitch?" he muttered.

I peeked out. D'Nard's back was to me. The bat head rested on the ground as he scanned the area, waiting for me to move into view again. He seemed confident, his hand relaxed on the handle, like the team's best hitter waiting in the batter's box.

A great anger took hold of me, something that surprised both Beth and Loser. I was angry at D'Nard, who approached the idea of hurting me with such nonchalance. I was angry at Maureen, who had tried so hard to destroy me. "This is my friend Beth Lousiere," she'd told the landlord, making sure I was identified. "Come out here and see the view," she'd urged, thereby getting my prints on her balcony railing. She'd written my name in big letters on her calendar so the police were sure to know she'd been expecting me. I was a murder suspect who would die a murder victim, and it was her fault.

It wasn't fair. Life wasn't fair. All I could do was fight back, and fight back hard.

Without stopping to think about it, I stepped up behind D'Nard and snatched the bat from his hand with a ferocious twist. He turned, surprise on his face, but I had already started my swing. All my fear went into that blow, and while the doorway shortened my range, I connected with his shoulder at about the same spot he'd hit me earlier. Exhilaration replaced anger when he staggered against the railing, howling in pain.

It didn't last for long. Like a bull gored by a picador, D'Nard accepted the pain and became even angrier than before. He straightened and came at me. I struck at him again, but the walls of the corridor made my blows largely ineffective. In the end I backed away, stabbing at him with the bat head. Grinning, he caught it easily in his meaty fist, twisting it out of my hands with half the effort I'd used to take it from him.

"Now we see who's boss," he said, and the tooth-diamond winked at me. "I want—"

I knew what he wanted, but he never said it. Movement behind him caught my eye, and my reaction caused D'Nard to turn. He was a little slow, and a hand grabbed his shirt and turned him into position for an uppercut that snapped his head back. He dropped the bat, which I removed from his reach, and Alex followed the first blow with another that sent him into the wall, where he slid partway down and shook his head, opening and closing his eyes as if to clear his vision.

"Cops are on their way, buddy," Alex told him as he rubbed his knuckles. "You might as well stay right where you are."

He didn't, of course, being amoeba-brained. Pushing himself to his feet, D'Nard ran at Alex, head down, intending to butt him. Alex moved lightly out of the way, and D'Nard stumbled onto the landing. His impetus almost took him over the edge, but he managed to stop himself on the rail with a grunt of effort. He turned back toward us, beyond knowing that he was already defeated, and came into the corridor again. "I'm gonna kill you both."

"Bet you don't."

D'Nard launched a fist at Alex's head, but Alex wasn't there when it arrived. The big man tried again, swinging this time, but he had no better success. His fighting methods were primitive and unlovely, and Alex defeated him with easy, almost effortless grace. A right to the jaw spun him around, and a follow-up left to the gut sent D'Nard to the floor. It occurred to me later that I might have tried to help, but I'd only have gotten in the way.

By the time the police arrived, D'Nard was sitting in the corner, nursing cuts, scrapes, and a terrible attitude. We ignored D'Nard's claims he'd done no one any harm. While a good lawyer might have made a case for him of extreme emotional distress and self-defense, he'd get a public defender. Having a few strikes against him already didn't bode well for his future.

Once Alex had been sure D'Nard was under control, he pulled me into a one-armed embrace, keeping the bat in his other hand as insurance. I couldn't remember the last time I'd felt so good about human-to-human contact.

"Are you sure you're okay?"

"Yeah. I'm good." His grip on my shoulder tightened, and I ignored the stab of pain it sent through the spot where D'Nard had hit me. The support of someone who cared about me outweighed a little physical pain. As long as Alex wanted to hug me, I was willing to let him.

Chapter Twenty-three

It was almost 3:00 a.m. on Sunday when we finished explaining things to the police. Alex put the full force of the Suggs Law Firm behind me, making the case for my innocence with reasoned arguments. We left Belle Isle with the understanding we'd see Detective Zender Monday morning to provide details she'd need to wrap up her case.

I asked Alex to drop me off at the office building. He was reluctant to leave me alone, but I was used to my own company. In fact, I needed it at times like this.

Unable to argue with that, he announced he'd come back later with lunch, but I reminded him there was enough food in the office fridge to last until Labor Day. He finally left on the condition I keep one of the firm's cell phones with me so he could call once we'd rested. Handing me his keys, he waited until I was through the building's front doors before driving away. I made my way to the roof, settled in a far corner with a blanket I grabbed on the way, and sank into exhausted sleep.

Alex's call came precisely at noon, leading me to think he'd made himself wait until then. I'd been awake for an hour, for the first time in years looking forward to the discreet little beep of the phone. Knowing he was only a few numbers away was comforting, even though I'd insisted I didn't want him with me.

I was painfully aware that my reason for not letting Alex stay with me was fear of what might happen between us. Fear had broken down my barriers, and I'd clung to him, waiting for the police to arrive with search lights and drawn weapons. In those tense minutes, when he simply held onto me, keeping me from collapsing to the ground, our relationship had moved to a level that made me nervous. Until I'd processed the night's events, I felt a whole lot safer with distance between us.

My weirdness paid off, at least a little, in the sense that honesty came easier when I wasn't looking Alex in the eye. On the roof of the office building, knowing he was miles away, I said more than I meant to.

"Did you get any sleep?" he asked when I picked up.

"Enough." For the first time in years, I hadn't heard the accusing voices of the dead in the night.

We talked a little about recent events, repeating what we already knew in the way people do when they've triumphed over something awful. Finally I said in what I hoped was a light tone, "You're making this coming to the rescue thing a habit. I guess you don't mind going above and beyond your duty as my attorney."

The tone of his response was equally light, but I felt an undercurrent. "Is that what we are? Attorney and client?"

"No," I admitted. "Attorneys don't face crazed men with baseball bats for their clients. I think you're in the friend category."

He didn't answer for a few seconds. "If that's what I get, I'll take it."

My voice turned unsteady. "Alex, I know you think there can be something more between us, but feeling sorry for a person is not a great basis for a relationship."

"Sorry for you?" He seemed genuinely surprised. "Beth, I've seen you take on bad guys twice now. You didn't curl up in a ball and give up either time. Why would I pity you?"

"Without your help I'd have died both times," I reminded him. "And there's Loser. She isn't someone I'm proud of."

"Why not? She's a survivor, and I'll bet she's taught you things you'd never have known as Beth Lousiere."

That was certainly true.

"As far as last night goes, you'd have found a way to escape that guy. You never quit, Beth. You keep coming back, whatever the obstacle." He paused for breath before adding, "There's no reason in the world to pity you, and every reason to admire you."

In those few words, Alex showed me two things. The first was a different picture of myself. Loser was part of me, but only one part, and she hadn't done so badly, given the circumstances.

The second thing I'd sensed before, but the blurry thought had turned clear. Alex was a man unlike any I'd met before. Knowing how messed up I'd been, he still believed in me. In turn I had to believe it was possible we could be together, if not today, then someday.

That was too much to deal with at the moment. Again summoning a light tone, I said, "Okay. You're allowed to admire me until some other female catches your eye."

Probably guessing I'd gone as far as I could in the emotional department, he switched topics. "Sure you don't want me to bring you lunch? Mexican sounds good."

"I'll see you tomorrow," I said with mock sternness. "Now go do something relaxing. Enjoy the rest of your Sunday."

Early Monday morning, Bert's Lincoln pulled up outside the office. A few minutes later there was a great deal of noise on the stairway to the roof, no doubt a signal for me to get decent before he appeared. Taking a page from Alex's book, he'd brought coffee and doughnuts, which we shared in his office before anyone else arrived. Once he was satisfied he knew everything I knew, Bert surprised me by proposing a celebration. "You're proven innocent, Beth." Looking over his glasses at me, he added a little guilt. "It's simply good manners to ask those who helped to share in the celebration."

It was another tiny push toward social integration, but he'd been so good to me that I said, "I guess you're right."

"I am." Eyeing my clothes, which had suffered substantial wear and tear during my weekend adventures, he added, "If you tell me where you hid your things when the police came, I'll have someone fetch them so you can freshen up before the day begins."

A year ago I'd visited Bert's office in duct-taped tennis shoes and a smelly flannel shirt, and he'd made no suggestion I should "freshen up." I took his offer as evidence I was on the road to normalcy and therefore expected to make a decent appearance. "I'll get them right now, before anyone else arrives."

"All right." Taking up a pad and pen, he said, "I'll make some lists for the party. We'll have your former partner and his wife, Alex and whichever woman he's seeing at the moment, the couple from the restaurant, you, and me." He started writing the names down. "That will be eight, a perfect dinner party."

I turned in the doorway, giving him a grin. "If you want to include everyone who helped, there'll be a few more." His brows lifted as I added, "And you'd better make it a picnic. These guys aren't the type who'll be welcome at a nice restaurant like the Tobacco Company."

It was comforting to have Alex beside me as we entered the police station. His light touch at my back reminded me I was there voluntarily, especially when we were shown to the same room I'd escaped by trickery a few days before.

Detective Zender came in right behind us, again carrying a folder. This time, however, she tossed it casually on the table as if she had its contents committed to memory. "Mrs. Lousiere, Mr. Bronson, please have a seat."

We sat. She didn't. There was an awkward silence, and I guessed she was trying to gauge our attitudes. I might play the role of an outraged, wrongly-accused citizen. The respected Suggs Law Firm might sue the department for harassment. Zender was probably supposed to find out how things were going to go.

"Mrs. Lousiere, Mr. Bronson, the Richmond Police Department regrets any inconvenience you suffered during this investigation." She stopped, apparently trying to read my expression.

I decided to meet her halfway. "It's okay. I'm sorry I—um—left the other day."

Her eyes met mine, and after a second she grinned ruefully. "That was embarrassing. I've never lost a suspect before." Taking in my much-improved appearance she added, "I underestimated you."

Alex shifted slightly in his chair, tacitly encouraging the detective to get down to business. She took the hint, sitting down opposite us and adjusting the folder with the tips of her fingers so it was aligned with the table edge. For twenty minutes she led us through the events of the last few days, listening carefully as Alex explained and I added details when necessary. When she finished, Zender looked at me directly.

"I'm sure you know by now that Maureen Daley was a very disturbed individual."

"Will her death be ruled a suicide?" Alex asked.

Zender nodded. "I think so. She was desperate, no money, no job, no friends." She looked at me. "I don't know what you did to focus her anger on you—"

"Nothing," Alex said firmly. "As you said, Maureen Daley was disturbed."

"Yes." Opening the folder, the detective leaned in, squinting until she found the spot she wanted. "We spoke to a woman named...Aisha who says Maureen duped her into helping with Ms. Minier's abduction. When she realized it wasn't a joke she objected, but Ms. Daley threatened her life—Blah, blah, blah." Zender closed the folder, rolling her eyes, and I let out the breath I'd been holding. I'd expected Aisha to lie but hadn't been able to predict what sort of spin she'd put on things.

"Aisha isn't honest, but I doubt she'd knowingly assist with murder."

"Good to know." Zender's tone turned irritated. "Detective Marshall released her with her promise she'd remain available for further questioning. She's since disappeared, along with a man who's apparently her boyfriend."

"Billy."

She shrugged. "It doesn't matter. We might have charged her as an accessory, but who'd testify with Daley and Minier both dead?"

Alex returned to his main concern. "Ms. Lousiere is cleared of all suspicion?"

She nodded. "Evidence at the house where Minier was

held clearly supports the account you gave the officers." Zender leaned toward us, eager to make a point. "We'd have figured it out eventually. Things didn't make sense."

"Like what?" I asked.

"Items in Daley's apartment weren't knocked out of place. They were set there."

Imagining the scene, I recalled the overturned lamp's bulb and shade had been intact. "She couldn't make noise for fear a neighbor would come to see what was going on."

"Right. Besides that, the M.E. says the fall wasn't right."

"Not right?"

Zender made one hand into an imaginary railing and her pen into a figure next to it. "When a person falls off during a struggle, she usually goes backward." The pen mimicked the path a body would take in such a case. "Daley fell forward. In that case she should have grabbed the railing to try to stop herself, but she didn't." Laying the pen aside, the detective put both hands on the folder. "They figure she stood on the railing and leaned out, working up the nerve to let it happen."

I pictured Maureen on the balcony of her dingy apartment, hating me so much she'd die to hurt me. Should I have been kinder? More of a friend?

Alex squeezed my hand under the table, and I grimaced in an attempt at a smile. Maureen had made my destruction her goal. The cost hadn't mattered one iota, and nothing I'd done or not done would have changed things.

I rose from my chair. "Thank you, Detective Zender for giving me some peace of mind."

Zender glanced at Alex as he, too, stood to go. "It was the least we could do after arresting you twice in two days."

As we left the police station, I was surprised to see Manville leaning against a wall in the lobby. He was off-duty, wearing jeans, a plaid shirt, and boots with substantial heels. Alex stepped between us like a guard dog, dwarfing Manville despite the boots. "What do you want?"

Leaning past Alex, he spoke directly to me. "Can I talk to you, Beth?"

"Alex, do you mind waiting in the car?"

He wasn't happy about it, but he went, giving Manville a look that promised dire consequences if the upcoming conversation upset me.

When he was gone, Manville seemed unsure how to proceed. This was important. He'd made the effort to learn when I'd be here and come on his free time.

"What's up, Manville?" I asked. My tone was more "get on with it" than friendly.

"I—uh, I'm—I mean, I came to say I'm sorry. I didn't treat you right, and I was wrong."

The apology surprised me, but I put it together: first Zender's regrets, now Manville, almost groveling. The RPD was nervous.

Soon everyone would know I'd committed no crime. The public and the media were likely to turn their outrage onto the department, asking how such a travesty of justice had occurred. It wouldn't necessarily be out of concern for me, more from the desire for a good story, but it would make things uncomfortable for the police.

I couldn't have cared less what the media said or the public believed. Looking at the now-penitent Manville, I felt only dislike. Certain of my guilt and vocal in his views, he'd arrested me, harassed me, and generally treated me like garbage.

"You were wrong about me. How many times a day do you make the same mistake?"

He bit his lip, apparently tempering his first response. "You know how it is out there. All the scumbags we have to deal with every day."

"Here's an idea. Don't assume a person's a scumbag until you know that's what he is."

His lip curled. "It wasn't just me. Everybody thought you did it. And Maureen kept saying how lucky you were you never went to prison."

"Lucky?"

Movement outside caught my eye and I saw Alex pull up in the BMW, his gaze anxious as he peered toward us.

"I have to go." I headed out the door, but Manville followed.

"I just hope there aren't any hard feelings, y'know?"

Without looking at him I said, "I won't file a complaint, if that's what you're worried about."

Obviously relieved, he stepped ahead to open the car door for me. "I appreciate it, Beth. I mean, you don't want to keep this going now you recovered. Let it be in the past."

First I was "lucky" and now I had "recovered"? I didn't feel lucky, and I'd never fully recover. I had the truth, which has to be enough sometimes.

"You got one thing right," I told Manville. "I sincerely hope you and everything about you is in my past."

As he stood glaring at us, we pulled smoothly away from the curb. After a few seconds Alex gave me a sideways grin.

"You go, Beth!"

On the ride back to the office, things I'd been thinking about began to come together in my mind. For the first time in years, I was free of suspicion. The tragedy that had disabled me was explained, though not forgotten. I could go back to Beulah, but would I be happy there? Was I willing to leave my friends to people like Manville, who assumed they were worthless? There might be something I could do, something I was uniquely qualified for.

At the law firm Alex and I reported what we'd learned at the police station as Bert made disgusted sounds at the depths humanity can sink to. Once Maureen had been fully discussed, I asked, "How much money do I have?"

Glancing at Alex, who shrugged to indicate he wasn't in on it, Bert replied, "I've told you, Beth, you'll never have to work again."

"Do I have enough to fund a project?"

He gave me that over-the-glasses look. "What sort of project?"

I explained about the downtown mission called Get Up! and Jonanna Booker, who had lots of good ideas. "She operates on almost nothing, and I'd like to help her out." Not sure they'd understand, I added, "To help the people I care about, the ones like me."

"A place like that requires a lot of money," Bert cautioned.

"I know, but I don't need much. I could get a job."

Alex had been chewing on his lip as he listened. "Will you let me put in a share?"

I'd expected counter-arguments, not support. "You?

Why?"

"Let's just say Loser made me look at the homeless differently."

Again I wondered if Alex really understood. "You can't fix us," I warned. "There aren't any easy solutions."

"I know. But it will make us both feel better if we try."

Bert cleared his throat. "I think it's doable, and I might want to participate as well." A little too casually he added, "Charities are a good write-off until they overhaul the tax code, which won't be anytime soon." He turned to his computer. "Let's see if the agency is viable before we approach Ms. Booker with an offer of support."

As we left Bert's office, I asked Alex, "Why would he want to help? He does a lot of charity work already."

He smiled. "He might think if someone like Ms. Booker had been around when you needed her, things would have been different."

I thought of my days as Loser, when I'd found a sense of purpose in cleaning Verle's kitchen. I thought of Mabel, who with a stable home had found peace. "Everybody can do something," I told Alex. "But sometimes they don't know what it is."

"So we help them find that out, right?"

"Right."

Moving to his desk, Alex made a shooing motion. "Go make yourself useful at reception. I'll never get any work done if you keep looking at me like that."

My party was interesting, to say the least. Bert arranged a picnic for twelve at a pavilion in Byrd Park, and he chauffeured me there himself in his Lincoln Town Car. I'd made an effort to look good, choosing capris and a matching top. I worked at fixing my hair and even added a tiny bit of makeup. While it seemed a little disloyal to my street friends to fuss with my appearance, I didn't think they'd resent it. Beth was in control, and everyone who knew me saw that as a step forward.

Alex was there when we arrived, wearing a grin that showed he was pleased with himself. Beside him was David, the boy from Belle Isle, wearing the same ragged clothes, but with hands and face scrubbed clean—well, almost clean. His grin was every bit as big as his new hero's.

I was surprised to see him, since he'd disappeared by the time the police arrived on the island. "I went looking for him Sunday afternoon," Alex told me, "but I never found the shelter. I'd brought along a bag of cookies as a gift, so I left them near the ladder at the power plant with a note inviting him to come today."

He put a hand on David's shoulder, and the boy's grin got even wider. "Knowing our friend is an experienced scavenger, I figured he'd find them before anyone else did, and sure enough, he was waiting at the bridge today when I went to pick him up."

Remembering the old hag's comment about David's past, I wondered what the boy had thought when he read the invitation. He must have sensed Alex wasn't the type to lure him into dark corners, but now, as guests started across the grass to join us, his expression turned nervous. He moved so close to Alex he was likely to get stepped on.

Bert quickly sized up the situation and devised a way to put David at ease. "I wonder, young man, if you'd agree to keep the guests' glasses filled with iced tea and punch. I generally pay twenty dollars an hour, and the caterers are quite busy, so I'll take it as a personal favor if you help out."

Actually the two women had already loaded the table with food and were just chatting as they waited, but David eagerly took up the job. He got each of us a drink, and after that we could hardly take a sip without getting a refill.

Jake and Sasha arrived first, then Verle and Flo. I got hugs from everyone but Verle, who offered a punch on the arm that was just as good. I had to relive my adventure, but Alex was more than willing to be the storyteller, adding sound effects and acting out the more exciting parts.

He was just finishing when the guys from the All-Aid joined us. To their credit, neither guests nor caterers turned a hair when Bubba's crowd-sized voice announced their approach. I guessed Bert had warned that these guests would be non-typical for a catered affair.

They were a little late, no doubt having spied out the situation from a distance before showing up, as Loser would have done. Howard wore a battered pink Panama hat, and he'd tied a slightly wilted helium balloon to his scooter in an effort to look festive. Penrod stumbled along beside him, one hand on Howard's shoulder and the other over his mouth. Bubba led the way, boots flopping. "Lookit, Howard!" he shouted from fifty feet away. "They got shrimp."

"I think that's everyone," Bert said calmly. "I'll tell the ladies we're ready to begin."

As he went off, I looked around, trying to spot the woman I'd invited personally. There was no sign of her, and I felt a stab of disappointment.

Bubba and the others stood a few feet back from the table,

aware there were niceties to be observed before they could eat. As I joined them Bubba said in a tone of wonder, "All that to eat, and shrimp."

"Go ahead, guys. No sermon before the meal today."

"Whatever you say, Loser!" Bubba took a plate but paused reverentially to savor the moment. "You ever had shrimp, Howard?"

Maneuvering his scooter up to the serving table, Howard left Bubba in second place. "'Course I have, idjit. Everybody's had shrimp." He began loading his plate.

Bubba followed suit, asking, "Where does shrimps come from, Howard?"

"The ocean." Howard continued work on the small mountain he was building.

"No, they don't." Bubba's face scrunched in denial.

"They do too."

"I betcha they don't. On my sister's TV they showed how to make Shrimp Scampi one time. I axed her, and she said that means they come from Scampi. That's in Italy."

Howard's expression turned even more disgusted. "Well, Italy is shaped like a boot, so there's ocean all the way around it."

"Oh." Bubba thought about that. "A boot full of shrimps," he said. "That'd be somethin', wouldn't it, Howard!"

David stood off to one side, holding a pitcher in each hand. "Put those down and get something to eat," I told him. The boy obeyed, stepping into line behind Bubba. Alex joined him, pointing out the different dishes and urging him to try them.

Penrod had stopped at a tree just outside the shelter. "Come in," I urged. "Fix a plate." He hung back, gauging the distance between the table and the tree. "Here," I said, offering the shoulder that wasn't black and blue. "I'll walk with you."

Putting one hand on my shoulder, he pressed the other to his stomach. "Thanks, Loser."

Once they had their food, the guys sat down at a small table at one side of the shelter. David chose to sit with them, probably more comfortable with people as tattered as he was. He ate self-consciously at first but soon surrendered to pure enjoyment.

At Bert's urging, the rest of the guests moved through the serving line. I was pleased to see that each of them tried in some way to let my street friends know they were welcome. Verle started it, since he knew the guys from the neighborhood. Holding a plate heaped with ribs, he stopped at their table and chatted briefly. Flo, wobbling behind him on ridiculously high heels and carrying a much lighter plate, smiled and nodded a lot, setting her long earrings spinning. When they sat down at a table a few feet away, Verle looked back at David and said something to Flo, who nodded sadly.

Alex also stopped to greet them, and Bubba said loudly, "Hey, it's the guy with the car!" He slapped Howard's shoulder. "This guy has a Beemer, Howard. Honest!"

"I know that, idjit! Ain't he been driving around for a week looking for Loser?"

Bert, Jacob, and Sasha paused to introduce themselves. Jacob didn't mention his profession, saying only that they were old friends of mine. Howard answered for everyone at the table, telling them I was "something."

Jacob glanced at me and winked before acknowledging, "She certainly is."

After I'd filled my own plate I joined Jake and Sasha, catching up on preparations for their daughter's wedding, now less than a month away. Sasha made me promise I'd come, and I told myself Eddie would probably enjoy a trip to Richmond. As we talked, she kept glancing at David, who was watching Bubba's antics with a bemused expression. Finally she asked, "Is the boy homeless?"

After I explained who David was and what he'd done for me, she looked to Jacob. He nodded at her in tacit understanding before saying, "Sasha and I have been thinking of becoming foster parents. The girls are gone now, and we miss having a kid or two around. Do you think David would want to come and live with us?"

I thought about the miles of red tape they'd have to cut through and the emotional damage David had to deal with, but I guessed they could handle it if anyone could. "I'll bring him over when he's done eating, but from the looks of that plate, it'll be a while."

Once the main meal was finished, Bert cleared his throat to call for attention. "I promised Beth there'd be no speeches, but I feel we must acknowledge she's beginning a new phase of life. She's been through a lot, but today she faces the future without a cloud of guilt overhead. While we can't celebrate so much tragedy, we can find peace in knowing justice has been served." He raised his glass of iced tea. "To Beth's future."

All around me, glasses were raised in salute. Looking at the odd collection of people toasting me, I blushed with embarrassment but also with pleasure. I was all they had in common, but each had supported me in some way.

"Beth, would you like to say something?" Bert asked.

It was a test. As all eyes turned to me, I froze for a second.

Finally I said, "I love you guys. There's ice cream for dessert."

They clapped then, maybe for my new-found confidence, maybe for my admission of affection, maybe for dessert.

Once the ice cream was gone, the party began to break up. Verle and Flo left first, claiming they had to get back to the restaurant. I led David to Jacob and Sasha's table and left them to talk. As Jacob spoke earnestly to the boy, Sasha folded her arms against her body as if fighting the urge to reach out and embrace him.

The caterers began packing up their belongings. Bert and Alex stood together, ostensibly talking, but I guessed they were giving me a chance to say good-bye to my street friends. While it wasn't something I was good at, it had to be done.

Bubba, Howard, and Penrod were still seated at their table, but the mound of dishes and debris had been cleared away. As I took the seat David had vacated, Bubba and Howard lolled against their chair backs, looking a little nauseated. I guessed they'd overdone the shrimp. Maybe everything.

"Hey, Loser, that was really good," Bubba said around a not very decorous burp. "You can have a picnic every week, and we'll all come."

He was clueless, as usual, but Howard and Penrod knew what was up. Neither met my gaze, and Penrod's lips moved in his chant, silent but comforting: *Choose an awkward moment.*

"Bubba," I said softly. "I'm going home tomorrow."

"Home?"

"To West Virginia. I have a house there, with Mabel and a boy I take care of."

"Yeah?" Bubba's forehead wrinkled. "When are you comin' back?"

I herded some crumbs on the table into a pile. "Well, I might visit sometimes."

He finally got it. "No more picnics."

I shrugged. "Not for a while." Loser reached out from the depths of my mind, stopping the words that were in my heart. Instead I said, "I'm glad you all came today."

"We'll come anytime you want us to, Loser," Bubba said. "We like you."

"And not just because you buy us food," Howard added, his tone almost angry.

"Nope," Bubba agreed. "Loser's a good person. Right, Howard? Right, Penrod? She's a good person, and we're always gonna be her friends, even if she lives someplace else."

Bubba looked around the table, proud of himself. It was ironic that the one of us with the least understanding was the only one who could put his feelings into words.

The guys left then, soon followed by the Graumans and David. In a quick update Jacob told me that Bert had promised to start the process of making them the boy's legal guardians. The waves Sasha and David gave me as they got into the car were almost casual, and Jacob hurried after them. They had a new focus, and I wished them well.

The pavilion was almost empty when the guest I'd been missing hurried toward us. Jonanna Booker, looking gorgeous and a little out of breath, apologized for missing the party. "I was all ready to lock up when an emergency landed on the doorstep," she explained. "I guess when you run a help center, you have to be ready to help."

"This is Alex Bronson, and this is Bertrand Suggs," I told her. "They're my attorneys."

"I see," Jonanna said, but her expression said she didn't.

"We have a proposal for you." I turned to Bert. "Will you explain?"

As Bert talked, Jonanna's eyes went misty. "I can't believe this," she said when he finished. "I can't—" Words failed her, though her mouth kept trying to form them.

"If you have the time," Bert told her, "we could go to my office now and discuss the matter more fully."

Jonanna agreed, still a little confused. Bert led her to the Lincoln and helped her in like the gentleman he was. The catering van pulled away, which left Alex and me. "Need a ride back to the roof?" he asked.

I cringed at his knowing I slept atop the office building. The voices had been silent for three nights, and I hoped I was past that torment, but I hadn't yet gathered the courage to try sleeping inside.

"I'd appreciate it, since my escort seems to have taken off with another woman."

It surprised me that I could joke about being abandoned, but such things were easier when Alex was around. Tuned to my moods, he seemed to know at any given moment what approach to take.

His expression turned serious. "No man in his right mind would pass up a chance to spend time with you, Beth."

Of course someone had, but the pain of Darrin's betrayal was fading. He'd been a flawed being, as I was. It was the combination that had been wrong, not him or me.

As we left the park and started for the law firm, Alex returned to the topic of our joint project. "I really like your friend Penrod. Do you think as an investor I can influence Ms.

Booker to hire him in some capacity?"

"We could suggest it." I looked out the window for a while, watching Richmond pass. "It might not work out for him." In a burst of honesty I added, "It might not work out at all. I hate to see you invest your money in this because of me."

He shrugged. "I can't keep going around beating up deadbeats to assuage my need for justice."

"I didn't think that was such a bad thing," I told him. "Justice sometimes needs a helping hand. But how will you ever afford that row house you've always wanted if you keep giving away large chunks of money?"

Alex turned toward me and said seriously, "I don't need a house right now. I'm waiting."

Something told me I shouldn't ask, but I did. "Waiting for what?"

"For you," he answered. "Sooner or later, you're going to be ready for a man in your life, and I intend to be first in line when that happens."

Dear Reader:

If you enjoyed this book, please consider placing a review somewhere others will see it, since authors rely on word of mouth to spread the news of a new book or series. No one does that better than happy readers! Thank you for supporting what we writers love to do!
Peg

If you liked *Killing Despair*, there are two more Loser Mysteries.

Killing Silence (Book #1): Loser sleeps on the streets of Richmond, Virginia. She washes up in gas station bathrooms, eats when an opportunity comes along, speaks less than thirty words per day, and spends her waking hours in front of a local drug store, watching the world pass by. When the father of a child Loser is fond of is accused of murder, she wants to help, but can Loser the Loser pull herself out of her own pain to help catch a killer?

Killing Memories: needing to recuperate from the stress of her adventures, Beth goes home to West Virginia, where her foster mother has left her their former home. Another of Marta's foster daughter's shows up, sending Loser back into danger.

Website: http://pegherring.com

About the Author

Peg Herring reads, writes, and loves mysteries. As an educator she once set the school stage on fire (just a little one). As a driver she's been so lost that she passed through the same town in Pennsylvania three times in one day. Family and friends have lost count of how many times she's locked herself out of her house. As the award-winning author of several best-selling mystery series and standalones, it's much safer if she sits in her office and writes, either as herself or as her younger, hipper alter ego, Maggie Pill.

Visit http://pegherring.com for Strong Women, Great Stories

Books by Peg Herring

Available at major booksellers in print and e-book formats. Many are also available as audio books. Series are listed in order.

***

The Kidnap Capers (Suspense with cozy tendencies)
KIDNAP.org
Pharma Con
The Trouble with Dad
***
The Simon & Elizabeth Mysteries (Tudor Era Historical)
Her Highness' First Murder
Poison, Your Grace
The Lady Flirts with Death
Her Majesty's Mischief
***
The Loser Mysteries (Contemporary Mystery/Suspense)
Killing Silence
Killing Memories

Killing Despair

***

Clan Macbeth (Historical Romance, Medieval Scotland)

Macbeth's Niece

Double Toil & Trouble

***

Mercedes Maxwell Suspense Series (with Historical Implications)

Shakespeare's Blood

Charlie Dickens' Documents

***

Standalone Mysteries

Somebody Doesn't Like Sarah Leigh (contemporary cozy mystery)

Her Ex-GI P.I. ('60s-era mystery)

Not Dead Yet... ('60s-era paranormal mystery)

***

Maggie Pill's Cozy Mysteries

The Sleuth Sisters Mystery Series

The Sleuth Sisters

3 Sleuths, 2 Dogs, 1 Murder

Murder in the Boonies

Sleuthing at Sweet Springs

Eat, Drink, and Be Wary

Peril, Plots, and Puppies

Captured, Escape, Repeat

***

Trailer Park Tales

Once Upon a Trailer Park

Twice the Crime This Time

Visit Maggie at http://maggiepill.maggiepillmysteries.com

www.ingramcontent.com/pod-product-compliance
Lightning Source LLC
LaVergne TN
LVHW091029080826
845145LV00002B/413

* 9 7 8 1 9 4 4 5 0 2 4 5 4 *